General Pershing's

Other Daughter

Christian Strayhorn Spence

DEDICATION

This work is dedicated to:

The General Pershing of my life, James Darrell Strayhorn 1928-2010

My Russian inspiration, Fatimate Chardanoff 1934-

GENERAL PERSHING'S OTHER DAUGHTER

TABLE OF CONTENTS

General Pershing's Other Daughter

PART I: INNOCENCE

CHAPTER 1

To change is to discover that we are creatures of self-control; that we are not fated into our circumstances and chosen to fail. The mind is a powerful machine and can easily convince the soul of lies and fallacies. These untruths build upon one another until one creates another person, someone they do not want to be. Humans call this person me.

So who are we really? Are we the person we become through our environment and experiences, are we the person we choose to be, or is there a being that lives deep down inside of each one us that is our destiny, that tugs at our heart when we least expect it?

Some say life, at some point, comes full circle. It is my hope that every human being will in his lifetime find the person that emerged from his mother's womb, rather than the person this world has conditioned him to be. What follows in these pages is the journey of my soul, not the events some call my life.

CHAPTER 2

My father used to tell me that every moment contained within it a story. Every wink, smile, grin, snarl, and wince meant the future had just changed course. The key to one's own destiny required controlling the emotions of those surrounding us. He often quoted Napoleon to me as a child.

"A leader is a dealer in hope," he would say.

Then he would add his own touch,

"Who cares if the followers will actually see their dreams come true, what matters is that they believe in you Julia, that they believe you will deliver them."

My father, Jacob Patterson, lived and breathed for the military. With a slender, strong, and handsome physique, the looks of a young Paul Newman years before the movie industry, he celebrated his eighteenth birthday, so I heard at least twenty times in my eight years with him, by marching two miles to the closest New York City army recruiter in the summer of 1915. He stormed in the front door of the recruiting office, shaking the door as if it had not been opened in the past ten years, and yelled,

"I want to join up with the infantry for when that damn Wilson stops being such a pansy."

The recruiters looked at each other as if an atheist just walked in the front door of a Roman Catholic Church looking to join the Crusades. Atheist or not, a healthy eighteen year old body that could have appeared on a recruiting poster, would always be handy, especially with a war in Europe brewing. Later in life, I always vowed that a divine force intervened to make my father a 1910's American rather than a 1940's German.

My father's best friend Olli always swore that he once had a mellow side; that he could even be sweet on occasion, especially when it concerned my mother. She changed his ways, or so I often heard.

Apparently Father enjoyed the life of a real doughboy in France during World War I, once his dreams came true and finally got deployed. With his sharp good looks and a clean military uniform, he fell in love, or at least infatuation, a dozen times or more while enlisted in France.

As Olli would tell it,

"Your father would walk into a country village on the way to the trenches, into a tavern in a city, along a roadside after the war, into the home of some Frenchman and his family, or even into the library and leave with a new love. Every time he would declare that she was the one, until somebody's heart got broken, more often than not, the beautiful young girl who had fallen for the immaculate American infantryman."

I often thought that Dad first adopted his Napoleonic theory of building hope and faith through lies and persuasion, always telling people what they wanted to hear, as young women stared at him desperately in love or at least desperate for a savior. According to Olli, my mother was the first and only woman, or human being for that matter, to replace Dad's mind with his heart, and he did the same for her; they took the planning, perfectionism, and obsessions and opened each other up to new experiences and emotions they never before allowed themselves to feel. Perhaps they learned from each other something too many of us lose as a child, along with our innocence, without even seeing it slip through our fingers.

Daddy only talked about my mother when he was drunk, so he talked about her often. Upon reaching his fifth or sixth drink he would start,

"Your mother was the most beautiful spirit this earth has ever seen, with the legs of a gazelle, the patience of a saint, and the heart of King Richard III."

I knew not to ask questions, because the moment I raised awareness of my presence would be the very moment he would simply say,

"Another time, another drink."

After The Great War, my father stayed in France, not because he loved the place, but simply because he did not know what he wanted to do with his life. He contemplated returning to New York City to work in the family bakery in the Bronx, but he believed that he had too much talent to throw it all away standing behind an oven for eighteen hours a day like his father. The longer he could wait it out in France, the better chances he had of seeing his natural math abilities discovered by engineers seeking to rebuild Europe. Naturally talented in the fields of math (especially calculus), physics, and design, my father had a lot to offer the world. I discovered these talents for myself when he momentarily forgot about the haunting spirit of my mother.

After about a year of doing any odd repair job he could find, going from home to home, usually only receiving the pay of a night's sleep and a few good meals, Dad found a permanent job in Paris working for a small engineering company. He was far from making the money he knew he was worth, but at least it was permanent, and it did not involve yeast and ovens.

The young Jacob Patterson possessed his charming good looks, his militaristic attitude, and his energy for greatness, and the girls still flocked to him; that is until he slid on a piece of loose rock while surveying a building damaged from the war, for the engineering company. He knew immediately that his twelve-foot fall had seriously damaged his leg. Upon being rushed to a former Russian doctor, he discovered that his leg was indeed broken. Within seconds he realized that breaking his leg was the best thing that had ever happened to him, because at that moment, in walked my mother, Leeana Serenova. In that moment, for the first and only time in his life, my Dad discovered the true meaning of love.

Leeana, a newly arrived immigrant from Russia, barely a woman, yet old and wise beyond her years, had just arrived in Paris completely alone, aged eighteen. The year: 1919. Leeana's parents truly believed in the Czar's power in Russia. They believed in the monarchy, and they like many fellow Russians despised Rasputin. In 1916, Leeana's parents began talking to friends of theirs whom migrated to France before the Great War. They feared correctly that Rasputin would bring down the Romanov Dynasty and ruin the destiny of Russia, and they arranged for Leeana to move to Paris and work as a nurse as soon as she turned eighteen.

By the time 1919 came around, Leeana jumped at the opportunity to move. The Russian Revolution terrified her. It wasn't that Mother was anti-communist, she simply sought to avoid the war and revolution that engulfed her life, and she wanted to move to a place that seemed to hold a chance for a real and steady future.

The family she moved in with served as doctors in Russia, but of course lost their license to practice medicine in France. They were currently studying to become official French doctors, and saw people who could not afford doctors and those in the surrounding area who trusted them. They gladly accepted Leeana, who had been taught medicine, French, and English by her grandparents who were both doctors in Russia. She assisted in the routine exams and problems that arose in the office.

Leeana, the woman who would become my mother, maintained two beautiful, silky black braids, always straight, perfectly parted, and pinned at the bottom, stretching down her narrow hips. She had the face of an angel, which never saw the touch of makeup. She dressed like a woman twice her age, with every wrinkle pressed out, and every skirt at least knee length. Her style was always a choice, never a demand or a familial requirement. She believed in simplicity. Needless to say that when my father first laid eyes on the beautiful eighteen year-old Russian, it proved to be a sight, he unfortunately, would never let himself forget.

Maybe the simple fact that my mother had no interest in Father provided the excitement and spark he needed in a woman. Just as Mother had never felt the touch of a man, Father had never felt the thrill of the chase.

As soon as they set Daddy's leg, he started his typical American charm. My mother, however, was no fool. She had a brilliant knack of reading the intentions of people, and she saw Father as an American taking advantage of his handsome features and popular position. In other words, she saw my father as he was. Yes he was attractive, smart, and funny, but he only wanted to have fun, and Leeana had not moved across the continent to play games.

Jacob refused to give in to Leeana's bluntness and refusal to go out on a date. He returned to that Russian medical office in a beat up old apartment building in Paris every day, seeking Mother's surrender. Every day, she would give him the same response,

"The only way I will court a man is if I have my father's permission. If you want to see me so bad, then here is my father's address. Write him a letter, and when he says it is okay, I will say yes."

Jacob continued to go back to that office every day, and after about two months of harassment, he walked in and once again said to the beautiful Russian,

"Would you like to have dinner with me tonight?"

Leeana reached in the pocket of her skirt, pulled out an envelope blushing and began to read:

Dearest Leeana,

Oh how I miss you these days. Of all of my girls, you were my first, and have always been my most responsible. I miss you watching over my diet, I miss you giving me practical advice, and most of all I miss your beautiful smile, which does not come out nearly often enough.

Your mother and I have worked so hard for you to have a good life, and with every moment you exceed our expectations. You are brilliant, proper, beautiful, and destined to be a success, and although it hurts to let you go not knowing when I will see you again, I know that you Leeana were a gift to the world, not to me. I must share you.

There is only one hope I have for you, which you have not already demanded for yourself. I wish that, rather than reinforcing your success, I had forced you to be a child. Yes, I want you to be a strong, independent woman, but I want you to remember your happiness. No one is perfect, and although you try to make your life that way, your life will never be complete without having met the love of your life. Open yourself up to happiness and peace Leeana, because of all things in this world, happiness and memories are the things you will always have, no matter where life takes you.

A young man has written me a letter. I believe you know him as a Mr. Jacob Patterson. He may not be your destiny, or even a twinkle in your eye, but I want you know that it has always been my dream for you and your sisters to find love and happiness at some point in your life. The choice is ultimately yours, but if a man is willing to write a letter to some old man living on the dreams of his children, asking for an evening with my beautiful and proud daughter, I must give my blessing. If you escort this young man to dinner, then he will have answered a prayer of your father, not that you fall madly in love as I love your mother, but simply that he will be a starting point in showing you how to live your life to its fullest.

Do not grow any older Leeana, or I'm afraid I will be the child and you will be the parent. A life worth living requires that you remember that moment when you were five years old and told me your dreams. In that moment your dreams did not involve success, control, and infallibility, but that moment involved love.

I will always love you my dearest. Never forget that, and remember of all the people in this crazy world, it is you who I would trust my life with.

Love Always,
Papa
May 8, 1920

"Pick me up at six and don't be late," Mother said as she turned and walked back into the examination room.

That evening was the last night my mother ever called my father Mr. Patterson. For three and a half years, my father would go pick up my mother after work. She, always dressed in her finely pressed skirt, a classic blouse, her hair in braids, and a beautiful smile, would meet him on the sidewalk. She taught Daddy great patience. She was different than any woman he had ever been with before. She demanded respect, was brutally honest, and stung with the sharpest intellect of anyone in Paris. Unlike other girls, she demanded that her date take her to the library or to classic

Parisian locales during their evenings together, and she always required that Father return her to her sidewalk with an evening kiss by 10:00 every night. Olli always claimed that Jacob Patterson never knew what he was getting into when he asked Leeana Serenova out on their first date together.

During their time in Paris together, Jacob and Leeana often met with some of their friends, Olli Zingre for one. Olli was born in Switzerland, yet his mother dragged him all across Europe, as she often fell in love and married. Because of his mother's marital progression, Olli swore that he would never get married. Olli rarely dated, but occasionally I would catch him talking about a girl named Maria, who I often thought was the true love of his life.

Maria had never been married, and was raising a three-year old little boy whom she loved with all of her heart. It seemed that Olli was the only man in all of Paris who was willing to have a serious relationship with Maria, because of her illegitimate son. Olli could have cared less. He knew very well what it was like to be an unwanted child, and he did not want that for Patrick. I once heard Olli say, "No child should have to live for the sins of his parents."

Jacob, Leeana, Maria, and Olli were inseparable. Olli knew more about France than my parents put together, and he became their guide. Olli always wanted to help somebody, no matter the cause, even lost causes. That is my guess as to why he cared for Maria so much; simply because she needed somebody to care about her and Patrick. Olli truly loved Mother and Father and believed in their love. He had known my Dad a year and a half before the Russian doll came into the picture, and he knew before anyone, that my father would never be the same. Olli would tell me,

"I saw your father go from being a playboy to being at the mercy of a beautiful Russian nurse. She could get him to do anything, but it was magical how she never had to ask."

In the winter of 1923, Jacob received life-changing news from New York. Apparently my grandfather was dying with tuberculosis, and distant relatives wrote asking Father to come home to see Grandfather one more time and take care of the family business. Jacob knew that he would never be able to leave the one woman who made his world go around, Leeana.

My mother and father married in a civil ceremony a week upon arriving in the United States of America. Grandfather's last moment of happiness involved his oldest son's wedding. Leeana worked in the family bakery, and my father got a job working with an engineering firm, which specialized in perfecting transportation in New York City.

Olli came to visit a couple times before I was born and once after my birth. He came under the title of a visiting professor from Switzerland, where he was working as a professor of Human Geography at the University of Zurich where Albert Einstein once attended.

My parents immediately wanted a family. Olli would tell me as he tucked me in how excited my parents were to know they were finally going to have a baby. He would talk to me about the joy my parents felt on January 30, 1925, when I made my first appearance in this world, and how he knew that my father loved me with all of his being. Little did anyone know that within six months, my father would face the death of his heart.

CHAPTER 3

Immediately Olli was named my godfather, and after little deliberation, I was named Julia Josephine Patterson. Mother always acknowledged Father's love for the military, and she accepted that without the war she would have never met Jacob Patterson; therefore, she allowed Father to name me in honor of the World War I General John Joseph Pershing. He wanted us to have the same initials, and as you can tell, he gave me almost the same middle name. My father would never leave Europe, and Europe would never leave my father.

Apparently, Pershing had been married with three daughters and a son. In 1915, however, a fire killed his wife and three daughters. Only his son survived. My name was presented to me as a memorial honoring the daughters of my father's hero. From the moment I entered the world, I would have a legacy to fulfill, one that would drive me and haunt me throughout my entire life; a legacy that honored me as an American yet possessed my soul to save the world.

Six months after my entrance into this world, my mother would face her exit. The only thing Daddy was grateful for was the realization that Mother did not have to suffer. She had an undetected aneurysm in her brain, which took her immediately. I could not remember anything about Mother directly, except for an occasional aroma that reminded me of something I had never really known.

I learned everything about my mother from pictures, from Olli, or from my father when he drank himself into a stupor. One time as I rustled through old boxes in a hallway closet of our Bronx apartment, I found a letter from my Russian grandfather to my mother. It read:

Dearest Leeana,

Have I ever told you just how proud I am of you? You have become quite an astounding woman. I am so happy for you and Jacob and your happiness, yet I am sad for the pain of missing you. But don't you worry about me my beautiful young girl. Your happiness makes me happy.

I feel like you have your life together for the first time, and it is hard to believe that you are not even studying sixteen hours a day! Isn't life wonderful when you let it be? You have found that five year old girl I remember, who sat on my knee, called me Papa, and dreamed of one day falling in love, traveling the world, and living in a world of peace. I used to worry that the Great War took all of that away from you, and I thank God every day that Jacob was able to help you remember the person you were born to be, rather than the person you created. He allowed you to feel again after all emotion had been drained from your body through war.

Do not misunderstand me, dearest Leeana. You have developed your God given talents to perfection, with which I am bursting with pride, but it was not until your letters mentioned your Jacob that I saw your God given emotions and feelings develop to perfection.

No matter where life takes you my dear child, remember to never stop feeling. No matter the pain, the ugliness, or tragedy, remember it is better to feel both good and bad than not to feel at all.

Love Always,
Papa
January 8, 1924

As I read the letter, I came to believe that my grandfather must have been the wisest man in the world. To a five year old, it seemed like a simple request of my mother. I immediately ran the letter to my father, whom I thought would be thrilled to glimpse into his past. It was the only time I ever saw him cry, though I could sometimes hear him through his wall. It was then, still as a young child, that I first remember obsessing for hours about something that bothered me, which I followed immediately with the recitation of the Constitution in my mind, trying to remove or cover up bad thoughts. I had to make myself forget that emotion, that pain, at any cost.

I unconsciously rejected my grandfather's advice, and I shut down my heart. I could no longer take the torture of seeing my father in pain, and I stopped allowing myself to feel, by spending all of my free time in books, seeking to remove everything uncomfortable, and working on perfecting my life so I would never have to suffer as he suffered.

CHAPTER 4

"You're being raised by a group of rabid wolves Jules. All of the books in the world will never replace the necessary woman's touch, which only your mother could have provided." Olli would say this every time I punched a boy in the face for calling me an orphan, or for playing with the toy soldiers my father gave me rather than the dolls that still sat stacked in their boxes, never opened, organized by date of reception.

I went to live with Olli in Vienna on January 30, 1933, which not only marked my eighth birthday, but would go down in history as the day Adolph Hitler became Chancellor of Germany. I had been living with my grandfather's first cousin (on my Dad's side) for a month after my father passed away in December of 1932.

Even at seven years of age, it was clear to me for a year before Daddy's death that he was ill and getting worse. It started with a major decline in his weight. Always thin, Father became ghost-like. And for the first time in his life, he missed work, and not because he had the flu, but simply because he suffered from extreme fatigue. By the time we found out that Father had cirrhosis of the liver, he was bed-ridden and unwilling to give up alcohol.

He told me that Olli would make sure my dreams came true, and that unlike himself, Olli was strong and would always be there for me, even when he could not take care of himself. Daddy told me not to miss him, because he would finally be at peace with my mother, and he apologized for being a failure as a father. I never thought he was a failure, only a heart-broken man, doing everything in his power to raise a daughter alone. He told me he loved me and would watch over me, just as Mother constantly did from heaven. The last thing my father ever said to me was,

"You rule the world Jules, don't let the world rule you. There is a major difference between being great at following direction and being great at following direction until you must stand up for what you know is right. Be the one that is always fighting, whether that is with the mass or by yourself. You will know what to do. Live up to the name I gave you Julia, don't let General Pershing down."

Olli arranged to pick me up and escorted me to Vienna. He moved to Vienna in 1930 from Zurich to take care of the mother who always failed miserably to take care of him. Her last marriage to an Austrian factory worker moved her once again, and for the last time. Her Austrian husband passed away the year after I was born, and within three years she faced several serious health issues, including severe heart problems. To attest to the character of Olli, the moment he found out he packed up his things and moved across Europe to help his mother that never really was. Within a month Olli found work as a professor of Human Geography at the University of Vienna, or what the locals called Hauptuni.

Even though Olli's mother passed away the same week Father's cirrhosis of the liver took his last breath, Olli grieved more for me than himself. He treated me like a porcelain doll, which could break at any moment if handled wrong for the entire first year I lived in Vienna.

I absorbed languages from Olli as I sat in his university classroom everyday listening to his lectures in German. He also taught me French at home once he started home-schooling me. Every new word was to be repeated in English, German, and French. Once I mastered German, he would call me up to the front of his classroom and have me read his notes to his students, allowing me to add in my own touches. It made me feel so intelligent and mature to lecture college students, and I loved to see their faces as they took notes from a mere child. I especially enjoyed the discussion on the United States, because at those moments I was the professional in the room.

A student would ask,

"Professor Zingre, do you believe the United States will remain in isolation, or do you think the Great War changed their perspective on world affairs?"

Olli would say,

"Well, let's ask someone with experience: Julia?"

My father, even though constantly depressed and drunk, maintained his passion about his second love, war. And to make sure I understood everything that emerged from his fumbling mouth, Father constantly educated me. By the age of four I read at a third grade level, and by the time I reached third grade I could read at a high school level. College students, therefore, never intimidated me, because I maintained an incredible knack for understanding all perspectives. My father and Olli, for example, or even my mother and father, loved each other to death, but perceived the world and related their priorities in completely different ways. Having lived with a depressed alcoholic and then a happy-go-lucky professor, I became a self-professed expert on the subject of understanding a variety of views on life. Any question that came toward me in a class of 20 or 200 never scared me. Amazingly, I could answer most of the questions the college students would ask me.

CHAPTER 5

By the time I turned ten, Olli and I had been together for two years in what I consider to this day to be the most beautiful place on earth. Our neighborhood was in the 9th district of Vienna, also known as Alsergrund. Alsergrund served as the Academic center of Vienna, mainly because of its proximity to the University of Vienna. The 9th district also housed Liechtenstein Palace, where I would often go to think about how on earth I ended up in Austria. My home, however, would eventually be world renowned for being the home of Sigmund Freud until 1938, when he fled Nazi persecution.

Our apartment was small and cozy. The front door of our apartment, on the fifth floor of the Viennese apartment building, opened into the sitting room and kitchen. To the left of the door one would find the sitting room. Nice furniture and beautiful paintings, which Olli gathered through his travels across Europe, filled the apartment. None of it matched, but the beauty of the room and the paintings hypnotized everyone upon entrance. Our kitchen, to the right of the front door, simply had a small built-in counter where we always ate, behind which Olli never cooked. Everything we consumed came from some hole-in-the-wall eatery Olli discovered wandering through the city. Dinner proved to be the high point of the day, because what Olli brought through the door was always a mystery, but I could guarantee you Olli would not be cooking.

To the extreme left behind the sitting room extended the hallway. Olli's room appeared as the first door on the left. I was assigned the bedroom at the very end of that hallway, which was also the very end of the apartment. I loved my bedroom, because I always felt so safe. Unlike most people, I treasured the peace and comfort of being closed off in my own space away from the rest of the world. Between our two bedrooms, we shared a bathroom.

My favorite place in our apartment extended off the kitchen; our porch, or in reality our large fire escape, which overlooked a small café, a shoe repair shop, a bookstore owned and operated by Jews, a tavern, and a family owned general store. Often escaping there to process some obsession bearing down upon my soul, I loved to go out on evenings and watch the university students going to the tavern. I would pretend that I was on a date with a handsome future doctor. During the day, I often took a book out with me and watched the recently homeless go in and out of the stores looking for work, or watch the elderly make their weekly trip to visit the merchants. The age of the traveler determined the predictability of the routine.

My daily routine, which became increasing more fixed, included going to work with Olli in the mornings and sitting through his lectures on the demographics and patterns of human movement, studying and reading in my private cubby hole in the University library between lectures, and returning to our apartment for schooling from Olli until 6:00 p.m. Olli would leave me to my lessons and return with dinner, after which my most recent book would escort me onto the fire escape for my favorite time of the day.

I headed to bed at 9:00, my mind swarming with how much I could possibly learn in the library while struggling to overcome the most recent obsession that had no doubt consumed my consciousness. I would try to rationalize my irrational worry and when it felt like I conquered my problem, I would recite the Constitution to seal it away.

I loved to explore the topics of my past. I would look up information regarding American soldiers in World War I, alcoholism, cirrhosis of the liver, Russian immigrants, genealogy, aneurysms, bakeries, orphans, current events, General Pershing, and any other topic that could possibly provide clues as to who the hell Julia Josephine Patterson was supposed to be. I wanted assurance that I acted in a way that would please my father, whether that was trying to have the maturity of General Pershing or studying engineering. I absorbed everything I could possibly find to create the person I wanted to be, to never disappoint a soul.

The librarians loved to see me walk in the front door, usually because I carried with me an offering of some leftover meal Olli scrounged up from God knows where. I would simply leave my daily offering with a list of resources I wanted to indulge myself with and scurry to my favorite corner on the fifth floor of the library. I would set-up my notebook, pencils, and erasers in my little cubicle and seemed to always turn around at the precise moment a librarian approached with a stack of books neck-high.

One day, Ms. Gerg, one of the librarians asked me,

"Julia, don't you like stories about puppies and princesses?"

"When both of my parents died before I turned eight, I kind of gave up on the idea of happily ever after," I replied.

The librarian gave me a concerned smile and headed back to the reception desk.

Later that evening, while Olli and I were partaking in shepherd's pie, he said to me,

"So Jules, you've been spending a large portion of your time in the library, huh?"

"Yes," I said.

"Is that it, just a 'yes' with no explanation?"

"I didn't realize I had to explain going to the library. Why don't you go badger some other eight year old who is playing in a mud puddle?"

"Wow!" said Olli with a smile. "You have never reminded me so much of your father as you do at this moment." He paused and continued, "It is just that the librarian Ms. Gerg came to see me today."

"Ms. Gerg, is she the one with blonde hair or brown hair?"

"You do not even know the names of the people you see every day?"

"No Uncle Olli, I have more important things to do with my time in the library. You know I love to learn new things, and if I want to have a good life one day, then I need to get a head start."

"For Christ's sake Jules you are just a baby, give yourself a break." He took a deep breath and went on, "Anyway, Ms. Gerg told me that you mentioned something about the deaths of your parents today, and she was concerned about your compulsive studying. She told me that she had never even seen a University student work as hard as you do."

"Uncle Olli, please just tell me what you want me to do. Do you want me to stop going to the library, because I am such hard worker?"

"Of course not. I just want you to enjoy your youth a little. Play with some kids your own age, get dirty, go outside, hell Julia, get in trouble."

"How can you say that to me when you take me every day to your classroom full of college students?"

Olli grunted and said,

"Now you remind me of your mother. She could make a purple sky sound logical. I want you to read something."

Olli walked to his bedroom, closed his door, and after about ten minutes he returned to the kitchen counter with an envelope, which had apparently been opened at some point. It was yellowing, and on the outside it was addressed to a Ms. Leeana Serenova in Paris. Olli said,

"Do me the favor of a lifetime and take this letter to the library tomorrow and read it instead of trying to figure out how Lenin pulled off the Russian Revolution, okay?"

"Anything for you Olli," I said sarcastically.

Then feeling guilty for being so short with Olli I said,

"I love you Uncle Olli."

"I love you Jules," he replied on his way to our tiny little deck.

I would have joined the Nazi party if Olli asked me to, so reading some old love letter between my parents was a small request, though reading anything emotional proved to be difficult, because I learned to hate feeling the emotions and carrying the burdens of other people.

When I walked into the library the next morning, Ms. Gerg gave me a smile as I dropped off my daily food gift. As I rushed off to my cubicle Ms. Gerg stopped me,

"Julia, where is your list?"

"I have other business today Ms. Gerg. If you are concerned just give Uncle Olli a visit," I replied with a wink.

I made it to my usual spot, sneaking a few books here and there along the way, so that Ms. Gerg wouldn't tell Olli I read the entire time I was stationed in the library. Those books would be for the moment I finished reading the surely boring old letter Olli gave me. I settled in, with the letter still neatly inside of its envelope placed directly in front of me and the books I swiped along the way, stacked to the side in order of importance and theme.

I slowly pulled the letter out and immediately noticed that the letter was not a love letter from my father to my mother, but a letter from my grandfather to his oldest and most cherished daughter. It read:

Dearest Leeana,

I am so pleased for you Leeana that you have reached a place where your dreams can develop. You have always had such high

standards for yourself, higher than any good parent could demand of his children. I know that you have just arrived in Paris, and that you are yet to make friends. Do put that on your agenda. I know my precious, beautiful daughter, who is brilliant beyond her years, and who will one day change the world. I also know the part of her, which will close herself in a box believing that the world lies in a book rather than in the heart of her neighbors. Leeana, I know that you want to be perfect, and that you want to absorb everything this world has to offer, so please do not allow yourself to forget the part of you that also needs educational grooming: Your heart. Experience life Leeana; because reading about other people does not allow you to truly live their experiences. Live life for yourself, and make others intrigued in your story. The most educated and sophisticated person to ever walk this earth is yet to be discovered, because she has not realized that other people must be involved.

I am so pleased with you Leeana, my first born, and most dedicated to the fate of the world. I have no doubt you will make your mother and I proud, as you already have. You are so beautiful and have so much to offer. I know you are the one person in this world who will not fail others. Please Leeana, do not fail yourself.

Love Always,
Papa
March 11, 1919

At the first read of the letter, I was so proud of myself for being just like the mother I never knew. Heck, I never even knew her maiden name until that moment, yet I felt like I knew everything about her, because I was her. I reveled in the fact that I turned out also destined for greatness. It

22

took me years to realize that just like my mother, I ignored the advice my grandfather aimed to instill.

I would sit for hours in my bedroom on the weekends looking at pictures of my parents. They were absolutely gorgeous. Father had sharp, distinguished features, beautiful blonde hair, a neat haircut, and a smile that would knock you dead. Mother also had a natural beauty about her. She maintained a simple beauty that other women envied. If she had lived another fifteen years, Hollywood surely would have come knocking.

I unfortunately believed I was cursed. I was that girl with two beautiful parents, who turned out to be plain ordinary. It seemed like the worst features of my parents merged to make one boring combination. I gained my father's blonde hair and short stature and my mother's brown eyes and short round nose. My books allowed me to avoid people, not for the sake of avoiding nuisance, but for the sake of maintaining my self-esteem. The smarter I made myself, the more I looked down on other people for their vanity. Facts created a bubble around me that helped me feel good about myself and avoid the pain of childhood.

I always thought I was so smart and secretive for avoiding the vices and pains of youth. Olli, on the other hand could read my mind. He knew how and why my actions were motivated, and he never fought against me. I truly believe that Olli looked at me as a child who had felt too much pain at too young of an age to face a typical childhood, hence he never pushed me to be normal. He simply used my grandfather's letters to my mother to teach me the lessons of maturity and the mistakes too often made by the wise.

Olli never pressured me to do anything, because he understood that my soul pressured itself, and that I would eventually reach a point where perfection overtook me to create a new person. What Olli didn't realize is that I had already reached that new person. By the time I lived in Austria for two years, I no longer remembered the six-year-old little girl living in the United States. Of course I still had memories, but all of the innocence and joy of youth was gone. Everything now had a reason, purpose, plan of action, and solution. Somewhere along on the way, I lost the little girl who would talk to anyone about anything, who did not fear failure or embarrassment, who dreamed of getting married, living in a castle in England, while being a professional author. The day my father died was the day I forgot the person I was born to be. The day my father died, was the day I created a new Julia who would never feel disappointment again.

CHAPTER 6

"Julia, what happened?" Olli asked as I walked in the front door of his office at the University on an incredibly hot summer day.

"A boy who lives near Hauptuni called me an ugly orphan when I walked out of the library today."

"Julia, please explain the blood on your blouse," Olli continued as he ran toward me.

"Oh, when he called me an ugly orphan, I punched him in the nose, which then inconveniently flowed on my brand new blouse. Can you believe it Uncle Olli, that boy not only had the nerve to disgrace my parents, but he also lacked the integrity of keeping the blood on his own shirt rather than dripping it all over mine?"

"Julia, you should have told me rather than punching the boy. Even though he may have deserved it, he is a kid, and he makes mistakes."

"Sorry Uncle Olli, but the right hook my father taught me should be enough to protect him from future mistakes. Daddy always told me that in uncomfortable situations, I was the only person who could determine when the painful actions of another had to stop."

Even though Olli fumed with frustration over my actions, I saw a smile break when he said,

"Oh, how much I miss your father. Go clean up Julia, I will cancel class, and we will go home for tonight to talk about the likelihood of your jab showing up sometime soon."

Olli never scolded me, because he knew that every action, which emerged from me, had been through a complete analysis, even if the decision had been made in a matter of seconds. It was at this point that we entered our apartment, and within minutes, Olli handed me another letter of my mother's from my grandfather, and he said,

"You may be surprised to find out that you may have thrown your mother's right hook today, rather than your father's. The only difference is your mother knew how to use words as a weapon. Maybe that is something you should consider you little smart ass."

Then Olli just smiled and walked off to the porch to leave me to my letter.

Dearest Papa,

Let me first say that I truly do miss you with all of my heart, although sometimes I know my letters can sound quite dry. Jacob found the last letter I wrote you before I mailed it, and he said that it might be nice if I express some emotion to you. So Papa, I love you, I miss you, and no matter what my life becomes or how happy Jacob makes me, the love of my father will never be replaced. So there Papa is all the gushiness I will put in this correspondence.

Jacob and I are planning on moving to the United States and getting married, as I am sure you know. Jacob told me that you honored his request for my hand in marriage through the mail. I hate it for Jacob that we have to move because his father is dying, but that is life I guess. I dread the day I am faced with the situation. Though we are thousands of miles apart, you still fill in a void through your letters.

I encountered a situation the other day that brought a true smile to my face, as it reminded me of how witty you made me Papa, and how Mama would despise the moment someone offended me. I was reminded of the time when I came home from school with my hair colored green. The other girls used to make fun of me, because I never spent time in front of the mirror. Do you remember how I was always consumed in some childhood mystery? Then the especially mean girl, Anya, dipped my long braid into green paint. I told Anya, that at least I could have green hair and still be pretty, where she had to cover up her hair, body, and face with fakeness, and how I was content with myself and did not have to make others feel bad to be important. Then I added that my mind would lead me to better things, whereas her brain would only lead to digressing the human race. Do you remember Papa? I wish you could be here so that we could laugh together. That was the only time I ever saw Anya cry, and after that, no student would even speak to me out of fear. Though I would never hurt anyone first, it was refreshing to have to avoid the petty details of growing up, the gossip, judgment, and anger. I wish that our country would learn to fight with words rather than swords Papa. When will the world learn that the mind is more powerful than weapons?

Enough about me, how are you and Mama doing? Please write me soon, as I know you always will. You probably already have the next letter on the way, but I must stick to conventions and ask you to write.

Love you Atyets,
Your Leeana Forever
November 16, 1923

I stepped out onto the fire escape and saw Uncle Olli looking down at the street below with a concerned look. I interrupted the silence and said,

"So tell me Uncle Olli, how am I supposed to fight against people with words when Hitler is burning books in Germany?"

"Julia, you know that has nothing to do with punching that boy in the face today."

"But Uncle Olli, don't you see that it has everything to do with punching that boy in the face today. He will soon be a part of the Hitler Youth Movement everyone around here is always talking about. He is a patsy, a simple follower feeding on the pain of others."

"Julia Josephine, I think you should move to the United States in about 25 years and run for President. I would vote for you. For God's sake, can you not just enjoy life like a ten year old?"

"I know you are not bringing up my failure to live life through fake dolls and toys, and instead experience the world for myself."

"Okay Julia, just stop being so damn smart for a minute and listen to me. Some problems are not yours to fix. There are some things in this world you must live with, that you cannot perfect, and that you will never understand; and though you believe that knowing everything will allow you to live life to its fullest, knowledge is like anything else, too much is paralyzing."

I reflected a minute and was humbled. It suddenly struck me that Olli had lived in this world through the Great War and the death of his two best friends, among other things, in his thirty-five years of life. Although I had already experienced years of very intense pain, I forgot for a moment Olli's humanity. Olli's willingness to listen to an over-opinionated child amazed me most. How dare I treat this man as if he did not understand the world? That is when I said,

"Uncle Olli you are right. I would like to apologize for rushing to judgment on issues. Thank you for your advice. Good night."

"Good night Jules," he replied as if in a state of shock at my sudden change of attitude.

As I walked to my bedroom I yelled out,

"I love you Uncle Olli."

CHAPTER 7

I will never forget that date, September 16, 1935. That was the day I awoke to crying in our living room. A living room, which rarely saw guests, especially those expressing emotional agony. I reacted with terror and listened through my closed door. I refused to step into any situation in which I could not control, and certainly someone sobbing in our living room indicated a situation out of control.

Through the sounds of a woman sobbing with fear, I could hear Olli calmly trying to console a familiar voice. Within moments I made out the voice of Mrs. Spiro, the sweetest lady I had ever known. Unlike Ms. Gerg from the library who monitored my every move with concern, Mrs. Spiro and her family often encouraged my reading by giving me free books from their family owned bookstore on the street below our apartment building. I viewed Mrs. Spiro as the closest woman to my mother within my reach, though our conversations were often only educational. So the fear and anger that flourished out of her mouth terrified me.

"What has this world come to Olli?" she said while gasping for breath.

"I do not know Adara. The world seems to be closer to hell everyday, and the countries of the world, those that could do something about it, pretend it is not their problem."

"Will I ever be able to go home? Will I ever see my nieces and nephews again?"

"I'm sure you will Adara. This will all pass us by. They will only let Hitler go so far, and these Nuremburg Laws in Germany might just be the beginning of his inevitable self-ruin."

"I hope you are right Olli. You are the smartest person I know, and

I pray every day that you will always be a friend of my family, even though I know it is difficult to be a friend of a Jew right now."

"Don't be silly Adara, I am not as simple as some of our other neighbors, and even if I turned against you for some unseen reason, you had better believe that Julia will always stand up for you. She is a little dynamo when it comes to humanity. Sometimes I look at her and wish I could be more like her. She is so brave and only ten years old."

I suddenly started making noise in my room so that Olli and Mrs. Spiro would know I would soon be coming out to eat breakfast. I waited until I heard Mrs. Spiro gather herself and scoot toward the door before I pretended to drag myself toward the kitchen. As I made my way down the hall, Mrs. Spiro slid out the front door. I pretended to be ignorant of the odd situation that had just developed before my ears.

"Who was that Uncle Olli?"

"Oh that was just Mrs. Spiro. She wanted to discuss a book she had just read."

That was all Olli said to me for the rest of the morning. He handed me the breakfast he had conjured up from some local bakery. When I asked him what he had eaten, he said,

"I'm just not hungry this morning."

Then, in typical fashion, we strolled off to class for the day. I sat and counted the seconds until I could sneak off to the nearest paper stand and find out about these so-called "Nuremburg Laws" that had so frightened Mrs. Spiro. I wanted to know why she feared now, more than ever, for her family in Germany.

I had read Hitler's Mein Kampf, but really who in their right mind would believe the rubbish he put in that book? And who on this earth would ever help him enact a policy of racial superiority? As I read about the Nuremburg laws, my heart seemed to stop. How could intelligent people, who considered themselves civilized, believe that Jews were less than citizens? No wonder Mrs. Spiro panicked in our living room this morning; her relatives had just lost the status of citizen, not to mention the fact that she and her family were practicing Jews in what was becoming a scary Europe.

As soon as I grasped on the topic, I ran from the library, past Ms. Gerg, who was wondering where I was going in such a hurry, straight into the middle of one of Uncle Olli's lectures. I slammed open the door and yelled,

"We must protest Nuremburg!"

"Julia Josephine," Olli said in a frightened way as he ran toward me. He grabbed me by the shoulders and escorted me out into the hallway.

"Julia, we cannot talk about this here."

"I can say whatever I want," I replied.

"Not here you can't Julia. This is not the United States." He spoke in a tone I never heard him use, even when I used sarcasm to cover my feelings or intentions. For the first time I could remember in my young life, I was scared.

I turned around without uttering a word and headed straight home. I went into my bedroom, and without picking up a book, I took a nap. I was mentally exhausted, and I, Julia Josephine Patterson, for once in my life had no energy to think. I slept until Olli knocked on my door when he got home from the Hauptuni that afternoon.

"Julia?" he offered.

"Yes Uncle Olli?"

"Could I speak with you in the kitchen for just a moment?"

I popped open my door and Uncle Olli was already sitting at the kitchen counter waiting for me. I humbly sat in the chair next to him,

"Jules, I am so sorry for getting upset with you today. Sometimes I forgot that you are so young. However, we must not forget your ability to use words, and how powerful they can be in certain places and at certain times. I know that not too long ago I told you to use words rather than your fists, but we need to have a serious conversation about what is happening around us as we speak."

"Uncle Olli, I don't understand why you got so upset about me complaining about the Nuremburg Laws in Germany. I mean they are ridiculous. Hitler has lost his mind, if he ever had one, and I have the right to complain."

"It would seem so Julia, but we are living in a place and time when we cannot say what we believe is right and wrong. I know that is a horrible thing to believe or say, but for your safety, you must keep your political thoughts to yourself."

"What do you mean for my safety? Am I in danger?"

"You are such a smart girl, so for just a second think about something for me. Think about how close we are to Germany, and think about how the Germans just took away the rights of every Jewish person. Julia, my fear is that they are also taking away the rights of anyone who speaks against their policies, and I do not want my god-daughter to fall victim to the hatred of others."

"I appreciate your concern Uncle Olli, but I want you to think about something for me. I want you to think about my namesake. My father endowed me with the name Julia Josephine Patterson after the Great War General John Joseph Pershing, and I will not let my father or General Pershing down. If not me, then who Uncle Olli? No offense, but obviously not you."

Uncle Olli put his head down as if I had just stabbed him in the back and he said,

"Julia, I think you misunderstand me. There are other means besides words and fighting. You are smart enough to know that, and I know you are smart enough to know that you cannot help the world if you are dead or in prison. Make me a promise Julia?"

"Anything Uncle Olli."

"Promise me you will not do anything to hurt yourself."

"I love you Uncle Olli," I replied.

CHAPTER 8

In my eleventh year of life, Uncle Olli's life continued to be the epitome of predictability. He went to work, always with me of course, gave the same lectures on human geography, came home with dinner, and then schooled me on whatever eleven year olds were supposed to know. He had a few dates here and there, for the first time since I had come to live with him. I was happy for him, because I felt like I held him back from enjoying the opposite sex. I occasionally found letters in the mail from Maria, the only woman he ever really talked about from his years in Paris. It was the first time I realized that he even still talked with her and checked in on her son Patrick, who he cared so much about in Paris. It made me happy to know that I was not the only piece of his past left.

My eleventh year also consisted of the takeover of Ethiopia by Mussolini and a Spanish Civil War. Olli did not like to talk about the current state of affairs, so I would sometimes go down to the bookstore and talk to Mrs. Spiro. I learned to play off of her fears as a Jew to get her to talk about world affairs. I think she looked at me like I was the only person in the world who was willing to talk about the tragedy happening in Europe, and she desperately needed someone with whom she could share her fears. My heart truly ached for her.

Also in my eleventh year of life, Olli decided I needed to learn to "socialize" with some other kids my own physical age, though mentally I must say they were lacking. All of the local parents around Hauptuni knew Olli, and he had a reputation as an excellent teacher and educator. So when Olli decided to advertise his intentions of adding a student to my class of one, the parents of the boy I referred to previously as the bloody nosed idiot, since the day he called me an ugly orphan, became Olli's newest student. When I received this new information, I of course protested.

"Uncle Olli, you sold me out!"

"Julia, I picked him, because learning to get along with your enemies will make you a better person. NOW that is a lesson you need as an eleven year old that you don't already have."

I calmly replied to him as if I was his mother,

"I'm disappointed with you Uncle Olli."

Uncle Olli just smiled, and said,

"Jules, your parents would be so proud of you. You are a loner like your mother and a firecracker like your father. God how I miss them."

Thus began the torment of my youth-his name was Ari Prock. When Ari walked in for his first lesson, he immediately came toward me and said,

"Julia, I am sorry I said that ugly comment to you last year. I was just always jealous at how your Uncle let you walk around the University."

"Well your actions will have to prove you mean your apology; that you are not just throwing out rehearsed words your mommy taught you Mr. Prock," I replied.

Just then Olli walked in the room smiling,

"Ready to begin" he asked.

Ari, the little suck-up smiled and nodded. I simply did not respond.

From that moment forward Ari came to our apartment every day, as Olli taught him long division, how to write fiction stories, proper grammar, a very general and politically correct European history, and about weather, the earth, and the planets. My job was to simply be nice to Ari, while Olli provided me with constant critical thinking situations to analyze and lots of science work. Fortunately, I inherited my father's math skills, and I had a natural passion for history and writing, but I despised science. So after my lessons on analyzing and writing, there always followed a science lesson, which Ari and I both learned together, because in that area we were at the same level. In all actuality, Ari was my superior in science, though I would never admit that to him.

Ari and I fought over everything.

"Julia, why don't you lighten up a little," he would say.

In which I would respond with some sarcastic slap to the face. We never exchanged words in front of Olli, at least not on purpose. Of course there were times when I was so indulged in my own lexicon and wit that I never saw or heard Olli walk into the room. Ari sat in wait of these moments as if it was Christmas Eve and he was waiting for Ole Saint Nick to come down the chimney.

Olli would always look at me with irritation, and before he could start defending Ari, I would simply say with a grin,

"Words Uncle Olli not fists."

Of course he appeared frustrated on the outside, but I knew he was smiling on the inside. Olli lived for those moments where, if only for a matter of seconds, he could pretend my father and mother were speaking to him through my witty repertoire. Ari never stood a chance for a fair defense when it came to my emerging sarcasm.

CHAPTER 9

"How about that Jesse Owens," I asked Olli in his office at Hauptuni. "It's a shame though that it had to be a black man representing the United States in Berlin," I continued. Uncle Olli turned and looked at me, and for the first and only time in my life, I saw true disappointment emerge on Olli's face. He simply looked me straight in the eyes, and said,

"Julia Josephine Patterson I would like for you to leave my office now, go home and stay in your room until I get home. I'll make sure Ari's lessons are cancelled today, because, for once in your life, your wit will not help you escape from what we have to talk about. Now go and don't stop at the library!"

"But Uncle Olli, I love you," I replied.

"Go Julia, I can't look at you right now."

I humbly listened and walked out the door holding back my tears. I kept telling myself that Julia Josephine Patterson does not cry, that I was disappointing Father, Mother, and General Pershing. I could not be weak. I had to be strong. I did not know what I said to Uncle Olli to have him look at me that way, but I would make sure he never looked at me with such contempt again. What had I done?

I could not hold back anymore, and as soon as I entered the apartment out of the public eye, I broke down completely. I dragged myself to my room and fell on the bed. My mind was utter chaos and the tears soaked my pillow for the first time in the history of my Austrian existence. After obsessing over and replaying the situation in my mind, I fell asleep; and when I woke up four hours later, Uncle Olli was still not home. I began to worry about him. Did he hate me? Was I a disappointment? Was he avoiding me? Was he tired of me?

I did not know what to do so I sat in my room, just as instructed, obsessing about every word that had come forth out of my mouth. To pass the time, I did what I always did to relieve unwanted thoughts, I started to recite the United States Constitution in my mind, which I memorized out of respect for my dead father who I'm sure looked down on me each time I said those magic words, with pride emerging from his patriotic heart. I started with "We the people..." and by the time I got to Article 2 of the Constitution, I heard the front door open. Those ten seconds before Olli called my name seemed like an eternity.

"Julia Josephine Patterson, could you please come out to the counter please? We need to have a talk."

I nervously sat down at the counter having not looked up since I exited my room.

"First of all let me say, I love you so much. You are my daughter, and nothing you could do or say, for that matter, could ever change that."

I took in a deep breath of relief. Five minutes ago, my eleven-year old brain thought that Olli had given up on his hopeless orphan.

He continued,

"Julia, once again I conveniently forgot today that my genius god-daughter is only eleven years old. Regardless of that fact, I know that I can have a serious and educated conversation with you, which at this moment in time, I realize has become necessary. I need you to put aside the sarcastic banter for just one conversation today. Can you do that?"

"Yes, Uncle Olli, I certainly can and will," I replied holding back a new flood of tears. I was glad that he was doing all of the talking, and that I simply had to listen, because at the moment, for the first time in my life, I don't think I could have talked to Olli without bawling.

"You see Julia, I know that you are a product of your environment, as we all are. I'm afraid, however, that has created a mass of confusion for you. Very few people in this world are lucky enough to be the daughter of an American hero and a Russian turned French nurse, the god-daughter of a Swiss turned Austrian professor, and already a native of two countries, speaking multiple languages. You have seen so many great things Julia, and at the same time you have experienced way too much tragedy. I often feel for you, having to live with a single professor in a foreign country, with no mother figure."

"But Uncle Olli," I broke in.

"No Julia, please let me finish, you cannot deny the truth, and I have come to accept certain things in this world. Today you made a comment that I never thought would emerge from the lips of someone so dedicated to justice in the world." He fumbled his hands and continued, "Julia, you cannot choose which causes you will stand up for and which causes you will ignore if you are to truly be a voice of truth in this world. You have such good instincts about integrity and honesty, that it actually shocked me to hear you make the comments you released today about Jesse Owens."

In my mind, all of a sudden I understood why Olli had gotten so upset. What an ignorant statement I had made earlier. What was I thinking? I never considered that my comment against a black man was unjust. Wasn't that what everyone in the United States was thinking? I remember hearing comments like that all of the time when I lived there, and they often received a snicker or an outburst of laughter. At that moment, I realized for the first time, that the remark I made was equal to that of a Nazi making a comment about a Jew. How could I have said that after talking about discrimination everyday with Mrs. Spiro? I hated myself, and in my mind I started reciting the United States Constitution again, until I reentered reality and realized that Uncle Olli was still talking.

"Julia, what makes you better than him? Your skin color? And what makes you think you are better than Ari Prock? Your intelligence? If you want to make General Pershing, your mother, and your father as proud of you as I am, then you need to realize we are all human beings, and that you simply have an amazing gift given to you by God, which I'm sure was granted to you, because, no doubt, you will be in a position to change the world one day. Just make sure you change it for the better Julia Josephine Pershing."

Olli then caught himself, and said,

"I meant to say Julia Josephine Patterson. But let's stop and think about General Pershing and what you can learn from him today. I am certain you know that his nickname is 'Black Jack', but obviously you have no idea why."

Olli took a deep breath and continued,

"Early in his career, Pershing led a unit of black Buffalo soldiers in Montana against the Plains Indians. He gained the name 'Black Jack' because of this assignment, but also because he fought for blacks to be allowed in combat positions rather than just being cooks and servants. Julia, Pershing would have been ashamed of your comment today. I am not trying to be hurtful or ugly, but I know that when you look back on today in fifty years, you will be disappointed in yourself. Like all great generals, you must do what is right for people and you must learn to ignore stereotypes. I have faith that you will find the right balance.

"Now give me a hug and let's eat." I wrapped my arms around him tighter than ever. He continued, "I love you Jules, and I have something I would like you to read before you go to bed."

As he handed me another old letter, I simply replied,
"I love you Uncle Olli."

Dearest Leeana,

I have written this to you, knowing that you will find it on your train ride to a better future. I am so happy for you as you begin your journey; a journey into the unknown. I have no doubt in my heart that you will hit some bumps in the road, but that in the end you will have nothing but success and happiness. Your mother and I have wanted nothing else for you, but to find a place in this world of peace and a place in your heart of calm. I will pray for you daily, and I will write to you weekly in France. Remember to keep your head down, work hard, and live life in the moment instead of letting the world slip by. Most of all, you must never forget from where you have come. You were born into a society that has attempted to ruin your identity, to take away your person, to demoralize you into believing that you hold nothing special, nothing worth saving, accept for a warm body that can be wasted when the country needs you most and when you need your country the least.

You will encounter many people in your life Leeana, some good, some bad, some smart, and some stupid, but no matter whom you meet, you must remember one thing: We are all in this thing called life, together. Do not judge others, because you know what it is like to be judged. Do not stereotype those you meet, because you are stereotyped as a Russian. Every human being has characteristics that cannot be changed, whether that is height, wealth, race, disease, one's parents, or country of birth. Leeana I trust you to never treat people how you so often have found yourself treated in a society tearing itself apart with a smile. Be ahead of your time, and give every person you encounter a chance. Change the world one person at a time.

Your mother and I love you so much, and we hang our hopes and dreams not on our own lives, but simply on the life of our eldest daughter.

Love Always,
Papa
February 1, 1919

After reading the letter from my grandfather to my mother I felt even worse about my short lapse of judgment. I corrected that, however, by saying the Constitution to myself a couple times, and within an hour or two I pushed the guilt out of my mind, at least enough for the night. As I sat in peace on the porch, for the first time that day since I had been in Olli's office that morning, another concern popped into my mind. Was my grandfather telling me to be nice to that Austrian jerk, Ari Prock? I didn't hate him because of his race, looks, or disabilities. I hated Ari, because he had the genetic flaw of simply being an asshole. Certainly Grandfather could not blame me for such a just cause.

CHAPTER 10

"Ms. Gerg, here is my list for today. It is pretty short, only books on the development of poison gas in warfare," I said as I walked into the library. A few moments later she approached me with her typical half smile, half concerned look as she handed me my books in my usual cubby.

In reality I could not care less about poison gas, but it always spiced up my boring life to mess with Ms. Gerg at least once a week. I would gradually act normal around her, and just when I believed she saw me as a typically innocent child, I would ask her for a topic that made her question my sanity. Occasionally Uncle Olli would get a call from her, and I would smile slyly from across the room as he stared me down while talking to Ms. Gerg about her concerns for my unusual interests. Olli pretended to be aggravated, but in his heart I knew he was amused by my playful antics.

On this particular day, I had other things on my mind that I wanted to use my precious library time before I had to go home to the dreadful Mr. Prock. Simply put: my father. I dreamt about him for the very first time since he passed away. I wanted to take the time to think about the eight years I had with him, because I honestly avoided the topic mentally; it had been far too painful. I believed that if I could get everything out or purge all of my thoughts and memories, that the pain would never bother me again.

After two hours of frustration in trying to remember exact details, I felt farther away from the truth than when I started. I decided that the best way to remember without analyzing every single detail would be to write my dead father a letter.

Dear Daddy,

I'm twelve now, and I am starting to think about our short time together. I want to release all of our memories together, not memories of your existence, but memories of your pain. Don't get me wrong, I have plenty of images of you that make my heart flutter, that give me strength during the tough times, and that make me smile, but there are also memories that are too hard to keep. Daddy forgive me for forgetting these things after today, but I have chosen to remember you as the strong man you wanted to be, rather than the heartbroken man life made you. So here is a list of all of the things, I no longer wish to remember:

Hearing you cry through the walls of my bedroom

Drinking yourself to death

Blocking out everyone in your life who wanted to help you

Making people feel sorry for me, because you were either working or drunk

Watching you hide every picture of my mother

When you spilt coffee all of yourself in front of my classmates at school

When you told our neighbors to piss off

How you conveniently forgot to tell me that your liver was dying

When you got fired for going to work drunk

When you told me to forget my mother, because knowing her caused too much pain

Leaving me before your time

Daddy I will always love you, and nothing you have ever done will take away the fact that you cared for me with all of your heart, that you always looked out for my best interests, that you never hurt me, and that you always treated me like your baby girl. No matter the circumstances or pain we were experiencing, you took care of me. I want to remember you as the strong, controlled, brilliant engineer that you were for most of your life; the man who always picked me up from school with a treat in his hands, who took me on walks and out to dinner telling me how to succeed in the world, who read me to sleep at night, and who sat up with me all night when I was sick or had a bad dream. Daddy, I'm letting the bad go as of this moment, and I'm keeping you how I want.

This is the last I will think of these things above. I'll never look at them again. I am releasing them, and they will never again enter my mind. That is the last time I'm going to think about, don't think about it again Julia, that is the last time. That is it.

JJP

October 28, 1937

I said the Constitution in mind a couple times to change the direction of my thoughts; I picked up my things and walked out of the library. My brain needed some rest.

I headed in the typical direction of Olli's office, because his first class of the day was due to begin in about thirty minutes. As I walked across the University grounds from the library, I ran into one of Olli's morning students, who informed me that Professor Zingre had posted a note on his office door explaining that class would be cancelled for the rest of the week. Of course this conversation peaked my curiosity, because Olli never changed his schedule. The last time he cancelled class, he sailed across the ocean to pick up his orphaned goddaughter.

The first thought that entered my mind involved Ari. Would the bane of my existence be at the apartment, making it more difficult for me to inquire into the truth behind Olli's true intentions for canceling class? How would I get rid of him? Then I began to worry about Olli. Was he okay?

Had someone died? By the time all of these thoughts flashed through my constantly running mind, I caught myself running, and before I could slow down I was home.

I took a deep breath and entered the apartment, and before I could eke out a word I saw two suitcases leaning up against the counter, my jacket laying across the suitcases, and a book on poison gas.

"Relax Julia, I'll explain everything," Olli said the moment he saw a panicked look on my face. He continued, "We'll have plenty of time to talk about everything on the train to Paris."

Paris! I had no words to respond to Olli's sudden decisions. I walked with Olli to the train station in absolute silence, thinking of all of the possibilities that could explain this out of character move of my systematic godfather.

Olli handed me my boarding pass and we boarded the train. We had our own cabin, and as soon as we both sat down Olli began,

"Julia, first let me apologize for the rushed confusion. Something came up this morning, and I had to make some quick decisions. A friend from the past sent a telegram asking for a favor, and I obliged."

Olli paused, waiting for some type of response or reaction from me, but I had nothing to give yet. Surprised, Olli continued,

"My friend Maria, from my days in Paris, found a book I have been looking for in a used bookstore. She knows that I have been looking in every bookstore in Europe for this particular book for the past twenty years, and she has finally stumbled across it for me. Not to mention, it will be a great experience for you to see Paris for yourself, rather than through some book."

I immediately knew that Olli was full of shit. How on earth could he be canceling classes for the first time in his life, dragging his twelve-year old goddaughter across Europe, preparing for a trip in less than the three hours I was in the library that morning, and pulling himself out of the routine he participated in 365 days a year, for a book? Couldn't books be mailed? It was at that moment that I realized that the Maria Olli randomly brought up and wrote letters to was more than just a friend--he loved her.

Olli continued,

"It will be a good trip anyway. I haven't seen Maria's son Patrick since he was about twelve years old. Gee, he's sixteen now. Anyway, enough on that. So there is your explanation. See there is no emergency, just a favor an old friend did for me, and I owe her the respect of going to get this item in person."

Olli stopped and looked at me waiting for a response, an acknowledgement that I agreed with him, that this whole sudden event was not completely odd. I did that the best way I knew possible. I asked,

"So Uncle Olli, why the book on poison gas?"

Olli smiled and the tension in the train car subsided back to normal as he replied,

"I conveniently asked Ms. Gerg what your reading interests have been of late, and so here is an intriguing book I selected just for you."

I could see in his face that he was smug with himself, because he had found a way to get me back for tormenting Ms. Gerg by bringing a book I pretended to be interested in, which in reality I had no use for whatsoever. At that moment I realized that Olli was quite the little smart ass himself. I could also tell, that for the first time in my life with Olli, he was gleaming with happiness on his face.

We left Vienna at 1:15 p.m., and we arrived in Paris in the middle of the night, sometime around 3:00 a.m. I couldn't tell exactly, because I had been in and out of the phases of sleep since 9:00 p.m. or so. Olli, however, seemed as alert as ever when he tried to wake me at the train station. I ignored him, due to the exhausting circumstances of the day.

At least going to France would give me the opportunity to use the French Olli taught me daily. I could also add France as the third country I had visited in my young life. The best part would be enjoying my existence once again without Ari Prock, if only for a week.

I vaguely remember Olli carrying me off the train, and then handing me over to someone else. The next thing I knew, I was waking up in a strange room with twin beds. I could hear people talking in the next room, and I could hear noise outside of the building. I got my bearings and bounced out into the next room still in my clothes from the day before. Olli looked at me with a smile, and before I could utter any semblance of words, he said,

"Julia Josephine Patterson, I would like for you to meet Maria Bellew, a dear friend of mine and of your parents."

I smiled cordially, and as I was about to give some proper introduction and babble about nice to meet you, wow what a wonderful place, etc., etc. etc. Maria interrupted my train of thought, not yet been vocalized, to say,

"Olli Zingre, my God how much she looks like Jacob and Leeana at the same time. It is like seeing two ghosts from the past."

Olli smiled with a sense of pride on his face. His facial expression made me realize just how much I really was his daughter now.

"I'll have to take your word for it Ms. Bellew, because it has been four years since my father drank himself to death, and of course I have no memory of my mother. I guess I look like their fading pictures that seem to hold less meaning every day," I started when Olli chimed in,

"Maria you will have to excuse Julia, she is just..." when Maria cut in and whispered,

"As blunt as her father and as witty as her mother. Gosh how I miss

48

them. And by the way, please call me Maria."

Maria saw right through me, and I loved it. I felt as if she had known me my entire life, though we only met five minutes before. I realized just how much I had turned into my parents, and I was proud. Olli and Maria continued conversing as I sat at the table in awe of Olli's different personality, which I would later learn, only emerged around Maria. I sat wondering if this jubilant, excited man had existed around my parents as well, when a young man walked in through the front door of the apartment.

I sat in awe of the handsome creature walking through the door with a loaf of bread under his muscular arm. He looked like the perfect specimen of a human being. His face was chiseled and friendly, he was tall, and he walked with an air of confidence. He had a gorgeous smile with perfect white teeth. He put the squirmy Ari Prock to shame. I sat analyzing this new person entering the picture when Maria proudly said,

"Patrick, I would like for you to officially meet my friend, Julia Josephine Patterson. She is Jacob and Leeana's daughter, my old friends from Paris that I so often talk about."

Patrick, still smiling, replied,

"The infamous Julia, we finally meet." He took a bow and kissed my hand. "I feel like I already know everything about you from Olli's letters to Mom. Oh yes, and last night when I was carrying you from the train station to the apartment and you told me to put you down or you would kill me, I felt like I couldn't wait to talk to you when you were conscious. I bet you are full of surprises, aren't you?"

I asked myself-Just how often does Olli write Maria?

Patrick continued, "I have big plans for you while you are here. Olli has left your care in my hands, and I intend for you to experience every piece of history and art which makes Paris the most beautiful city in the

World. Stick with me kid, and you will have the time of your life; that is if you don't kill me first," he said as he tossed a wink in my direction.

Wow, he is charming too, I thought to myself.

"You know I vaguely remember your parents," Patrick said to me as we walked toward the Louvre.

"I was pretty young when they moved to the United States, but your father gave me my first baseball glove as his parting present, and then your mother argued that I needed something more educational. Your father whispered to me that there was nothing more educational. I just remember them being so kind and warm. Your parents, Olli, my mom, and me were the closest thing to a family I have ever had."

I wanted to pretend I didn't care as we walked along the cobblestone streets of Paris. As we passed cafes and small shops bustling with business, as people were flying by me on bicycles and talking in the most beautiful language in the world, as I viewed France in the daylight for the very first time in my life, all I could think of was how lucky Patrick was to have had a moment with my father at the peak of his life. Lost in my thoughts like usual, Patrick chimed in,

"He was my hero as a child. I saw him as the epitome of American independence. He had the war experience, the beautiful woman on his arm, and the looks of a real ladies man. But I guess you know all about that, don't you?"

I didn't dare want to disturb the immaculate image my father held in Patrick's mind, so I lied,

"Yep, that sounds just like the father I remember."

I knew it was odd that a little girl was striving to preserve the innocence of a sixteen-year old boy, but I assured myself that General

Pershing would have done the same. He would have preserved Patrick's faith, because that is what makes good soldiers, what maintains loyalty.

By the time I convinced myself that saving Patrick's memories had been the right thing, we were entering the Louvre. I was so enthralled by Patrick's hypnotic and vibrant personality, that I forgot to even look at the art. I had waited almost my entire life for this moment, when I stood in the graces of Da Vinci among others, but my priorities had amazingly changed in the past hour. All I could think of was digging through Patrick's vague memories of my parents. I had not yet realized that Olli had just as many memories, if not more, and yet I had never thought of asking him. What made Patrick different? It must have been his age or his innocence, which produced the ideal image of my parents, completely unflawed, just how I wanted to remember them.

"Isn't it beautiful?" Patrick asked as we stood in front of a timeless masterpiece. I could not answer him, and he looked at me with concern. "Are you okay Julia?"

I dropped to my knees and kept telling myself to breathe. As my heart pounded, Patrick scooped me up in his strong yet young arms and carried me outside, saying along the way,

"You are fine, just breathe. We will be outside in the fresh air and you will be fine. Just relax sweetie, just relax. You are okay, and you will be back to normal in a moment. I'm not going anywhere."

Patrick kept repeating words like these over and over again to comfort me, and by the time we were seated on a bench in a park about a block outside of the Louvre, I had retreated out of my very first panic attack.

After about five minutes of Patrick rubbing my back and repeating reassuring words, I said,

"I'm okay, and I'm so sorry to ruin your day. I have no idea what just happened. I was really enjoying myself and then I caught a whiff of something that I am sure I will never be able to forget for the rest of my life. Please don't tell Olli about this. He will worry needlessly, thinking that he has permanently disturbed my tender environment by bringing me across Europe, when that couldn't be farther from the truth. There has just been so much excitement in the past couple days on top of the memories that have been brought back. I am so sorry, I promise I will be fine."

Patrick looked at me and winked. Then he said,

"It will be our little secret. But you must tell me something."

"Anything," I replied.

"What smell brought on this rush of emotions and panic?"

I simply replied,

"I know it makes no sense, since I never really knew her, but Paris smells like my mother."

That day with Patrick would go down as one of the best days of my life, at least for the days of my life spent outside of the library. I barely even thought about Ms. Gerg and the library that day.

After leaving the park we stopped and bought lunch at a vendor on the street a couple blocks away from the Louvre. For the first time, I saw Paris. I stopped to look at the buildings lining the narrow streets, the French architecture, and I gladly uttered every word in French that day, even as Patrick and I ordered baguettes.

I felt so comfortable with myself and at peace for the first time in a long time, as the Paris breeze blew through my hair and as Patrick carried my tiny little frame on his back from place to place. He took me to the place he lived as a child, and to the location of the apartment my mother worked in as a nurse. He took me by the restaurant my parents went to on their first date, and to the park where he, his mother, Olli, and my parents had a picnic when he was four years old. The most enjoyable part of the journey, however, was when Patrick carried me into the old bookstore, which had been my mother's favorite place in Paris; where she spent hours combing through used books, picking out the perfect piece of authorship she would read next. It was in that place that I felt like I had found home.

Patrick just sat and talked to the storeowner about the weather, art, jazz, architecture, and anything else he could think of to keep himself occupied. He never once rushed me. He just sat there talking calmly and courteously until he crept up behind me and tapped me on the shoulder saying,

"Julia, we can always come back tomorrow, but we must begin to head home. Olli and my mother will start to worry now that the sun is going down."

I nodded my head in agreement as Patrick knelt down so I could take my last ride on his back for the day. Thank goodness I weighed hardly anything for a twelve year old. When we walked outside I saw that we had been in that little bookshop for almost two hours. Poor Patrick, I thought to myself, but the smile he started the day with never left him.

"Hold on Julia, it will be about twenty five minutes before we get home. We are a couple miles from where we started."

I put my head on his shoulder and just watched the people and the places stride by as we headed toward Maria's apartment. Nothing in the world could have felt better, when I heard,

"Boy she sure is tuckered out isn't she? What did you do to her Patrick?"

"I showed her Paris. That is a lot for a little girl."

I then recognized Olli's voice saying,

"You will learn soon enough that Julia is no ordinary little girl."

As I raised my head, trying to figure out what had happened, I realized I was once again waking up in Maria's apartment.

"Did you have a good day Julia?" Olli asked.

With an uncontrollable grin on my face as Patrick put me down off of his back, I said,

"The best Uncle Olli, the best."

As I walked toward my bedroom and my twin bed I heard Olli whisper to Maria and Patrick,

"I had better go tuck her in, she has been through a lot in the past two days. Did she give you any problems Patrick? She hasn't had much experience being out and about with new people"

Patrick responded,

"No, I had a great time myself. I'm not sure if I taught her anything or if she taught me everything."

That is when Olli said,

"I don't think I have ever seen her smile like she just did. Thank you Patrick, she needed it."

Then Olli entered my room and said,

"Goodnight Jules, I am so glad you are here to experience Paris for yourself. Your father, mother, and General Pershing would be proud.

CHAPTER 11

Have you ever been to a place that entered your soul and refused to leave? Paris came to exist as that place for me. The fall of 1937 was the very first time I felt possessed by a place outside of a book. Yes, the pyramids in Giza, the Mayan ruins, and the Hindu temples all grasped me from pages of old stuffy books, but Paris, yes Paris was the first place which Julia could leave, but which would never leave Julia. For the rest of my life, I would have Paris and Paris would have me. No wonder my father never wanted to leave.

Patrick and I spent the rest of the week in Paris in a similar routine. Patrick went to school in the morning, while Olli and I visited the bookstore, which once held a tight grasp on my mother. We would stop for lunch at a different place every day, in tradition with Olli's compulsion to scavenger hunt for food. We would return to Maria's apartment by mid-afternoon, and I would take a nap every day for the week we were in Paris. It was the first time in my life that I could find enough calm to actually take naps. Maybe that was one reason why I loved Paris so much; I truly felt at peace.

After my newly found naptime, Maria returned from work at the shoe factory, and Patrick marched in the door with a game plan for the day. Patrick would take me to a museum or a park or even the library. He even found the time to escort me to the famous tomb of General Marquis de Lafayette. We took a picture replicating Pershing's first visit to Paris, and I stood exactly where Pershing stood twenty years before in honor of the French Revolutionary War General. Patrick would usually chime in with a history lesson or a culture explanation on some Parisian experience, and usually to his surprise, I would correct him or have more information to add.

It was as if we had turned into best friends and confidants within days. I had never been around someone like Patrick before. He was different. I honestly think that is why Patrick enjoyed spending time with a child so much, because I was different than any person he had ever met.

Who knows what Olli and Maria did while Patrick and I absorbed all of the energy of Paris. My guess is that they were reminiscing and catching up on old times, under the intoxication of the years they had spent apart. They always appeared calm and collected around me, but I had my suspicions that they acted like a couple of teenagers in love when they were alone.

When Patrick and I would return around sunset, Olli would be setting the table for Maria's cooking. It was the first time I ever saw Olli eat home-cooked food, rather than something he bought somewhere. I think he would have eaten raw meat or become a vegetarian if Maria asked him to. I don't think that Olli ever stopped smiling in Paris.

The week flew by, and when it was time to return home, a feeling of sadness overwhelmed me, which I had not felt since I left America. Olli's decision to suddenly jump on a train and travel across Europe had been one of the best experiences of my life, and I would forever be grateful for that week of joy.

When our time was up, Maria and Patrick walked us to the train station. I wanted to cry with all of my heart, but I refused to let General Pershing down by showing weakness. I held back my sadness, and promised Patrick that I would write about the adventures of my Austrian existence. Patrick handed me a package and told me not to open it until I was sitting at home in my favorite spot: the fire escape overlooking the cobblestone street of reality.

I hugged Maria and I gave her all of the common courtesies of a well-treated guest. In reality, however, I had spent very little time with Maria, and did not have as much to say to her as I'm sure swarmed through Olli's mind. I conveniently started onto the train begging Olli to let Patrick help me find our cabin, so that Olli and Maria could have a last private moment until the next time; whenever that might be.

Patrick helped me put my suitcase away, and we found my favorite stuffed monkey to place beside me on the seat. Patrick sat with me at about 8:30 p.m. as we waited for Olli to wander his way onto the train. We were due to depart at 9:00 p.m.

From the moment that Patrick sat down, I began obsessing that Olli would run late, so I kept checking out the cabin door to see if he was coming. Patrick could tell that my nerves were on end about being late, as my nerves were usually on end about something completely unimportant.

To get my mind off the time, Patrick kept kicking at my foot in a playful way, when he finally said,

"Julia please tell me what it will take to get you to relax and enjoy the company of your new found friend."

I simply responded,

"Well, we have two options. First of all, you are bound to know by now that a good conversation about some world topic will always keep my mind occupied. Or you can let me open this package now."

That is when Patrick shocked me and said,

"So Julia, where do you fit into this current European picture? Do you think you are at risk because you are a Russian-American combination? Or do you think that Hitler isn't interested in exterminating your kind of people? Do you think I am at risk, because I am a bastard? In other words Julia, how do you plan to change this world and make us both safer?"

I sat there staring into Patrick's eyes with astonishment. I was speechless. I had no idea that my new friend had such a political mind. I had spent hours in bookstores, libraries, and historical sites with him, yet I had no idea that he had any concern or realization of this world. I had been so arrogant around him, and he treated me like a princess. Words couldn't even explain how ignorant I felt. I immediately began obsessing about how Patrick might despise me for my disposition, or how he might think I am an over entitled child, or how he truly felt happy he was finally getting rid of this brat.

"The infamous Julia, speechless?" Patrick said with his classic smile.

I had been sitting there processing my thoughts, and in the process I had forgotten to respond. That's when I began,

"Patrick, I am so glad I met you. It is refreshing, though rare, when I meet someone who helps me remember that there are other people in this world. So let me tell you how I plan to change the world. I plan to change the world by…" and that is when Olli finally showed at the door.

"I hate to break up all of this brain power, but we are now a few moments from departure," Olli said.

Patrick stood up, shook Olli's hand and offered a few words, which I cannot remember due to the adrenaline of the moment. He then turned to me, patted my stuffed monkey on the head, and reached down and picked me up with a huge hug. He kissed me on the cheek and whispered in my ear,

"Remember Julia, don't open the package until you are home by yourself. And don't worry about my question, I have no doubt you will change the world. Just remember to find yourself first."

As Patrick turned and walked away, I fought the temptation to cry. Emotions ran all over me, emotions I had never felt before, or at least could not remember. I found myself dwelling in a pool of sorrow, of immediate loneliness, and emptiness. Now that I knew Patrick, how would

I go on without him? How would I be able to get back into my routine after the best week of my life? I realized that I would have to figure out a way to continue, because I could not let General Pershing down.

The train rolled out at 9:07 p.m., and Olli began to talk to me. About what, I have no idea, because I was already dozing off from exhaustion. I held my monkey in my right arm, and the package Patrick gave me sat on the seat beside me, which I kept my left hand on. When I woke up at 6:00 a.m. to go to the bathroom, Olli had obviously thrown a blanket over me at some point in the night, and was wide-awake staring out the window. I came back to my seat, still half-asleep, and slept all of the way until we reached the station in Vienna at 1:00 p.m.

Olli and I got off the train, got our things and began to walk home. I was still groggy and unable to think or even function properly. Olli carried all of my things, except of course for my very special package from Patrick.

On our walk back to the apartment, I began to wake up. I posed the question to Olli,

"How did you sleep? Hopefully you got as much rest as I did."

With a grin, Olli replied,

"I didn't sleep a wink. My body is still coping with all of the excitement of the trip. I haven't had that much fun in a long time. I see that you also seemed to have a wonderful time. That is a trip we will definitely have to make again soon."

I smiled and wondered why we had not made the trip before, and why Maria hesitated to ever make the trip herself. I saw Olli look at Maria the same way my father would look when he talked about my mother. For the first time, I envied that look and wished that someday a boy would look at me like that.

We picked up some food from the market on the way home, and

when we finally got home, we unpacked our things. Olli headed to his office at Hauptuni to play catch-up with preparing for the week's lessons. He told me not to wait up, that he was going to pull an all-nighter. I personally wondered when he planned sleep, but I didn't ask questions. I was more concerned about opening my gift from Patrick.

I waited until dark skies appeared once again. I wanted the moment to be perfect. It was as if I was setting up this moment as some historical marker; as if what I was opening was a piece of my own personal history, and it had to be perfect.

What book had Patrick found for me? It had to be a book, what else could he possibly give me? Would it be about the Parisian experience, children of single parents, or something fun, like how to make snow angels?

I walked out onto my perch in the sky and got absolutely comfortable. I wiggled around in my chair until things felt just right; until the atmosphere spoke to me, and all seemed right and at peace in the world. First the people on the street below faded out of existence, then the noise, and finally self-awareness disappeared. All that existed was the package wrapped in newspaper surrounding an old ragged box.

I slowly unwrapped the newspaper without tearing a piece. It was not as if I was trying to save the paper for another day, I just didn't have it in my heart to rip something Patrick had given me, something he had put his effort into. I folded the newspaper neatly and placed it under the box, which was yet to be opened.

Excitement, panic, joy, and sorrow ran over me all at once. I knew this gift would be amazing, but it was impossible that my book would live up to the expectations I placed on its head. How could any materialistic thing encapsulate the memories I had accumulated in the past week?

As I popped open the top of the old shoebox, I broke into tears. All of the emotions I had been holding inside from my Parisian experience began to flow and there was no stopping it. I found myself sobbing in tears of joy and sorrow. I felt like a big baby, but I didn't care. I couldn't stop. Inside the box lay no book. Instead, there existed a different kind of learning tool, one I severely needed. It was Patrick's worn and scruffy baseball glove, the one my father had given him right before moving to the United States. Inside that box existed a youthful, happy-go-lucky side of my father I had never known. There could be no better gift. That box held something more valuable than any book I had ever opened. Inside that box, I found a piece of me, a piece of my father, a piece of Patrick, and a piece of Paris. It seemed like I had found the beginning of Julia Josephine Patterson in one moment.

I carefully picked up the glove out of the box as if I was holding the lost scrolls of the library at Alexandria. I held it against my chest, as close to my heart as I could get, as the tears gently began to dissipate on my cheeks. As I began to fall back into reality, I pulled the glove away from my body and examined every inch. I lightly tugged on the strings, felt the leather fingers, sniffed the center, and then slipped my hand inside so that I could pound my hand into the mitt just like the Bronx Bombers Dad and I used to watch in New York.

Something inside the glove did not feel quite right, so I examined the inside closely. With my fingertips, I pulled out a folded-up piece of paper. Patrick had written me a note!

Dear Julia,

I must say, you completely lived up to the rumors I have heard about you for past four years or so of my life. My mother has talked about Olli's brilliant goddaughter since you moved to Austria, but I actually had to encounter you to absorb everything you had to offer. In other words, you did not disappoint.

If you ever need anything, anything at all, please just write me at our address in Paris. Julia, I feel like I have made an amazing friend that I can trust for the rest of my life. Therefore, I offer something to you that you must never share with anyone, even Olli. I know that is tough, but I trust and believe in you, that you will not let me down, because in my mind, you are someone General Pershing himself would trust. If you ever catch yourself in an EMERGENCY in this chaotic world and cannot find me, please find Soren Ambler in Paris and give him the key words 1,1,9,9,14,14,20,26. Julia, you must never give ANYONE this key word, you must never use it in conversation, and please pretend it does not exist. I do not seek to scare you, but I know that you understand the current situation in Europe, and in case you need life-saving help, I will be there for you, even if you cannot reach me directly.

Place this letter in a special place, where you will never forget it, but place the knowledge in the back of your mind. Do not seek this person, do not research the key word, do not even think about a situation where you would need to use Soren Ambler. This is just to insure you never find yourself without a friend in this crazy world.

Thank you for being a new friend in a lost world. Of all people it is you I would trust with my life.

Patrick Bellew
Paris, France
November 4, 1937

Patrick's letter struck a chord with me, a chord of reality. Up until I read those words, it escaped my attention that there might be real dangers in Europe, that real threats existed, and that I lived in the midst of all of the change. I had the knowledge of this reality, but the fear came to exist in me for the first time. Before I read Patrick's letter I still felt protected by the mighty American shield I had lived under in New York. Now, I was fully aware that I was stranded in a Europe where I wasn't immune, where the freedoms I had understood under my father's red, white, and blue flag, no longer embraced me.

I immediately sought to follow Patrick's directions. I had to find the perfect hiding place, where the letter would never be found without my command. My first thought, was to place it under my mattress, but what if Olli were to flip my mattress??? That would never work. My next thought was in my special keepsake box, where I kept pictures of my parents, the letters of my mother Olli gave me, and other trinkets. That would never work, because that is the exact spot a stranger would look for special codes and documents. I had to think like a General. I finally decided to place my newest most precious item in my most precious place in the world: the library at Hauptuni. I could think of no better place to hide a treasure than on the fifth floor of the library.

The next day I made my way to the library before heading to Olli's class. My cubby, which always remained reserved for me by Ms. Gerg and the other librarians, would be the perfect spot. I rarely, if ever, saw other students on the fifth floor. I figured out how to unscrew the front, left leg of my home away from home, and I slide the note inside. I put the bottom piece back onto the desk so it would not wobble or appear tampered with. I would be the only person who ever knew of the note's existence, except for Patrick of course.

I exited the library and walked to Olli's first class of the day. I had no idea how long Olli spent in his office the night before, after we got off the train. I was so absorbed and enthralled with theories behind my letter and the glove Patrick had given me that when we got home, I fell asleep with both items in my arms. I just couldn't let go of Paris yet. When I woke up that next morning breakfast was waiting for me on the counter, as always with a note from Olli saying he would see me in class.

As I entered Olli's class, I stopped thinking about myself for a moment and wondered why Olli had to go to the office to do work the night before. He taught the same material over and over again for years, and it never changed. I had listened to the same topics, and even given some of his lectures for four years straight. I knew he didn't have papers to grade, so why on earth would he have pulled an all-nighter at the office?

I thought over these questions as I sat in the back of the auditorium where Olli's first class was held. I cradled the baseball glove in my hands, playing with the strings and smelling the leather. I sat and analyzed this piece of my history. Chills ran all over my body as I thought of how my father and mother once touched this glove, and of all of the memories it held for Patrick. For a nerdy twelve-year old, it was like I had just found my security blanket, my version of every little girl's teddy bear.

Professor Zingre walked in the door with the look of pure exhaustion on his face, an exhaustion I had not seen since he lost my father and gained a goddaughter. We were at the point in the course where he explained ethnocentrism, and how all races and ethnicities were equal, just simply different. I always loved this lecture, because interesting stories about rituals from other countries always popped up, and each year he changed them purely to entertain me.

As I sat in the midst of this year's version of the same old lecture, I found myself immediately disappointed. Olli simply explained ethnocentrism with a textbook definition, gave no examples, and moved on to the next topic. The rest of his lecture continued with the same blandness.

Since when did he take the conservative viewpoint of the world? His lectures had always been filled with excitement, discussion, and controversy. I came to the conclusion that exhaustion from our trip had overtaken him to the point of just trying to get through the lecture. But why would he have spent all night changing his lecture into a barrage of boredom?

In the midst of Olli's lethargic lecture, I went back to focusing on my glove and thinking of the wonderful trip to Paris, thinking of how I hid my special letter, and thinking of what Patrick must be doing at that very moment. Lost in my thoughts, Olli's lecture ended and within fifteen minutes his second, and last class of the day began. Regardless, of the newer version of his lesson, I was completely entertained and overcome with a sense of warmth simply remembering every word, glance, discussion, and waking moment in Paris.

Olli and I walked home from the University together, and for the first time he saw my new gift.

"Where did you get that?" he asked me.

"Patrick gave it to me, he said it was a gift from my father. Do you remember it?"

"Of course, he got it on his birthday one year. That is very exciting Jules, and very nice of Patrick to let you have it. He must think a lot of you."

"Well I think of a lot of him," I said to Olli.

Olli just smiled, the first smile from his face since we returned to Vienna.

"I tell you what Jules, how about you and Ari get an education today in a little American baseball? I am completely exhausted, and really need to take a nap, so how about I let Ari borrow my old glove and you all spend the afternoon outside playing a little catch?"

Despite the use of the word "Ari", Olli's suggestion sounded great to me. I had been dying to use a baseball glove for the first time, and I could always pretend the baseball was Ari's head. If nothing else, I could throw the ball as hard as I could at him. I smiled to myself as we walked up to our apartment building where Ari waited against the wall outside.

We went inside the apartment building and sat down in the living room, while Olli searched diligently for a baseball glove, he apparently had not touched for years. As Ari and I sat waiting, Ari started talking to me about all of his friends from his old school, and about this girl he thought was pretty, and about his parents not letting him spend as much time walking around the University as his friends were allowed. In one way, Ari's chatter struck me as immature and boring, but in another way, I thought it must be nice to have friends one's own age, and to have boys think I was pretty. Oh well, God gave me brains, and that was better than anything I was missing out on at a regular school with regular kids.

When Olli finally found a glove and ball, Ari and I went outside and walked to one of the courtyards on the grounds of the University. Neither of us had ever used a baseball glove before, so it was quite a learning experience. It became obvious within a few minutes, however, that Ari and I both were naturally athletic.

For a few hours that afternoon, Ari and I lost ourselves in a pool of fun. Ari forgot about his popularity, his attractiveness, his annoying as hell charm, and I forgot about my hatred for his arrogance. I do believe that Ari himself forgot about my stiffness and cold nature. For once, I enjoyed being a kid with another kid. We didn't talk about other people or school, we simply laughed. Don't get me wrong, Ari still annoyed me in general, I still thought he was a bit of a jerk, and I never doubted his inferior intelligence, but it was fun to let loose from Julia Josephine Patterson for the day.

PART II: AWAKENING

CHAPTER 1

Do you remember that day in your life, where all meaning changed? For some Russians, it was the day the reds killed the last Czar, for some Americans it was the day Kennedy was assassinated, for some Germans it was the announcement of the Versailles Treaty, for some Japanese it was the dropping of the atomic bomb, and for me it was March 1938. It was then that the soul of humanity seemed to disappear from the face of the earth, or at least from my reality. Most children begin their teenage years with hope and joy, and I was no different. The hope and possibilities of the future overwhelmed me, and life seemed to be holding everything I could possibly want. I was completely unaware of my happiness and privileged childhood, until it gradually began to fade away in one brief moment.

1938 started out as any other year. Fear of German aggression subsided to some degree in my mind, although that was wishful thinking considering the German occupation of the Rhineland. Hope of Nazi failure seemed to be the only optimistic part of my existence, and for the most part it would be the end of all optimism in my body for years to come.

Red flags flew into the air indicating that peace in my world found itself ceasing to exist. Still filled with an American mentality of immunity from world danger, I refused to let myself believe that my world could suddenly change. The reality of a peaceful world seemed to be the only piece of innocence I had left, and I refused to let it go.

CHAPTER 2

My thirteenth birthday would mark the last act of normalcy in my life for a series of years. On January 30, 1938, I celebrated my entrance into young adulthood with a surprise birthday party orchestrated by Olli. The guest list included Mr. and Mrs. Spiro, Ms. Gerg, who was so bitter it was no surprise she came alone, Mr. and Mrs. Prock, Ari's older brother Stefan, and Ari himself, with his newest little girlfriend Zala. Amazingly everyone brought me a book as a gift except for Ari.

The Spiros gave me a book on the history of Vienna, which I had already read. Of course I said thank you with a smile. Ms. Gerg gave me a book of fairy tales. When I opened it, I told myself she had wishful thinking, but of course I politely gave a nod of appreciation. I could tell Olli was entering a state of panic about some sarcastic comment I might make, so I held it together. Olli gave me an empty book, with blank pages for my writing. His gift is what you are reading right now. Mr. and Mrs. Prock and the gorgeous Stefan, who looked nothing like Ari, gave me a series of science books. I guess Ari told them how horrible I was at science, which made me question how much he talked about me at home. The card on the outside read,

"Maybe this will be your last piece in knowing everything."

Maria and Patrick sent a package from Paris, which contained my mother's all-time favorite book, *My Antonia*, by Willa Cather. Although I had read it before, I was unaware it had been my mother's favorite book, so I planned to re-interpret the book with this new knowledge.

Lastly, I opened the present from Ari. Having no idea what on earth he would get me, or what his mother had picked out for him, I opened the box with a sense of excitement, and boy was I shocked to find a beautifully sewn white button-up blouse, just like the one Ari bled all over when I punched him for calling me an ugly orphan. Before I remembered that I was the center of attention at my own birthday party, I cracked a smile, and before I could cover it up by rolling my eyes, Ari shouted out,

"I saw that Julia."

Zala looked over at Ari and asked him what that meant, and he just smiled and shook his head. In that moment, Ari pissed me off like never before. It was the first time I didn't have a witty, smart-ass response for Ari, and of course I couldn't just yell at him in front of all the people at the party.

Later that evening I sat on the porch watching all of the college students below dancing on the sidewalk outside of one of the restaurants playing music. I sat and analyzed every moment of the party that day; every reaction I made, the gifts I received, the impressions people probably gained, reinforced, or changed about me. Just as I finished reciting the Constitution in my mind to clear my head from breaking down the day any farther, Olli walked out onto the tiny little spot in the sky with me.

"So Jules, how did you enjoy your surprise party?" Olli asked me.

"It was wonderful Uncle Olli. I had a great time, but did you really have to invite Ari? I mean his parents and Stefan, were fine, but really Uncle Olli, my nemesis?" I responded with a wink.

"So birthday girl, will you dance with me?" Olli said as he looked to the street below.

"Of course, Uncle Olli, anything for you," I responded.

I stood up, and Olli took my hand. We waited for the music to change, and a waltz came over the radio. I was incredibly athletic, but a horrible dancer, so Olli just smiled as he tried to teach me the steps, and as I stepped all over him. I always dreamt of having a dance with my daddy, and dancing with Olli was as close as I would ever come.

In life, we often find ourselves wishing away time, telling ourselves, I wish it were Christmas, I wish I was eighteen, I wish summer would come, I wish this project was over with, and before we know it, we have wished our lives away, always waiting for the next thing and never enjoying the moment at hand. Can human beings ever be happy? Or are we always searching for the next thing to come?

I would argue, that like my thirteenth birthday, there are moments where peace possesses the body like a spirit. These brief tastes of bliss are not something a person can plan or create, because these flashes choose you. It is within these seconds of altered consciousness that life feels like a warm blanket on a cold winter's day, like being able to breathe after a long cold, or like dancing with your godfather on your entrance into young adulthood. It is in these moments that we realize life is worth living. I could think of no better way to usher in my thirteenth year of life.

CHAPTER 3

"Julia come have a seat at the counter please," Olli yelled to me from the kitchen.

It was 5:30 a.m., and as I crawled my way toward the counter from my bed, Olli looked at me and said,

"You know Julia you could have taken a few minutes to get dressed, fix your hair, act like a girl that I have to push out of the bathroom in the morning."

"Uncle Olli, by now you should know that I am a bookworm, and I have embraced my destiny."

As Uncle Olli sat there trying not to smile, I knew something was wrong. Usually Olli saw my banter as amusing no matter the circumstances, but today was different, he was troubled. In my heart I unconsciously ached for him.

"Jules, we have had this same conversation a million times, but today is different, and I need you to understand that. I really need you to reflect Julia. You must listen to me and you must trust me."

After a brief pause, he continued,

"Julia, can I tell you something without you getting mad at me, without you getting frustrated, without you looking at me like I have no idea what I am talking about? Jules as brilliant as you are, please realize that at this moment in our lives, I have some experience that you do not, and because of that I need you to humble yourself. Can you do that?"

Needless to say, there was no witty response to such a remark first thing in the morning. Olli hit me in the core of my being humbling me before I even had the choice to do it myself. Olli pointed out my only weakness, my ability to use words as a weapon, and challenged me to contain my only defense. I was helpless, and I simply replied,

"Yes sir."

Olli dropped the morning's newspaper on the counter and simply said,

"Julia read it. Let me know when you are finished."

As I read the words on the paper beneath me, my eyes went blurry with disbelief. Austrian Chancellor Kurt Schuschnigg and Adolph Hitler had compromised on Austria's future. The agreement included that Schuschnigg would release all political prisoners, including Nazis, and would allow a political party system in Austria, in exchange for Hitler not initiating military action against Austria. It became clear to me within seconds as my eyes glanced through the article, that Austria stood as Hitler's next target for empire, and I was going to be a helpless bystander.

I looked up into Olli's beautiful and sad blue eyes, and to his request simply responded,

"I am finished Sir."

"Jules, please let me tell you a few things, and I would like for you to think about your responses before getting defensive."

"Yes Sir," I replied, biting my lower lip.

"First of all, let me say that this is the only time we will discuss these things until I give you further notice, which means you are going to have to trust me. Some things are going to start to appear strange, and I need you to know that I am only acting to protect you. I fear our world is on the brink of becoming unsafe, and if we are smart together, I believe we will be fine, but you must not question my decisions, you must be aware of your surroundings, and you must not immediately give in to your instincts."

In my mind and in my heart I instantly felt terrified. I wasn't scared, or worried, or afraid of monsters under my bed; I was terrified of a reality I could not control. The world seemed to fall apart, and I felt like the actions in the newspaper were revolving around me and I was standing on the outside looking in. How could I live in such pure fear?

"Julia are you listening?" Olli cut in.

"Yes Sir," I replied as I tried to refocus my attention to the moment rather than the future with my chest tightening.

Olli continued, "As you well know, it is likely that Austria will soon become a Nazi country either by choice or by force, and as of today it appears that our Chancellor is not going to be strong enough to stand up against Adolph Hitler. This means we are going to be living in a Fascist country, where there are no freedoms, where you can be sent off to some prison camp forever, where you have no rights protecting you from doing as you please. Julia, I know that is almost impossible for you, being that you are from the United States, but I am going to demand that you act like a German."

"What, you have got to be kidding me! Hell no I won't," I yelled out without even thinking.

As calmly as anything else that ever exited Olli's mouth he continued,

"Julia, please remember where we started this conversation. We started with trust, and I need us to go back there right now please."

"But..."

"Julia, from the bottom of my heart, I ask that you please let me finish."

"Yes, sir," I replied once again gritting my teeth and keeping my mouth shut only for my love and respect of Olli.

"Julia you surely know how Hitler and his Nazis work, and you know that dissent is not tolerated. You may not be aware that six professors have already been dismissed from the University, because they were labeled "too liberal."

As Olli spoke a light bulb went off in my mind. I suddenly synthesized why Olli's lectures had suddenly become the epitome of boring since our return from Paris.

Olli continued,

"Julia a long time ago, I swore with my life to your parents that I would protect you, and Julia that includes protecting you from yourself. I know that you have a being that lives inside that tiny little exterior of yours that is a beast, and not just any beast, but a fireball of humanity waiting to explode onto the scene of injustice. That is why we are having this little talk now. In the case that war comes to Austria, I must know that you will act normal, that you will speak German, that you will lift your right arm to Adolph Hitler, that you won't research things that could make you appear suspicious, that you will not rebel against the machine."

"Are you finished Uncle Olli?" I calmly responded.

"Almost Julia. I have just one more thing to remind you of. It is unsafe for us to discuss any of these things if Austria is subjected to Nazi rule, hence we are talking about these issues this morning while we still have time. Julia, we must blend in, we must appear as no threat or opposition, we must pretend to be one of them. Do you understand what is at risk?"

I took a deep breath and found a starting point in the millions of things I wanted to say.

"Uncle Olli, I love you, and I would never want to insult you, so please take no offense to what I have to say."

Olli held back a smile with all of his might, as he knew he could not give into me at such a precipice in our lives.

"You promise you won't get mad."

"I promise Jules."

So I started,

"Julia Josephine Patterson was brought into this world in 1925 for a purpose. As I'm sure you will agree as a God-fearing man, I have a specific destiny in this world, there is a path that God has planned for me. And there is no way in hell that I am going to stand by and watch the world go to hell in a hand basket at the hands of Adolph Hitler. I will not stand idly by and watch myself become an agent of the devil. I know that you want the best for me, I know that you don't want any harm to come to me, I know you love me, but with all due respect Uncle Olli, you can't control my soul, my conscience, the fact that I must live with myself for years after you are gone. Anyone who doesn't do what they believe in is a traitor to their own spirit, an accomplice to crimes against humanity. Do you understand what I am saying?"

Olli looked at me with a different intensity on his brow than usual and said,

"Julia, I think this is the time to talk about something, and I might hurt your feelings, but it is a reality, which you pretend you are prepared for, so here it goes." Olli paused and brushed his hair back out of his eyes and began,

"Of all the facts, information, and books you have memorized, you have forgotten to learn about the most important thing in this world— yourself. Not to be harsh Jules, but you are traitor to yourself by your own definition. You cover yourself with brilliance, by using big words to protect yourself against emotion, to make others feel inferior. I have never mentioned it before, because of all of the tough things you have seen in your thirteen years of life, but Jules you have a problem, the same problem your mother had until she met your father. Julia, your habitual studying, your compulsive routines, your refusal to associate with people your own age, your resistance to discussing anything that creates emotion in your body—You are already betraying your own soul, regardless of Hitler and the Nazis. Everything does not have to be perfect, and until you remember that little girl four year old girl that told your Daddy about your dreams, hopes, and wishes, then you are already a traitor."

"But Uncle Olli," I replied in shock. How could he have known these things about me, and even if he had known them, why was he just now confronting me? Did he know all of my insecurities, the constant recital of the Constitution in my mind, the fear of giving someone a wrong impression of me?

"Julia, now wait a minute, I am not quite finished. I need you to realize that until you find happiness in who you really are, until you let go of all of those things you try to make yourself, and just exist as Julia Josephine Patterson, you are in no shape to stand up for what you believe in. I understand that you are well aware of what is right and wrong in this world, and that we will clearly agree that Adolph Hitler is wrong. However, you will be unsuccessful in your fight unless you stop fighting with your own mind. We both know that the majority of your time is spent in obsessive thought. Let it go Julia, and your mind will be much clearer to help others."

Olli's comments made me quite defensive, so I responded with an angry tone,

"Well, I think I am ready, and you have no idea what goes on in my mind. I am everything I hope to be and I have the continual duty of living up to the standards of General John Joseph Pershing. I love me Uncle Olli, and I will do what is right."

"We will obviously never agree Jules, so let's come to a compromise. Regardless of your intelligence, you are still a teenager, and you are still under my rules and my protection. I am going to ask that you follow my advice and directions until you are twenty years old. This way, I will be charged with all of the responsibility for your soul, you can live guilt free, and I will know that you are safe."

With no thought I replied,

"Sixteen years old. I am advanced for my age, so I have no doubt that I can function as an adult a little before the rest of my peers."

"Well this is a compromise, so my final offer is eighteen Jules. Give me five more years, and then you will be free to throw yourself into the hands of reality.

"Agreed, but at eighteen, I will be allowed complete control over the battles I pick to fight, correct?"

"Yes Jules, at eighteen you can bark up any tree you want, but until then, it is my right to protect you. Let's just hope that Hitler is gone by then. Now give me a hug."

I reached over the counter and held Olli as tight as I ever had. I knew he loved me, and was trying to save my life, but internally something wouldn't let me save myself. In some ways, it was a later reflection of that conversation that made me realize that Olli's decision relieved a major burden. He demanded five more years of innocence for me, five years that I never would have given myself. He took the choice of life or death out of my hands and told me I didn't have a choice. Olli healed one of the greatest obsessions floating around in my mind and temporarily gave me peace.

I decided that night, that I would try to break some of my compulsive habits, some of the obsessing, but I couldn't. My mind seemed broken. My thoughts and instincts didn't match the bodily reaction my thoughts gave me. In my heart of hearts I knew the truth, but my mind just wouldn't let my worries go.

That night everything cycled away from my worries about the Nazis and mounting a resistance, back to Olli's impression of me. Did he think I was crazy? Did he think I was arrogant? Did he love me? Did he hate me? After rationalizing each one of these questions, I said the Constitution in my mind until it felt right—exactly three times.

CHAPTER 4

Olli and I gradually turned into good little Austrian conservatives, or at least silent liberals. I became much less political in my reading and studying focusing my time on science books and teaching myself Russian in my special cubicle, as I figured such a time of limitation would be a great opportunity to make myself intellectually diverse. As for everything else, life stayed the same with visits to the Spiros' bookshop, my daily routine to the library and then on to Olli's now boring lectures, a walk home to our apartment in Alsergrund, and then lessons beginning in the afternoon with Ari. Of course Olli's lessons and selections were suddenly pro-German, and every time I had an urge to correct him, I could see in his eyes the existence of our agreement, the torment he carried for both of us.

Ari stayed the same through my incredibly tough transition. He came every day and studied his lessons, harassed me about my stiffness, talked about whomever his girlfriend was for the week, if you could even call them girlfriends, and maintained his careless and arrogant attitude, what I came to simply call "Ariness." That phrase would come to drive Ari crazy. Whenever Olli would make a mistake, I would just look at him and Ari and say,

"That's just your Ariness coming out," much to the dismay of Ari himself.

Olli would look at me with contempt, give me some lecture about treating Ari with respect later, and we would play the whole thing over again. I figured putting up with Ari for so many years deserved some type of amusement value.

Although life seemed pretty much the same, things around us changed beneath our feet. Vienna had become a magic carpet sliding out from underneath us without our awareness. More and more university professors lost their jobs as Olli's lectures became more and more conservative. Major political opponents, including outspoken supporters of Schuschnigg began to slowly dissipate from society, so slowly that no one really even noticed...

...But it was on March 12, 1938 that I came to understand the implications of every tiny little action I made. My father's words came back to me, and I really began to understand what he meant when he said that every action, look, or wink had a deeper meaning. One wrong turn for me could end my young life, and I would not have even had the chance to make an impact on the world.

It was on March 12, 1938 that I came to understand the quote made by the famous major league baseball player turned American Evangelist Billy Sunday in 1917 when he said, "If hell could be turned upside down, you would find stamped on its bottom, 'Made in Germany!'"

It was on March 12, 1938 that I ignorantly came to believe based on my sensory observations that everything made in Germany possessed evil qualities. I conveniently forgot the role the United States played after World War I in creating a people of hatred, lost pride, and revenge, dying to be acknowledged as fellow inhabitants of this world.

It was on March 12, 1938 that I questioned the sanity of not only the world, but of myself. What should a person do when the entire world seems to have gone crazy, and crazy becomes the norm; and you, the one soul who has a conscience, seem to be the crazy one? Questions come to exist about the nature of reality. Is anything normal? Do humans setup the system of normal, and if they do, are genocide and cruelty normal? Maybe the nature of man was evil...maybe I was the one who was wrong.

It was on March 12, 1938 that I had another of many panic attacks to come, because it was on that date that I felt like everyone else could live in the world but me. I felt like the entire world kept turning and people kept acting like people, yet I was stuck on the outside looking in. I felt like I was lost in a place that I could not escape, because I had no idea where the hell I was. Like all moments or hours of panic, it passes, and you remember your exact bearings in this world, and you feel completely lost in how you got to such a place of hysteria, but when it comes back, it always comes back with a bang.

It was on March 12, 1938 that the Nazi jackboots stormed their way through my neighborhood and over the innocent pieces left of my soul.

For it was on March 12, 1938 the German Anschluss of Austria took place, and Adolph Hitler officially declared the unification of Germany and Austria as one country. Segments of my heart seemed to perish as Nazi soldiers marched by our apartment building, German warplanes flew overhead, and crowds of mesmerized Austrians stood in the street cheering, rather than resisting; strangely betraying their own souls.

CHAPTER 5

"Julia, why don't you stay in the apartment today, since you are running a fever. I'm going to go by and cancel class and pick up Ari so I can be home with you," Olli said to me as I was preparing to head to the library on March 12, 1938.

I stood wondering what on earth Olli meant in regards to some mysterious fever, when I looked out the double glass doors which led to the porch and saw streams of German soldiers walking through my neighborhood and roaring tanks blazing down the cobblestone streets, as if anger and power were a symbol of beauty.

I realized Olli was making an excuse for me to not leave the apartment in the mist of Nazis. Remembering our special agreement I responded,

"Thanks for the break Uncle Olli, I really do feel weak."

Although I didn't really have a fever, the weakness was a reality. As Olli walked out the front door to make his appearance and pick up Ari, I ran toward the bathroom overwhelmed with nausea. My head got dizzy and I flopped out on the bathroom floor taking deep breaths. The feel of the cold floor began to ease my nerves, and that is when fear and adrenaline kicked in and completely obliterated any physical impairment. The sound of leather boots clicking in sequence created a murmur in my heart, for every time I heard a noise my heart seemed to skip a beat.

I was no longer sick with worry, but I was consumed with fear. Every sound, creak, or door slam seemed a million times louder than normal. Every movement I made and corner I turned in the apartment led me to believe that some Nazi stood behind me, ready to drag me away forever. Externally I seemed fine, but internally I was shaking, my muscles were tensed, and I was afraid to move. Like a little girl, I wanted Olli to come home. On that day I actually embraced Ari's presence, because it meant that I would not be alone if Olli had to run an errand.

When Olli and Ari finally arrived, the noise at the door scared me enough to crouch down behind the kitchen counter. As the door opened, I recognized the voices, and popped up. When I came up from behind the counter, I had to tell myself to breath, and then I explained falsely that I dropped something on the floor. I walked over and gave Olli a hug. The warmth of his body was the only security I had left in the world. I completely forgot that Ari existed. As I held on to Olli with my life, Ari, with an arrogant smile, squeaked out,

"So Julia Patterson does have emotion. Where is my hug?"

As I lifted my hand to make a corrective gesture to Ari, Olli grabbed my hand and said,

"Well we have wasted enough time, let's begin our lessons."

The lessons for the day provided an amazing amount of relief. With loads of work to complete and science equations to analyze and balance, I did not have much time to worry about my fears. We all worked together at the kitchen counter, and I went wherever Olli did, following him around the apartment like a puppy. I constantly badgered him with questions like, "Where are you going? What are you doing? Are you leaving? Do you need my help?" I sought any excuse to be as close to him as possible.

As night fell, my anxieties heightened, because I knew Olli would be out searching for food and walking Ari home. Olli never knew just how terrified I was. I wish he had known, but I would have never admitted weakness.

"I'll be back in fifteen minutes max. Your parents asked me to keep you for supper tonight Ari, so make sure you both wash up and stay out of trouble until I get back," Olli said as he grabbed his jacket and walked toward the front door.

Internally, I could not deny the relief that I would not be alone for those fifteen minutes, even if in the company of Ari.

"So Julia, what do you think of all this?" Ari asked as he sat back in his bar chair, which leaned up against the kitchen counter.

"Think of what? The miracle of how you learned to walk and talk?" I replied knowing good and well he was referring to our sudden union with Germany.

"Why do you have to be so damn mean to me? I made a mistake a long time ago, and although I'm sure you never make mistakes, I know you have it in you somewhere to forgive me," Ari slung back.

I looked Ari dead in the eyes and replied,

"Ooh big words from such a small man."

"What is your problem?"

"I haven't got a problem, I am perfectly content with who I am."

"Bullshit! If you were happy with yourself then you wouldn't be such a jerk to me. Fix your own problems without taking them out on me. I'm sorry your parents are dead, but that doesn't give you the right to treat me like I'm dirt," Ari said with a deep breath.

There existed an obvious sigh of relief that he had finally told me what he thought of me. On the brink of tears I simply looked at my feet and said,

"I guess no one is as perfect as you Mr. Prock."

"Julia, I didn't mean what I just said…"

I cut him off to say,

"At least I know what you really think of me now. You think you know everything---you and your fancy little friends who care only about who likes who, who has better and more expensive things, and where you are going to meet to make other people feel bad. One day you will realize what pain really is, and that is when I am going to sit back and look justice straight in the face. Because Ari Prock you are not..."

That is when Olli came through the door with a fake smile.

"Food is served," he said as he laid the food in the chair by the door to hang up his jacket.

When he looked up he said,

"Everything okay boys and girls?"

"Everything is great! Let's eat," I said sarcastically staring at Ari in a stream of anger.

Supper took place in complete silence as everyone had their own minds to sort out. I'm sure Olli sat contemplating his existence in the new Europe, while Ari sat making a list of ways he was better than me.

I sat re-analyzing every moment of the earlier conversation. I hated that anyone would look at me the way Ari described, and I hated even more that he was right. I only knew how to protect myself against him by demeaning him, and I knew that was wrong, but that was the only way I could think of keeping my own self-esteem. To me, it seemed like he lived in a world of teenagers that had great social skills, enjoyed hanging around each other with no objective, sought to party, and wanted to have a good time. For me, these things were unnatural, even alien. They only interested me to a small degree, yet I felt left out of them. How would I ever have friends my own age? How would I ever fall in love one day? How would I ever learn to exist in a social setting? I wanted to be comfortable in the world of my peers, but because I was not equipped to be young, I looked down upon them, and Ari took the brunt of my dilemma.

About an hour after supper ended, Ari's parents arrived at our apartment building to pick him up. I could not explain the excitement that I would not be left in isolation with my thoughts once again while Olli made the short trip across Alsergrund.

Rather than making my typical journey to the porch with a good book or my journal, I went to my bedroom. I was not yet prepared to look below my feet and see German soldiers marked with swastikas on MY street. How dare they invade my corner of the world!

Although Olli existed less than 200 square feet away, terror overwhelmed me once again. I would learn that night was always the hardest time during war. Nothing I could do or think made me calm, so I got up and moved my twin bed next to the bathroom wall, which separated the two bedrooms in the apartment. I sat in bed in a ball with my arms hugged around my knees holding the baseball glove Patrick had given me as a security blanket. With one hand I rubbed the leather strings rhythmically trying to calm my nerves. My other hand found its way to the wall. I wanted to be as physically close to Olli as possible. I sat wondering if this was a big enough emergency to contact Patrick. I still had the secret information he had given me in my cubby in the library. I quickly debated the choices in my mind, before I realized that this moment did not meet the necessary qualifications to call Patrick into action.

That night seemed to be one of the longest of my life. Every time Olli would get up to go to the bathroom, which seemed to be quite a bit, or whenever I would see a light in the hallway, I would savor a moment of peace. Knowing that Olli was awake kept me somewhat comforted. I finally fell asleep that night only by focusing on the happy memories of my week in Paris. Two hours later, I awakened as the sun crept through my window.

In the days immediately following the Anschluss, I gradually learned to assimilate myself into the new world that had been created in front of my eyes. Imagine walking out your front door expecting to see the same pictures you hold in your mind; the man walking his dog, the college students dragging themselves out of bed into a coffee shop, an author walking into the bookstore below your feet; and then imagine one morning you walk out the door and everyone seems to be part of some great, life-changing event, and as they act like things are completely normal, you are searching for what was your life.

I waited a few days to test the waters of my new environment. I waited until Hitler sat safely and happily back in Germany, having pronounced to the people, "The entry of my homeland into the German Reich," from the balcony of the Hofburg Imperial Palace. I waited for the 600,000 Austrian Nazis to get back to their daily lives. And, I would keep waiting for the people to realize that all change is not necessarily good, especially when that change is Fascism.

In my heart, I knew that there were Austrians who were confused, who only voted in the staged plebiscite to be a part of Germany out of fear. I had to tell myself that the politicians, religious leaders, civil servants and the elite believed that a union with Germany would protect them. Yet, to my dismay, I sat and watched the cultural center of Eastern Europe dissipate into vulgarity, I watched dissenters disappear, I watched the Gestapo take control of the streets, I watched over 200,000 pictures of Hitler magically appear, I watched a sea of swastikas emerge on the streets below me as if blood streamed for the red and black symbol of hatred, and I watched Germans emerge from everywhere-hotels, restaurants, shops, and even the library.

My first day leaving the apartment on my own resembled jumping into a cold swimming pool; you can't wade your way in or it is too cold, you just have to throw yourself in, trusting that you will be okay, letting your body adjust faster. I used this philosophy as I reentered the new Vienna.

I walked straight to the library past young German soldiers, looking almost like my father in his younger years, listening to their playful discussions and envying their ability to enjoy the day. I realized that I seemed normal to them; that I did not stick out as a threat, which relieved some of my terror. For once, it seemed nice to be ignored by the opposite sex. I just wanted to be invisible.

As I passed Ms. Gerg, I gave her my list, full of books about German history and leftover food from the night before. I figured that the Germans would think I wanted to learn about them, but in reality I wanted to conduct research on trends of German aggression and motives. Ms. Gerg brought me my books as usual and said,

"Julia, I was getting worried about you. It seemed like you had fallen off the face of the earth."

In my heart, I felt like I had fallen off the earth, but I calmly replied,

"No Ms. Gerg, I hate to upset you, but I had the strangest fever that just wouldn't go away. It made me too weak to go out, and you know how protective Olli is."

Ms. Gerg gave me her typical wry smile and load of books then headed down the stairs back to the checkout counter on the first floor.

Regardless of the presence of the Nazi's, the fifth floor remained quiet, with the exception of the occasional student searching for a very specific book that just so happened to be in the stacks on my floor. No doubt existed that my secret note waited for me in the safest place in Vienna.

That day I did not make it to Olli's class full of facts about German superiority. I had planned to go and grit my teeth through another lecture full of propaganda, but as I left the library, a sight appeared before me that I would never forget, no matter how many times I tried to erase my memories by reciting the Constitution.

I walked out of the library, reading the book in my hands, when I bumped into a crowd of people. When I looked up from my book I saw, kneeling down below the crowd, a group of Jewish Austrians on the ground scrubbing the cobblestone streets, surrounded by Nazi's smiling and pointing as if they were watching a movie. Absorbed in complete and utter shock, I looked across the courtyard, and was paralyzed when I saw Adara Spiro and her husband, scrubbing the letters of the past Chancellor's name off the streets below their fingers. Emotional pain consumed my body, and I felt completely helpless. I wanted to break into the center of the crowd and grab the Spiros and drag them to their feet and restore their pride. I wanted to take them home and give them a warm cup of soup and tell them that everything would be okay, but I knew I couldn't. How could I stand there and take on over two-dozen Nazis? What would I do, beat them with my book? I knew that, like Olli had told me years before, I would have to find a way to change my environment without fists and even without words.

I ran home, skipping Olli's lecture, and entered my room crying. I slammed the door behind me out of anger. For the first time in my life I felt rage. I was pissed off, so pissed off that I punched a hole in my wall. I hoped that Olli would cancel class and be home any second, but in reality he would never do that anymore because that would make him look suspicious.

I finally felt so restless in my room that I walked into the kitchen, forcefully pulled out a kitchen chair and threw myself down in it. Tapping my foot, my arms crossed, my muscles tensed, and my jaw clenched I sat and waited for Olli to walk through the door, so that I could demand action.

When Olli finally arrived, I found myself disappointed. I jumped out of my chair ran to the door and said,

"Mr. and Mrs. Spiro are being forced to clean graffiti off the street. What are we going to do?"

Olli looked at me with sad eyes and a blank stare and said,

"Who are Mr. and Mrs. Spiro?"

In my mind, I prepared what I wanted to say. I wanted to yell at Olli at the top of my lungs about how he had invited them to my birthday party two months ago, about how he bought books from their bookstore below our apartment, about how he had promised them his allegiance in the event of a crisis. I guess a lot happens in three years, because it was not so long ago that I awoke to Ms. Spiro crying in our living room about the Nuremburg Laws.

The expression on Olli's face made me question for the first of many times to come how much he was pretending and how much he was becoming one of them, an agent of the devil. The Olli I called my Uncle would never betray himself like he did the Spiros, or would he? It would take years for me to truly understand his motives, for Olli to reveal the reality of his heart to me. And boy, would he be more complex than I could have ever imagined.

That day in the courtyard near my home would go down as the day Adara and Georg Spiro ceased to exist in Vienna, and as the day I learned to repress memories. No matter how hard I tried, how many times I said the Constitution, how many times I tried to rationalize that the Spiros were okay somewhere, I could not shake the thought of two of my dearest friends in the world being reduced to sub-human standards and vanishing into thin air. I kept thinking of the people standing around watching the display of demoralization as if it were entertainment. They stood there on the cobblestone streets humiliating some of the people who made Vienna so great, resembling spectators in the arena in Ancient Rome. I always wondered how on earth people could cheer and watch as human beings fought and died before their eyes, and after that day, the extent of human cruelty and desire for power became crystal clear.

That day I learned to treat memories like clothes, getting rid of those things that didn't fit right and keeping the things that made me comfortable. For the next ten years, I would learn to purge the memories that were too tight, itchy, uncomfortable, or short and keep only the thoughts that made me feel comfortable, beautiful, and good about myself. Needless to say, I tried to stop letting myself think about the Spiros that day, and I succeeded to some small degree. I liked to call it mental survival in a time of war.

Emotional survival, on the other hand, required a complete physical shutdown; a shutdown, which finally converged that day. In times of stress and life-changing crisis, we close ourselves off to all experiences and feelings, because we know that almost everything happening is going to make us feel bad or inferior. When we look back years later, we see that our experiences and existence were worse than realized, and we wonder how we ever made it through. In reality, we survive, because we have vaccinated ourselves against life. Of course, this process is unconscious, and we only realize our reactions years after the fact when crisis occurs again and we feel ourselves crawling back into a shell of immunity.

The day the Spiros disappeared from my world is the day that my mental and emotional self-realized that living as Julia Josephine Patterson in 1930's Austria was just too damn hard. Any emotion I had left after all of the death and pain I had seen in my short life, was too much emotion. That day on the streets of Vienna concluded my ability to carry the burdens of others for a long time to come.

As the days rolled by, Olli became more and more distant, and it drove me crazy. He still hugged me, told me he loved me, took care of me, smiled at my jokes; he was still the same Olli, but he no longer possessed the honesty I had grown to love. I knew he acted secretive and aloof to

90

protect us, but at times I came to question his sustainability as a person of resistance. Most of all, I wondered if Olli would have stood up for his beliefs, for the Spiros, and for the good of society if he didn't have a thirteen year old goddaughter to worry about. In a desperate search of an answer, I snuck into Olli's room searching for any detail or clue, which would reveal Olli's true motives. For once, my obsessive worry helped me, as I returned everything I touched to its exact spot. I went through papers, letters from Maria, which I did not have time to read but noted the existence of, souvenirs from across Europe, and medical and funeral papers from when Olli's mother died in 1932.

I felt reassured by Olli's character when thinking about how he completely changed his life, moved across Europe, and took care of his mother day and night when she got sick. She always treated him as an inconvenience to her promiscuous lifestyle, yet he gave her his life for almost two years. Olli had displayed the utmost honor and loyalty toward his mother, more so than any person I had ever met, so it temporarily reassured me that Olli would always do what he thought was right.

I continued to quickly and nervously scrounge around Olli's perfectly arranged room, when I found a woman's shoebox in his closet, and since no woman, besides Adara Spiro and Mrs. Prock, had ever entered our apartment, I could not resist looking. Inside the box, I found the remains of correspondence between my grandfather and my mother. Surprisingly, I also found the smell of my mother. Inside that box was the scent that had given me my first panic attack at the Louvre, the scent that often struck me at the oddest times in the oddest places.

I put my face as far down inside the shoebox as I could, trying to inhale memories I no longer had. As I yearned to see my mother, to be a carefree American, I remembered my need to hurry before Olli came home, considering I had slipped out of his lecture about fifteen minutes early, and it was nearing twenty minutes that I had been searching his room. Seeing a name that I did not recognize on a piece of paper in the box, I grabbed it without even thinking.

Dearest Leeana,

I miss you so much darling. I continue to pray that Paris finds you well and that you are experiencing new and great things daily, although I am almost sure that you sit somewhere studying life from a book. I give you my continuous lecture: Live life instead of hearing about it.

I have wonderful news to share with you in regards to the family. Zouriat is getting married in October. She is just a baby, but she is engaged to a wonderful young man named Ismael. Isn't it hard to believe that one of your younger sisters is getting married? I hope that you will soon find the happiness your sister seems to have committed herself to. You were always so serious and she was always searching for the next moment of fun. Could my two oldest children have been any different? I would never tell your sister, but she could have just a little more of your wisdom. You my dear, have more gifts than you know, and I would not change you for anything in the world. Matter of fact, you might just be the most perfect child a parent could ever desire. But, enough about Zouriat. The family will be talking about her wedding every day for the next eight months or so. I envy that you are so far away.

Mikhail just turned sixteen, and he is already talking about joining the military. I look at him and realize that he will never settle down. He is always getting into some kind of mess, and he has a strong desire to travel. He is a true loner, and in some aspects he reminds me of you in that way. I hope that he will wait until he is eighteen to join the army. I have no doubt that at some point in the near future he will try to forge papers. Mikhail is so stubborn and it is impossible to talk to him about what war is like. He has no idea. Unlike you, so aware of your environment, Mikhail can only think about playing soldier, without even considering the point behind war.

Kiril follows Mikhail around like a puppy. Whether Mikhail is working in the field or walking into town, Kiril is right on his heels. Kiril doesn't realize yet that he doesn't have it in his being to be as remote and isolated as Mikhail. He is such a good boy, with a happy-go-lucky attitude, and what a ladies man. At only thirteen years old, there is always some girl hanging around the fields while he is out working. Sometimes when I am sad or tired I simply look at Kiril's smile and innocence and find solace in knowing that he is content, and will always find a way to be happy.

Kristina has changed tremendously in the past year. I can tell that she misses you most, probably because Zouriat is such a priss. Kristina likes to play rough and tumble with the boys. She is always dirty from being out playing in the fields. Mother goes crazy every time she comes into the house with mud on her feet or with blood dripping from her knees where she fell chasing a boy. She is just like you were at eleven years old, only she does not care as much about books. Let me just say, that she holds her own in a world of boys and our family princess, Zouriat.

And then there is dear little Vitali. He asks about you almost every day. I don't think he understands where you have gone, but I promise to you that he will understand when he is old enough. He surely is Mother's baby. She still rocks him to sleep every night, and to the dismay of the others, he gets the lighter load of work and extra food at supper. When he gets in trouble, he pouts and Mother always comes to his rescue. Mikhail is the toughest on him, pulling him around, hating to watch him while Mother is completing chores. I think that Mikhail would sell him if he were offered a pretty penny. Little Vitali is already complaining about Zouriat's wedding and how he has to carry the rings. He is most upset that the wedding is in the same week as his eighth birthday, and that he, for once, is not the center of attention.

Oh Leeana, I cannot express to you how much we miss you. I miss you more than anyone, and if not, than I cannot imagine the pain they feel. You are a jewel in the crown of this world, and though I miss you, I have no doubt that giving you a life, where you can explore the world and yourself, was the greatest gift I could have ever given you. Write soon!

Love Always,

Papa

February 16, 1920

Sitting in my room reading and re-reading my newly discovered family and I heard Olli come in the door and yell out,

"Jules, I am back from class. Are you feeling okay? I saw you leave early."

"Fine Uncle Olli," I replied. "I'll be right out."

From previous letters, I knew that my mother had siblings, but I had no idea how many. I also learned that each of my aunts and uncles possessed qualities that I had inherited--some more than others of course. I especially related with Mikhail and Kristina, and oh how wonderful it would be to meet them. Were they even still alive? Would they be the same or completely different? Had war torn away their innocence as it had mine? It even seemed like that letter helped me learn a little more about myself, and I wanted to learn even more. That afternoon actually gave me a break from the world and allowed me to be a niece, daughter, and granddaughter.

Sadly, I adjusted to my existence in a society filled with strangers. I found the strength to find my way back onto my porch nightly, usually reading my latest book or watching the show below my feet. It saddened me, however, to no longer see families wandering in and out of the stores below, only men in uniforms. The music seemed to stop, although sound played in the background. The dancing ceased to exist, though people still swayed to the noise.

Gradually I permitted myself to stop being so afraid of the world outside my door. I never found comfort and peace as I moved about Vienna, but I taught myself to live without terror in my heart. I walked directly to where I had to go, I didn't stop to chat or wander in the park. I answered any questions directed to me, and I stayed on my schedule; the library to class to home where tutoring would begin to the porch at night.

By winter, life seemed pretty typical, though I began to worry, because I had not heard from Patrick since the Anschluss. I figured that communicating would be too dangerous in a time where there was certainly no privacy, and I sought to remain under the radar, so I made no efforts to contact Patrick myself. I knew in the back of my mind that I always had his emergency contact.

Just as always, as things began to calm down and life seemed to resume a normal path, another blow struck my heart, and this time the blows kept coming.

It started with "Kristallnacht" or the night of broken glass. The

Nazis smashed what was left of the Spiros' bookstore and every Jewish owned business in Vienna. The word "Jude" appeared randomly across Vienna, as graffiti marking the lives of Jewish Austrians by Nazis acting like dogs marking their territory. The glass that lined the street below my window disgusted me, because it symbolized the destruction of millions of people.

The Spiros' bookstore most of all tore me to pieces. The glass that lay within my old stomping grounds and outside on the sidewalks might as well have been the broken pieces of my heart. I walked by the store thinking of the memories I had in that place, and the worry I still held for the safety of the Spiros. A sensation ran over me, which made me feel lonelier than ever and reminded me of when I moved from the United States.

If you have ever moved to a place, somewhere that is not home, and then gone home to visit, you have a feeling of emptiness. You feel like everyone has moved on with their lives, yet you stand looking for the moment when you left. Your favorite places are gone or have changed, and you wonder in your heart if anyone even remembers that you once existed there. If they do remember, you question if they remember the things the way they are captured in your memory. Moments that shaped your entire world, which exist as snapshots in your mind, are forgotten as mere side-thoughts to those who you left behind.

As I walked by the Spiros' shop that morning, I felt all of those things. I wanted someone to remember, to acknowledge the way life used to be. Damn it, I wanted Olli to say that this world had gone to hell. But all of that showed itself in broken pieces of glass under my feet.

Did the memories of the Spiros' bookshop ever exist in reality the way I had saved them in my mind? Would there ever be another human being who could vouch for my experiences? I felt all alone in the world, because who knew what people would conveniently decide to remember about me, about the Nazis, about the Spiros, and about right and wrong. Thank God I had allowed myself to shutdown emotionally months before, because the full extent of the pain would have killed me instantly.

CHAPTER 6

The next test of my patience came almost exactly a year after the Nazis marched their way into my life. On March 15, 1939 Hitler continued his conquest of Europe by forcing his way into Czechoslovakia. For the first time I began to see people question the German presence in Austria. The thirty percent of Vienna that maintained Slavic origin did not handle the treatment of their fellow Slavs in Czechoslovakia as well as their recent reunification with Germany. Though no one decided to stand up and argue against it.

When the news first rang in my ears, surprise no longer overwhelmed me. I actually felt justified in predicting the world's descent into hell. It felt good in a way, to look at all of the traitors surrounding me and think that they were getting what they deserved. I wanted to scream from the rooftops, "I told you so," but that would have been the dumbest thing I could have done, and I was far from dumb. My self-awareness constantly urged me to practice humility, because me being right meant the suffering of millions of people, and trust me, this was one time it would have served me to be wrong.

Being lost in my thoughts and desiring something, not knowing what that could be, I went to the courtyard outside of Liechtenstein Palace and found a seat among what was left of the people of Vienna. The enormity of the palace gave me a sense of security. I felt small in a world that aimed to get rid of those who appeared big. I sat with the intention of thinking and finding something to ease my restlessness, when in reality I needed to stop thinking. With my head bowed down, I felt a tap on the shoulder and the words,

"Julia, are you okay?"

As I looked up completely confused as to who speaking (knowing that Olli was in class brainwashing Austrians) I saw Ari Prock standing above me.

"Shouldn't you be in the library figuring out ways to make me look dumb," Ari said with his typical charismatic smile, which I despised.

"I should be, but I just needed something different today," I replied.

Ari sat down beside me, and I scooted over to give him plenty of room.

"Julia, you know I really don't understand you. I know that you are not originally from Austria, and that you have been through some tough things, but really I just don't get you."

Ari paused as if he were looking for some response for me. After an awkward moment of silence I looked over and said,

"You just wouldn't understand Ari. Honestly, no sarcasm, no anger, no grudges; you just wouldn't understand. Just as I will never understand you and the things you enjoy and why you act certain ways and do certain things, I don't think you will ever understand me."

"Never say never," he whispered with a wink and an offer. "Can I walk you over to Olli's class? It is about time for his second lecture to start."

"No thanks, I want some more time here, but I'll see you at the apartment later. Oh yeah, please don't tell Olli I was out here. It is not that he would care, I just need to have some secrets," I said, but this time I had the wink and the smile. "What would Olli think if he knew I talked to you without pointing out your stupidity. He would think I was growing as a person."

For a brief moment that morning, Ari seemed like a decent person, as I was able to forget his constant annoyances. But that all came soaring back as his true colors emerged once again that afternoon. Somehow on the day that the Germans came to occupy Czechoslovakia, Ari cared only enough to find himself a third girlfriend in less than four weeks. As my heart ached for the world, Ari only ached to steal a kiss from his newest love.

Back at the apartment, I stood in the doorway of the porch watching the limited action of the academic quarter, which now seemed to explode with Nazis rather than students, while Olli changed out of his work clothes. In the distance I saw Ari courting some new girl, incredibly pretty, but obviously dumb. Actually she could have been a genius, but kissing on Ari, automatically made her an idiot in my book. As Ari oozed Ariness and eventually left his new toy for the week and headed upstairs, I completely forgot the humanity he had displayed earlier in the day. He was just a damn dog.

CHAPTER 7

With Ari only concerned about pinching some new girl's ass, the Spiros disappearing from the free world, Ms. Gerg still being the bitch she had always been, Patrick off the charts, and Olli concerned with appearing inconspicuous, I ached for a real conversation. I needed something real, something grounded, because my heart seemed to float away from reality. I began to question the nature of reality and the nature of man. I spent my time in the library reading some of the great philosophers-Descartes, Hobbs, Locke-just to name a few. Like all philosophy, however, there are never real answers, at least not satisfying ones.

The world is a scary place to be when you can no longer tell what is real and what is an act. You begin to question if everything is an act, even when people are not performing. When nothing seems real, life is one hell of a frightening existence; and for me, panic attacks became more and more frequent, as reciting the US Constitution no longer served to relieve my stress and help me get rid of unwanted thoughts.

I began to face new irrational fears as my nerves sought new methods of dealing with anxiety. All I really needed was someone to talk to, and I found increasing solace in my mother's letters. They seemed grounded in the reality I remembered. I learned that sneaking into Olli's room, grabbing a letter, and replacing it with the last one I had lifted, helped me remember a world that had not yet gone crazy.

Dearest Leeana,

Do you even still call yourself Leeana? It seems like forever since I was so blessed to see your face my dear child, but at the same time, I feel like it was just yesterday that I watched you board a train. I know you have changed so much, but I will always hold the image of you the day you left in my mind, and until I see you again, you will be eighteen years old. Although your little sister Zouriat is married with two beautiful babies, I still struggle to believe that my oldest child is married and expecting a beautiful baby. I wish I could be there to hold my newest grandchild when he or she is only moments old. I wish I could be there to shake Jacob's hand as a proud new father. I promise you Leeana, I will hold my granddaughter in my arms one day. That is right, I said granddaughter. Though you do not know yet whether you are having a boy or girl, in my heart, I know it will be a girl, and she will be just like you. She will show you just how frustrating it can be to have a child smarter than you. She will be my first granddaughter, a wonderful addition to Zouriat's two twin boys, Pasha and Nikolai. I bet she will be able to rough them up if they ever get out of line.

I miss you so much darling, but I know that you are happy, which makes me happy. Thank you for always writing promptly and keeping this old man's soul alive. My thoughts will be with you over the next few months. Having watched your mother give life to six children, and your sister give birth to two, I know that you will be fine and handle all things to come with a level of mastery, because it is you Leeana, who can handle anything this world throws at you.

Love Always,
Papa
September 7, 1924

My God, he was talking about me. My grandfather, Vladamir Serenov knew that I existed somewhere in the world. Did he know I lived in Austria now, did he even know that Father died? What information did he have about the pieces of Leeana's life after my mother died? I never even considered the fact that my grandfather might still be alive somewhere. I believed I was an orphan, without any real family left, when in reality a piece of myself existed somewhere that I could not touch. Those people in the letters-Pasha and Nikolai, my first cousins-lived somewhere with the same amount of blood from my grandfather that I held, yet they might as well have been dead.

I found myself denied contact with the Soviet Union, a society swiftly closing itself off to the world and making enemies along the way. One thing I felt certain of was the fact that my grandfather might have been right about my gender, but he was wrong that he would ever hold me in his arms. I imagine September of 1924 held the hopes of a different world, and boy did I ache to live in that world again. For it was in that world that the Great War had ended, creating hopes that war would cease to exist, but in reality creating wars for years to come.

What astonished me most was that my grandfather's letters provided the foundation I needed, the remembrance that sanity existed somewhere in the world, even if only in villages on the outskirts of the Soviet Union. Grandfather, who I mentally referred to as Papa, just as my mother had, relieved my panic, because he helped me remember the existence of good, rational people on our planet. Papa became my anchor, in a role I assume he also served my mother once.

I sat in my room holding the amazing letter, I sneakily discovered, which revealed an astonishing epiphany about my entrance into this world, when I heard a knock at the door. There were never knocks on our door, so it initially startled me. Alone in the apartment, because I had left the University after Olli's last class while he held office hours; and sure Ari did not stand at the door, because he barged in wherever he went, I composed myself and headed down the hall through the living room. Excited and nervous about who could possibly be in the hall to change my daily routine, I opened the door to find a German Nazi standing in front of me.

Forgetting to breathe, I just stared at the swastikas, feeling completely guilty, as if he could read the hatred in my heart. I felt like he could see through me, and that he had come to take me away forever.

After a brief pause, he bent down toward me and put a fake smile on his chubby cheeks, and said,

"Hello little girl, is professor Zingre here?"

I coughed out a breath, and found a few simple words to say,

"He is over at the University, but his office hours end in about ten minutes. I'll be glad to tell him you came by."

"That is okay, I'll just wait," he mumbled out as he pushed his way past me and sat his fat ass down in an armchair in the living room.

I sat wondering if I should speak, wondering if I should try and go to the University and warn Olli of the situation, contemplating how hot the Nazi must have felt in his full uniform in the middle of June. As I sat at the kitchen counter, feeling awkward, not knowing what to do with my hands or posture, wondering if we were in trouble, I analyzed the man sitting in my midst. I looked for some sign of attractiveness about him, but I came up short. He was fat, sweaty, over-confident, and had a horrible complexion. And how dare he call me "little girl" I thought to myself. Hell, mentally I was eons older than him. My anger continued to build upon itself as I portrayed myself with a sarcastic and bitter smile.

After approximately fifteen minutes of awkward glances, surface conversation, and intense thought, Olli walked through the door. Expecting a shocked look to appear on Olli's face and eagerly awaiting his response to a Nazi sitting in his living room, I ended up being the shocked one.

"Herr Lilienthal, Welcome! I was not expecting you for another thirty minutes or so. Have you been here long?" Olli said with a smile.

"No professor Zingre, just a few minutes. Your beautiful daughter, is it, let me in. I hope you don't mind, but I was over in Alsergrund taking care of some other business, which I finished early. I had no idea you lived in an area so absorbed with Jews for so long, but I am working on helping you with that problem."

Olli nodded and replied,

"Well thank you for coming. I am glad you met Julia. She is my goddaughter. I hope she used her proper manners."

"Oh yes, she seems like a wonderful little Austrian girl."

Olli continued,

"I received a message from a wonderful member of the Nazi youth movement here in Austria, Stefan Prock. I hear that we have important business to talk about, and I am eager to discover what has prompted a man of your stature to visit little old me."

I wanted to puke. I could sense the flow of shit coming out of Olli's mouth, and I wanted to smack him back to reality, but I knew everything Olli said had to have some alternate purpose, hopefully for the better of society rather than its ruin.

Settling in, waiting for this surreal conversation to come to a head, Olli looked over at me and said,

"Darling, could you excuse me and Herr Lilienthal for some grown up talk?"

Grown up talk, yeah right! I thought to myself. I could tell that our Nazi friend probably had the IQ of a turtle and likely moved just as fast. Completely pissed off, I rose to my feet and with the biggest sarcastic smile I could conjure up, I said,

"Yes Professor Zingre, anything you say. I will go braid the hair of my dolls. Do you think it is possible we could shop tomorrow for a new doll to add to my collection? I want one that looks just like a beautiful German girl!"

Olli nodded at me, and I could tell that he steamed with anger at my tone, though the Nazi in the room would have to gain a few brain cells to pick up on my demeanor.

"Julia, we will see how your lessons go today, and if you do real well, we can get a doll that looks like your best friend Ari."

In my mind I smiled and said, touché. I felt reassured that Olli still held a piece of himself somewhere, that underneath this whole charade lie sabotage.

I made an exit to my room, playing the role of dumb little Austrian patsy. Luckily, Olli had yet to figure out my ability to hear everything that happened in the apartment from my bedroom, or perhaps he relied on that simple fact.

"So Herr Lilienthal, how may I be of service to the German Reich?" Olli asked.

"Well Professor Zingre, we have been taking an interest in your area of expertise, human geography. The Reich has been observing classes at the University, and obviously you are aware that cleansing has begun of the liberal saboteurs brainwashing our Aryan students. We have had party supporters in every classroom, and all reports have displayed your loyalty to the Nazi party."

"Thank you. It is a sense of pride that my work has been seen and approved by the party," Olli chimed in.

"We are here, however, to talk serious business. We have a project that will change the world, and we believe that you are the foremost scholar in the area we are interested in exploring. What do know about the field of human eugenics?"

I knew that eugenics had recently appeared on the world scene as the newest scientific fad. Inspired by Charles Darwin and Francis Galton, the scientific community in almost every progressive country in the world had become obsessed with this idea that the human race could be perfected by selective breeding and forced sterilization in an attempt to create a more intelligent people. More specifically, I knew that our chubby Nazi wanted to use Olli and his knowledge of human geography and the patterns of human movement and achievement to prove German superiority.

"Wow, what an interesting topic. I have done extensive research and find the topic intriguing. The idea that we could improve the human species is breathtaking. Imagine what our grandchildren would be capable of," Olli responded with false enthusiasm.

"Well the rumors I hear of you must be true. You seem quite informed on the subject. I am sure you are aware of the conferences and University programs being developed in other countries, and the greatest country in the world cannot afford to fall behind in such monumental times."

"Of course not," Olli replied. "Just tell me what role you want me to play in the German program."

"Wonderful! I knew you were a patriot. I think you will be intrigued to learn of some of the projects we have brewing." Lilienthal then leaned over and said, "You can even have subjects from undesirable groups to experiment with. You just say the word."

Followed by a wink from Lilienthal, Olli replied,

"What a wonderful freedom that will be. Can I complete this work out of the University here?"

"I am sure that can be arranged. Your research is one of the Reich's priorities, so you just have to let us know what you need. The ultimate goals of your research will be to prove the genetic superiority of our people and figure out how to weed out those that impair our society. We know that this will take several generations, but we must get ahead of the competition. You have free reign to experiment on live or dead subjects, impose sterilization, implement compulsory euthanasia, or even change social policies of marriage. We only demand your loyalty and that you keep your work confidential."

"I honor your trust, and I will not disappoint you or the party," Olli replied.

The conversation continued with all of the typical courtesies; handshakes, pats on the back, words of thanks, kissing ass, etc., which I mostly ignored once again lost in my thoughts.

In my room, my mind bubbled with all of the new thoughts that had emerged in the recent conversation in the living room. I tried to analyze the meaning behind every word, but there was too much. I stayed in my room, trying to reason what Olli had really meant, rationalizing our initial conversation about acting like Germans, calculating the possibilities of Olli's turn to darkness when Ari arrived for our lessons, and Olli called me out of my room as if nothing unusual had taken place.

CHAPTER 8

As the days rolled on, Olli's office hours increased, and quickly months began to fly by. Learning to control my anger better and trying to teach myself breathing techniques to assist in easing my panic, I contained the emotion that stirred inside my being to the best of my ability. A miracle in my opinion, from where I had started my young, opinionated, life. I was proud of my nonchalant response to a Nazi sitting in MY living room, and I felt that I might just make it through the war.

That is until I completely lost self-control once again and screamed from the top of my lungs on Friday, September 1, 1939 in our living room.

"Great, we have Poland! What a dream come true Uncle Olli. I wonder how many Jews we can get rid of now. Your value should sky rocket in the academic world. Think of all of the subjects you will have to test. If you are lucky they will let you experiment on babies that they are ripping out of some mother's arms," my tirade began just a few minutes before the time for Olli to leave for class.

"We have Italy and the Soviet Union on our side. With the United States sitting around sucking their thumbs, we are set to take on the world. Long live Hitler," I continued.

Olli, noticing the panic on my face, ran across the living room to the apartment door where I was standing and grabbed my shoulders and said,

"Julia, I understand."

I stood shaking, trying to pull myself loose of Olli's grasp as he continued to repeat,

"I understand. Jules, I understand. Look at me in my eyes, I understand. I understand. I understand. I understand. Listen to me. I understand."

"You will never understand my excitement right now Uncle Olli. I think you have forgotten just how exciting these events are, and I cannot contain it anymore," I continued as we spoke in a kind of sarcastic code.

Olli could tell by the expression on my face, my shaking, and my demeanor what I really meant, and all he could say without putting us both at risk of being viewed as traitors was,

"I understand, it is exciting."

The sympathy written all over Olli's face brought me some ease. Though Olli said nothing that compromised his surface allegiance to the Nazi Party, I could see for the first time since we had talked in the kitchen over a year before, that my Uncle Olli still existed inside the shell of the decorated Nazi Professor.

As part of the teenage drama that summarized my life, which I could not escape no matter my IQ, I stormed off to my room and slammed the door.

"Julia, I have to go to class now. Don't get overwhelmed with your excitement for the recent events. Maybe you should stay home today and soak up all of the glory our country is feeling," Olli yelled back toward me sounding like there existed a twinge of pain in his voice.

Once again, he sought to protect me from myself, because who knows what words would have accidentally spit out of my mouth had I walked into a world where Germany had just destroyed the existence of Poland.

Ari arrived less than an hour after Olli left for work, and three and a half hours earlier than usual. From my room, where I still sat sulking from my argument with Olli, I heard the door open and close. Hoping Olli had returned to whisk me away to some other world or another time, hoping that I was waking up from a dream to find myself a baby in my mother's arms, I walked out into the living room completely taken aback to see Ari so early.

"What are you doing here," I bitterly snapped at Ari.

"Did you get lost? Or did you just forget where you were headed?"

"Oh Julia, that wonderful charm of yours is always so welcoming. To think, I should have asked Olli to pay me for keeping an eye on you."

"What are you talking about?"

"The elusive Julia, I am speechless that you don't know everything."

"Just shut up and tell me what the hell you are talking about. Why are you here, and what did Uncle Olli have to do with it? Or is that too much information for you to understand at once? I can go slower."

"Fine. He asked me to watch out for you. He said that with all the commotion going on right now, and with him so busy with work, it would be better if I followed you around. He claims that a young lady such as yourself should no longer be wandering around Vienna alone."

"What!" I screamed looking away from Ari.

"I know, you a lady?"

"Kiss my ass," I paused thinking about my new situation, and then continued, "So does that mean that you will be going with me to the library, to Uncle Olli's class? Damn, why doesn't Olli just give you a leash?"

"Why is it such a big deal? It isn't like you have any friends anyway. I am probably at risk for developing a vulgar language problem."

"The problem is that I have been stuck dealing with you every day for the past one thousand one hundred and twenty seven days since our tutoring began, and I have just learned that not only do I have to pretend to like you around my Uncle Olli for three hours a day, but now I must tolerate you every waking hour of my life."

"Did you just figure that in your head in ten seconds?"

"You are impossible Mr. Prock. Just stay out of my space," I replied as I walked back toward my room.

"Gladly," Ari retorted back at me.

Once again, Olli had sold me out. It was obvious that he felt he couldn't trust me to uphold my part of the pact we had made, and honestly, I didn't blame him in retrospect. My anger continued to grow, and although I personally knew that I would never do anything to hurt Olli, he couldn't tell that by my reactions.

I wanted to contact Patrick, and I debated going to the library and pulling out the hidden letter and attempting to find him, but I knew that would be incredibly risky. Any window I had once had to take Patrick up on his offer had slid out beneath my feet as it suddenly became clear that a European War, if not another World War, lay at hand. I was on my own mentally and unfortunately completely bogged down physically.

Coming to the realization that I no longer had any freedom, I stayed in my room sulking, preparing in my mind the perfect words for Olli when he came home. I tried to sleep while I waited, but that was to no avail. My mind raced about the events of the day; Poland's tragedy, Olli's reaction to my fit of anger, and Ari's assignment as my bodyguard. My life completely changed once again in the matter of a day.

In the process of letting my mind take over my body, as usual, I entered into a mode of self-realization. My self-awareness and in-depth thought showed me that I had become a teenager. I liked to pretend that I lived in a place above the angst and frustration of most teenagers, that I had no rebellious tendencies, that I always followed directions, and that I did not share the emotions of others my age. In reality, however, I realized that most of my frustrations toward Olli and Ari and the world, for that matter, had to do with my hormones changing. Yes, Nazi occupation, being an orphan, and lacking social skills all played a crucial role in my recent outbursts, but my entrance into young adulthood had amplified my responses, no matter how much I wished to deny it.

I continued to search for a sense of peace, when Olli entered the apartment. I couldn't believe four hours had passed since he walked out the door.

"Where is Jules?" Olli asked Ari, who still sat in the living room. God only knows what he was doing for four hours.

"She stormed off to her room in her typical manner right after I showed up. She has been in there ever since."

"Did you tell her?"

"Yes, and she was not happy to hear it."

"I'll talk to her about it," Olli said as I came running out of my bedroom, trying to resist my temptation to yell considering my recent moment of self-awareness.

"So nice of you to include me in the choices of my life," I started.

"Jules, I have only requested the services of Ari for your protection. I can't be with you everywhere you go."

"Yes, but you could have told me before you sent the ass of Austria here," I said with an increasingly angry tone.

"I am standing right here," Ari chimed in.

"At least he is aware that we are talking about him," I continued.

"Julia Josephine Patterson, stop being so rude!" Olli then added.

"Listen, can we please focus on what is important here?" I attempted to re-direct the conversation.

"You cannot take away my privacy."

"Eighteen Jules, eighteen," is all Olli uttered.

Remembering our original agreement, I just turned and sat down in the chair by the door, completely speechless.

"If it only took one word to do that to Julia, I would have tried it years ago," Ari said as he sought one more dig to get under my skin with

Olli protecting him.

"Shut the hell up," I replied.

"Kids, listen. Stop yelling and get out the book we are reading, we still have lessons to get to. You are going to be spending a lot of time together, and I will no longer tolerate disrespect in my presence. Do you hear me Julia Josephine?"

"Yes sir," I replied gritting my teeth.

Olli pulled out his copy of the book we were using to study atmospheric and weather properties and began to read. Sitting across the living room from him, I could see the stress on his face, and I felt bad for him. I was selfish. This man held the world on his shoulders, trying to balance the forces of good and evil, and protect his teenage goddaughter at the same moment. So consumed with my own problems, I had conveniently forgotten that Olli never slept anymore and spent hours upon hours at the University. The unintentional look on his face provided enough evidence for me to keep my mouth shut for the rest of the day.

CHAPTER 9

Two days after Poland faced its most tragic historical moment, the Second World War officially began with England, France, Australia and New Zealand declaring war on Germany, hence Austria, hence me. Stuck in the middle of a war, where I did not belong in any sense, I vowed to not put any more stress on Olli. I would deal with Ari in my own way, and I would learn to take care of my own problems. Olli had enough on his plate, and nothing he or I could do to would change our circumstances. It may have taken me a year and a half to actually hear what Olli had to say to me at the kitchen counter, when our freedom appeared to be in danger, but I prepared myself to no longer put pressure on my godfather.

The idea of actually being at war also helped pull me out of my shell of fear. When asked by German soldiers for directions, I would tell them the wrong way, while Ari would correct me. As we stood arguing, confusion would consume the faces of Nazis who apparently regretted ever asking Ari and I for advice. Though minute, I hoped the little things could somehow make a difference. I stole every opportunity available to act dumb and create chaos. Ari actually helped me create confusion without even realizing his involvement. He was my pawn, as he looked at me like I had just lost my mind. Though it killed me to act like a ditzy teenager, it was the only way I could think of to fight in the war without using words or fists.

By winter, my efforts seemed to be useless as the German offensive teamed with the Soviets to divide Poland and rob it of all pride and integrity; and as the Soviets continued on their trail of terror to attack Finland. I learned to stop throwing fits, because Olli was never around

115

anymore to listen, and no doubt Ari would turn me over to the Nazis in a heartbeat. I kept my anger to myself and let it bottle up beyond belief. When I look back, I wonder how I did not explode or have a coronary. With Patrick and the Spiros' out of the loop, I had no one to turn to, no one I could talk to. I felt like I would go crazy, so I kept myself immersed in books.

Reading approximately six hundred pages a day, I found myself sitting quietly amongst millions of pages of long silent books, and to my delight my peace provided the best possible torture for Ari. Unlike the times when we argued, watching me read added no excitement to Ari's life. So when I would get really pissed at Ari, I would wake up extra early and stay extra late at the library. Ms. Gerg would give him about thirty minutes of discussion time, he would wander around the stacks near my cubby on the fifth floor, and finally he would sit down and try to talk to me, aiming to get me to leave the library and go somewhere else, anywhere for that matter. I would conveniently ignore him, with my face in a book, refusing to acknowledge we even existed in the same world. He often tried staring at me to break my concentration, randomly laughing, hoping that I would ask what was so funny, or start making noises at me wishing I would yell at him to stop. In all honesty, I actually enjoyed Ari's company, because torturing him became the highlight of my dreary existence.

As we returned home at the end of the day for our lessons, as I no longer attended Olli's classes mainly due to resisting an outburst, Olli would ask with a strained and impartial look on his face,

"How was your day kids?"

I always responded,

"Wonderful Uncle Olli."

Ari never responded, and I prided myself on having figured out how to burst his bubble. Finally, I felt like I had learned how to be like General

Pershing, using wisdom and patience to win the battles of everyday life. Though the world seemed to be getting worse rather than better, I reveled in a sensation of accomplishment, of learning how to influence people and the world by my example rather than by my fury. What I didn't realize at the time was that my tactics were not the cause of Ari's aggravation, or at least not the main cause.

As I concentrated on breaking Ari as if he were a wild horse, Uncle Olli shifted his role as educator. So enthralled with his work at the University and for the German Reich, Olli had talked with Ari's parents and manufactured a new teacher-student relationship.

It was determined that Ari and I would exchange goods, and neither Ari nor myself were asked about our willingness to participate in this new structure.

"Have a seat kids," Olli said in the presence of the Prock family as Ari and I walked in from the library at our usual time on a Wednesday afternoon.

"What are you doing here? Shouldn't you be at work?" Ari directed toward his parents.

"We have something we need to discuss with you. Olli came by to see us this morning, and he has requested that your school schedule be changed. Due to his important work for the Reich, we must make some adjustments"

"Am I going back to regular school?" Ari asked.

Unconsciously I hoped not, though I would never admit it. Having gotten used to being around someone all of the time, life would seem very lonely. Even if Ari drove me nuts, it was nice to be around another person.

"No son," the Procks continued.

"Olli has explained to us your arrangement with Julia, and how you are escorting her about as she is a young lady who should not be wandering the streets of Vienna by herself. Your job is very important, and we support you learning this responsibility as a young man. Professor Zingre believes that Julia needs that same responsibility."

In my mind I had been laughing at Ari as his parents talked to him about his future; that is until my name popped into the picture. What did I have to do with Ari's development? He was only in my life for the purpose of learning from Olli.

Olli then chimed in,

"Yes Julia, we have talked about the current circumstances, time constraints with my new role at the University, and all of the time you and Ari are spending together. We have decided that you will be Ari's teacher. For science, I will create weekly packets of independent work for the both of you, as you will teach lessons in the other areas. In exchange, he will continue to escort you around Vienna."

At the exact same moment Ari and I looked at each other and yelled out,

"No!"

"There will be no debate or discussion. I am the teacher, and with the consent of Ari's parents, I am making a decision. If you choose not to follow through, then you will be banned from the library Julia, and Ari you will be denied access to the University grounds. This is not a game."

By the look on Olli's face, nobody dared pose a question. His reaction and statement scared me immediately, because it spit out of his mouth like fire, with the demeanor of an enraged Nazi. Maybe the stress of work had finally taken its toll on Olli's patience, as his nervous expressions indicated a side that rarely emerged. Regardless of the foundation behind his eruption, keeping my mouth shut obviously proved to be the choice of a genius or a first grader. And just to irritate Ari, I simply said,

"Yes   sir."

CHAPTER 10

Dearest Leeana,

Breathe my dear child, breathe. Take in every moment and breathe. Think of nothing but the air flowing in and out of your chest and through your nose. Let the world fall away as leaves fall from a tree in the midst of autumn. Do not question where you will end up, simply enjoy the freedom of the fall. STOP...Take a step back and breathe my dear child, breathe. Inhale the quiet of the forest in the middle of winter and feel the cold in your lungs. Hear the wind whip past your face brushing your hair into your eyes. STOP...Take two steps back and breathe my dear child, breathe. Feel the sun on your face on the first warm day of spring. Absorb the warmth seeping through your skin as the smell of pollen enters your nostrils. STOP...my dear child...STOP and breathe.

The words in your last letter reached to the depths of my heart, because among the words you chose to employ I heard the sound of distress. Not distress in a manner of boredom or woes about the path of your life, but the distress of worry for others. Unlike my other children, it is in you that I have known since the day that you entered this world that you feel the pain of others. You carry the burdens of the world and could personally care less about yourself.

I have known this for years, but Leeana it was not until I read your last letter, that I realized that you have finally become self-aware of the burden you carry, and I have a secret for only you Leeana; I carry the same burden, and I would have never wished this upon my worst enemy, certainly not my daughter. You spend hours upon hours a day analyzing everything. You struggle to get rid of bad thoughts when you see people in pain, replaying things involuntarily over and over again in your mind. Though you have moments of happiness, you lack finding peace, because you absorb the pain of those around you. I want you to know my dear child that you are not alone.

It took me years to understand a way of controlling my pain and worry. Before I had a method that actually worked, your mother used to complain of my mood swings, the ability of anything and everything to steal my attention, and my lack of mental presence in every discussion. Simply put, my mind was always somewhere else and not by choice, but simply by obsession.

Just as I have learned, my child, you must learn to find a place of sanity and calm. For me it is forgetting myself and teaching myself to breathe. I repeat these words in my mind finding a place of solace, and knowing nothing but the sensation of my own breath. Practice Leeana. Practice finding peace in yourself, forgetting everything else around you, and I will promise you that the anxiety and panic will begin to get better.

I love you my darling, and I think of you daily. I must say I am sorry for passing this dreaded trait onto you, because I know the misery it can cause. You must be strong and let yourself move on with the present, not dwelling on the past. Learn to breathe for yourself Leeana, not for others.

Love Always,
Papa
September 18, 1920

My grandfather's words struck me to the core. Although, I had not yet reached the point of self-awareness he referred to with my mother; the

September 18th letter of 1920 saved me from certain despair. Gradually the outward stress of the world had increased with the start of Germany's takeover of Austria and the beginnings of a Second World War. Not realizing the impact of these events on my soul, I ignored the fact that my obsessions and analysis of every detail in life had tripled in intensity. My mind never stopped working, so I began to employ the skills my grandfather had suggested almost twenty years before to my mother. At first these strategies seemed useless, but the worse I got, the more I tried, and slowly these attempts to leave the world behind, if only for a moment, became easier.

First the disappearance of the Spiros, and then becoming Ari's teacher increased my need for perfection. I had to make sure I could control my environment and avoid more pain. With Ari, that meant I always had to appear smarter than him, which forced me to be on my toes. I never felt like I had down time, as I always struggled to one-up him. This new burden increased the importance of following Grandfather's advice.

So overwhelmed with the world and myself, my only salvation lie in those old, yellowing letters, which held the key to maintaining my sanity and dissolving my panic. In retrospect, I would come to believe that God gave me those letters to help me deal with my gifts, the good and the bad.

CHAPTER 11

"Get your preppy ass over here. Stop staring out the window at all of those little tramps, have a seat, and get out your book," I yelled toward Ari as he stood at the porch door in a daze looking onto the street below.

"What's your problem?" Ari continued.

"Heaven forbid I spend five minutes during our class time relaxing and observing the world. Maybe you could learn something yourself by getting your nose out of a damn book and experiencing life."

"Well, asshole, if you have already forgotten, your parents would agree with me. Maybe that is why they have made me your teacher, and put the dependence of your education and ability to function as an adult on my skills to teach you. So piss off," I yelled at Ari as I ran out the front door of the apartment and down the stairs, knowing that according to the contract between him and Olli, he would be forced to follow.

Sure enough, Ari followed, but his legs couldn't even come close to approaching my natural speed. My mother may have had the legs of a gazelle, but I sure did run like one.

It is rare that a human being lets everything go and runs as fast as the physical body will allow, and on that day when I finally let my legs go, I felt free for the first time in a long time. It was as if I could fly as I dodged people walking on the sidewalks, ignored the movements of the town, and for once cared less about what anyone else thought of a teenage girl running through the streets of Vienna like death approached from behind.

"Wait up. Julia, stop running. I'm going to tell Olli. Please stop.

Just walk, I'm coming. Julia please," I heard echoing from the Ari's mouth about thirty yards behind me.

I couldn't possibly stop now. The exhilaration of the cool air filling my lungs provided a high that I could not contain. The sensation of the cool on my skin and the heat in my blood made me feel alive. Was I cold? Was I hot? I had no choice, I had to run. Ari had no choice, he had to follow.

Unbeknown to Ari, I operated under a plan. I did not randomly decide to run from the apartment in rage or annoyance, I had a lesson to teach him, one of Pershing proportions, and along the way I discovered a sense of pleasure only nature could provide.

Slowing myself so that Ari could stay within sight of me, I ended my journey by entering the Votivkirche, a cathedral built in Vienna in the late nineteenth century. A fairly new piece of architecture added to the history of Austria. I found the front door, slowed down and entered with reverence.

Breathing in life for the first time in a long time, I walked my way to the back pew facing the altar. I sat on the far end of the wooden bench and observed the magnificence of the windows, the white sandstone, the marble pillars, and the neo-gothic design. Having passed the cathedral almost daily, I had become immune to its beauty.

Sitting in the presence of God for thirty seconds while Ari found himself huffing and puffing with his heavy breath filling the air in front of his face, a cold chill ran down my spine as the sting from the cold of the bare pew pierced my body. Ari approached preparing to ream me for my carelessness, when he suddenly became aware of his location. He solemnly sat down beside me, and just as he caught his breath, he began to whisper. I interrupted, bowed my head, and said,

"*Lord hear my prayer. May the words from my mouth provide wisdom beyond my years and may the spirit of this place open the minds of those present. May the humility needed for me to inherit the earth fill my spirit, and may the actions through the course of this day create growth for all of those involved. Allow my choices not be in vain, and help me to hide myself and my words to provide a voice of reason and strength, through the name of your son Jesus Christ. Amen."*

Ari sat with his head still bowed when I finished. Looking at his hands, he was speechless--just how I wanted him. I intentionally held the awkward silence for about forty-five seconds and then began,

"Sometimes we get so caught up in ourselves that we forget the enormity of the world. Look at us sitting here in this marvelous place, having forgotten all morning the impact of this very site on the face of Vienna. Do you know why I brought you here?"

"I don't know why you do anything," Ari answered with his head still facing down, his hair falling in his face, and shivering from the cold.

"On this day eighty-seven years ago, Austria's Emperor Franz Joseph found himself stabbed and bleeding from the neck on this very spot. The strength of the collar on his military uniform saved him. As a thank you gift to God, his brother, Ferdinand Maximilian Joseph, began a campaign to fund this very church, and as you can see his efforts were not in vain. This place is the epitome of living life rather than reading it from a book."

I paused to give Ari a moment to think and continued,

"Ari, how dare you accuse me of not experiencing life when you have no idea the significance of the very place in which you live? How dare you accuse me of being boring and ignoring the world, when I can speak four languages fluently and pieces of two others? How dare you accuse me of not living when I am an orphan that if anything has lived too much in my life thus far? How dare you judge the work I have put into my education and consider your knowledge of the secular things and vices of life superior to my knowledge of the harshness of the world?"

Again I paused and gathered myself,

"Today, February 18, 1940, brings a question to my mind. As we sit in this place and eventually walk back to the apartment, I want you to think about this question, and your assignment will be to write me an essay on your answer. Complete sentences only with an introduction, body, and conclusion with defending points to each of the arguments you make. So Ari Prock: Will the military uniform that once saved Franz Joseph save Austria once again, or this time will it lead to utter ruin? I'll meet you outside, no running this time, when you are ready to head back to the apartment and look at what it really means to live."

I slowly got up to make my exit, giving Ari time to think in the isolation of the cold and overwhelming cathedral. I wanted him to feel alone, to feel the need to walk outside into the sun, to feel like he needed the information I had to offer. About to leave him, as the only soul in the massive church, he grabbed my hand pulled me back down to the seat beside him on the pew. The touch of a boy's hand made my body tingle, even it if was the hand of my nemesis.

Waiting for an apology, which he no doubt had been working on in his head, Ari caught me completely off guard when he quickly reached up and gently grabbed both sides of my face. With his thumbs, he pushed the hair out of my eyes and pulled my cold lips to his warm face. He made my entire body feel warm in the middle of winter in Vienna. Without a single thought or analysis, I was in shock.

After what seemed to be an eternity and a split second at the same time, my mind came back to earth from complete paralysis, and I pushed Ari away. Not knowing how to react, especially considering I didn't know how I was feeling, I looked at Ari and said,

"I'll see you outside in a few minutes. Give me a few minutes."

I stood up with my knees knocking together and my hands shaking, not from nerves; only God knows from what. I pulled myself outside and sat down under the closest tree.

A million thoughts ran through my head, and I couldn't figure out which one to start with. Matter of fact, they all ran together, and my obsessions were uncontrollable, all coming at once. I tried to sort through the feelings, the touch, the confusion, and the motives behind Ari's actions. Was he trying to manipulate me? Did he like me? (No that possibly couldn't be it, he was way out of my league.) Was he attempting to get me to shut up? Did he want something? Even if I did like him, he was a Nazi, and I could never become attached to someone with such a lack of moral fortitude. The kiss sure did feel good though, and there were sparks...at least for me. But he had to be using me, right? I was a dorky nerd. He was gorgeous and charming, while shifting from girl to girl. He had to be using my weaknesses of being completely awkward around boys and wanting someone of the opposite sex to notice me. He had slumped so low as to use my emotions as a human being against me. What an asshole! Or could he really like me?

With my head in my hands these thoughts swarmed through my mind, and I could not use any of my typical logic to work through it. It is amazing how the mind loses complete control when it comes to the heart.

I came to believe in those few seconds that Ari attempted to manipulate me with techniques perfected with lots of girls before me. Trying to find my bearings, I glimpsed up to see Ari heading towards me with his hands in his pockets. Oh my God was he handsome. I had never formed a crush on him, because I knew he used girls, and on top of that, someone like him would never be interested in me. Through my stream of consciousness, I focused on the fact that Ari quickly approached, and my heart lost control. I had forgotten to breathe and my heart pounded erratically. I couldn't speak, so I pretended to ignore him coming. What would I say? I decided that I would say something completely off topic to draw his attention away from what had just happened. I would ask him what he planned to write about in his essay, and pretend that the past ten minutes never occurred. When he finally reached me, we were all alone on holy ground in the midst of an Austrian winter, and rather than following the plan my brain just laid out, I yelled,

"What the hell were you doing in there?"

"This…" Ari barely eked out, when he more gently than the last time touched my face and drew his lips once again to mine. It felt too good to push away this time, so I let him kiss me, refusing to let myself think about anything else, while my stomach seemed to flutter away using a mind of its own.

This time I waited for Ari to stop the action, and when he finally pulled back he still stood within six inches of my face. His face never looked so angelic. I saw his eyes for the first time. I saw his humanity, and for a brief moment I forgot the world in which we lived. That is until I saw in the distance a black and red flag with a swastika hanging from a porch, and I remembered the reality of my situation.

"Julia, let me explain my actions," he started and before he could explain anything I whispered in his ear,

"There is nothing for you to explain. You are a Nazi, and even if it kills me or if I get dragged off to some camp somewhere, I will NEVER fall for the charm of some Nazi trying to manipulate me. You are trying to use me."

That was all I could say in public without putting myself in danger from a bystander hearing me and turning me in as a traitor. Seeing that red and black flag had convinced me that Ari, like all Austrian patsies only aimed to use me and throw away the pieces of my heart.

Ari looked back at me like I had taken a knife and stabbed him in the heart, and for a brief moment looking into his eyes, I felt bad. What if his actions had been sincere? So what, I thought to myself, he had been brainwashed by jackboots and angry speeches, not to mention he had no real grasp on what he wanted. I would just be his latest girl to use and leave behind, and that would be no way for me to start my life with the opposite sex, even if I wasn't the most beautiful creature the world had ever seen; even if no man ever loved me.

"Please meet me tonight at 9:30 in the library on the fifth floor. The night librarian will be sleeping by then. Please Julia, I will sneak out of the house, and you know for a fact that Olli will be in his office until well after midnight. If you meet me tonight, I will never bother you again if that is your wish."

I simply replied,

"Make sure you have your essay finished tomorrow," because at that moment I had not yet decided whether I would show at the library.

CHAPTER 12

Ari and I parted ways with a silent understanding that our day as teacher and student, enemies, or anything else for that matter, was over. He walked me home in silence and then left, to go where, anyone could guess. He definitely would not go home, because Stefan would tell his parents that Ari left school early. I figured that he would probably go tattle on me to Olli at the University about not being willing to teach him and running away or some bullshit like that. I sat in my room for the remainder of the afternoon reading about Napoleon waiting for the moment Olli walked through the door with a lecture about my commitment to hold up my end of the bargain, but the door never opened.

A million thoughts ran through my mind, and even though I wanted to think about how good Ari's touch felt, I tried to ignore the events of the day. Being obsessive over everything in my life, forgetting my first romantic encounter worked to no avail.

I kept replaying every detail of the day from the moment I ran out of the apartment. I analyzed the thoughts that must have run through Ari's head, the feelings I felt, where my plan went wrong, and everything that built up to the first kiss in the church. I re-created the atmosphere repeatedly in my mind just trying to get back a piece of the feeling that overwhelmed my body when Ari's lips first touched mine.

I tried saying the Constitution continuously in my mind to let myself forget the day, but it was just too much. My compulsive urges could not control the swarm of thoughts running through my brain. One memory led to another and though I tried to move on and erase the day, everything came back to me recreating that unimaginable feeling in my gut, that twinge of excitement and panic at the same time, and that shaking on the inside that only came when I recounted my first kiss perfectly in my mind.

I finally convinced my brain to prioritize and forget about my own interests. To be like General Pershing, I would have to push my confusion and hormones out of the picture. I needed to think clearly and make wise choices, and that meant deciding what would happen at 9:30 without re-analyzing my trip to the Votivkirche.

Though I told myself I had to make a decision, in reality my decision occurred the moment Ari touched my hand. No doubt I would find myself in the library. The question yet to be answered, however, was how to manipulate Ari once I got there.

I decided that I would show up thirty minutes late. If he really needed to talk to me he would wait at least that long. Plus the irritation would make him vulnerable. I would let him talk and say whatever he had to say because I must admit my mind felt a bit of intrigue. I knew that I had to show strength, because his charm or another kiss could weaken me, and that would ruin my position of control.

At 9:50, I looked both directions in the hallway of our fifth floor apartment building to make sure no one could see me sneaking out. I knew that Olli would still be working, but just in case, I left a note on the door in the event that he came home early. The note read,

Uncle Olli, I got hungry and went out to find a snack. Don't worry, I'll be back soon. I love you! JJP

Realistically only about a two percent chance existed that Olli would ever see the note. He had not been home before midnight from the University for over a month. Surely I would be home in time to take the note down before Olli ever knew of my departure.

I stepped out into the hallway and quietly shuffled my feet down the back stairs of the apartment building. The noise entering the building blasted from below as the restaurants and bars below teemed with noise from German soldiers. I definitely invoked no risk of waking up the neighbors.

Once I exited the building I decided to take the back way to the University. I did not want to get stuck in the fray of drunken Germans looking for some entertainment, and more importantly I did not want to risk running into Olli. I walked as fast as possible, without looking conspicuous due to the temperature, or running the risk of being bothered or stopped by someone, and I arrived at the back entrance to the library at 10:07 p.m.

I walked up the back stairs tiptoeing past the first and second floors. I did not want to wake up the nighttime librarian who slept through ninety percent of his time in the library. Ms. Gerg always talked about how she wished they would fire him, because of her repeated responsibility checking-in all of the books and making sure no one stole anything while he worked. To Ari and I, the night librarian seemed ancient, and as long as we were quiet, we had no worries of him interrupting our meeting.

By the time I reached the landing in the stairwell on the fifth floor I paused to catch my breath before I walked into the library. It was then that my heart started pounding, and for the first time ever, I actually felt jittery when thinking about seeing Ari.

I entered the door expecting to hear Ari chew me out for being late, but instead I entered to see him looking absolutely vulnerable. He sat in a chair beside my special cubby with his legs spread to a width longer than his shoulder span. His head faced down, his hands crossed, and his cheeks red.

"I didn't know if you'd show. I would have waited here for you all night," he said with his head still facing down. He had never looked so appealing, but I pushed that out of mind to stay focused, because I had to be loyal to General Pershing. I could never feel that way about the enemy.

"You have a lot of explaining to do Ari. I know there is no way in this world that you would desire me, that you would kiss someone like me. I am boring to you, I am irritating, and I am just too plain and un-lady like for your apparent tastes. I will not let you manipulate me to get whatever it is you want."

Ari looked up at me with his big brown eyes and said,

"You're wrong Julia. Don't you see you are the beautiful one? You are different than the others. You are the one that is out of my league."

"I'm not stupid Ari. I know you are charming and used to getting your way with girls. I've seen you use them up and throw them out over and over again. You probably have a girlfriend right now. Not to mention I could NEVER trust a Nazi. It could be the death of me to say that out loud in the world right now, but I have to finally say it to your face. You are nothing but a murderer in waiting."

"You wouldn't understand."

"Understand what? Peer pressure? Family pressure?"

"Julia I can't tell you. I wish more than anything in the world I could, but I can't."

"You can do what you want, and you are choosing not to tell me something. Trust me there is nothing you can choose to say that would make me feel the sympathy of a Jew killer."

"Stop it Julia. Damn it, stop calling me such horrible things."

"I will stop when you prove to me you are not a follower, that you are something different."

Ari stood up and looked me straight in the eyes, and once again he touched my face. It made me feel so warm, that I almost forgot we were arguing. He lowered his voice and said,

"Is there anything I could tell you to change your mind about me, or am I about to reveal something to you that will make no difference?"

"You can tell me you are not a Nazi. I know that isn't possible considering your parents are trying to sign you up for the Nazi Youth with your older brother, so I guess no there is nothing you can tell me that I need to know."

Ari paused briefly and responded,

"Julia I am not a Nazi."

"Bullshit," I spouted and then lowered my voice remembering my location and the intensity of my words.

"And by the way, why are you so intent on convincing me that I should like you? What do you want? Do you want easier lessons? Is it the fact that you can't stand the idea of someone not liking you? Why are you trying to use me?"

"Make me a promise Julia. You are the most honest person I have ever met, and I am going to trust my life in your hands. You must know that what I am about to tell you could ruin my family, and I know that you always do what you believe is right. Can I trust you?"

"Ari, I may have a lot of shitty qualities, but I will always do what I know is right. Now if your secret is not what is right in my book, then I will not keep it. Regardless of how I feel about you in any way, I will do what is the best thing for my conscious."

Ari reached over to me and put his hand around my waist. He pulled me close to him; closer than I had ever been to a man. Even Olli didn't hold me like that. This was no bedtime hug.

"You can't even tell Olli," he whispered in my ear.

"Not a soul on this earth can know, or you will not be able to live with yourself Julia. Believe it or not I know you."

I took a deep breath and prepared to push him off of me, thinking he was prepping to tell me some crap like his parents were forcing him to

Spence

be a Nazi, when he said,

"The Spiros are still in Vienna Julia. They are living in a room that the builders of our house never finished, that is not even on our floor plan. That is why we look like the perfect little Nazi family. We have to so that we don't disappear. My parents, Stefan, myself, Olli, and now you, are the only people in this entire world who know, and if anyone were to ever find out, we would all be killed. That is why I couldn't be honest, but I can't stand to lie to you anymore."

Then with a solemn pause he said,

"Julia, I am falling in love with you."

I fell to my knees in relief for the Spiros and in awe of Ari's confession. How could someone love me? How did I know for sure that he still did not have a plan to manipulate me? So I asked with a shaky voice,

"How do I know you are telling me the truth?"

"I'll do anything to prove it to you. Maybe it will take time, maybe something else. I was hoping that me sharing the biggest secret of my life would be enough to satisfy your doubts. If not, then tell me, and I will do it."

I suddenly felt incredibly selfish. I would have never told him a secret like that, and yet I still questioned him. I was a hypocrite, and I felt guilty. In all honesty I always found Ari attractive, but I never considered him a possibility because of his personality and tendency to be enthralled with beautiful, ditzy girls.

"What about all of those other girls? You have a new girlfriend every week. Why should I believe that I am special, that you haven't already told them the exact same thing? How do I know that you don't use your secret every day to suck girls into a web of deception?"

"Julia, I haven't had a girlfriend since that day we talked at

Liechtenstein Palace. Matter of fact that girl I walked home, I broke up with later that night. It has been almost a year since I have even looked at another girl. Believe it or not you stole my heart that day on the plaza.

"How is that possible?" I replied still sitting on the floor below Ari's feet.

He knelt down and answered,

"It is simple. You are beautiful, brilliant, independent, and passionate. All of those things make you the sexiest girl I have ever met. Being around you all of the time has made me see who you really are, and you are adorable. I have been working up the courage to telling you for a year, and in that time I haven't been able to do it. You intimidate me, and I was too afraid that you would reject me, and of all the girls in the world, I couldn't handle being turned down by the one I really care about. Why do you think I agreed to follow you around Vienna for free?"

When I thought about it to myself, I realized that I had not seen Ari with any girls since that day at the palace. I pulled my head up from looking at the floor and saw just how close he was to me. This time when he pulled my chin up towards his face, I did not panic or get lost in my thoughts. I simply enjoyed the moment, and nothing in my life had ever felt so good. I have no idea how long we kissed, but it seemed like forever, and yet that wasn't long enough. When our faces separated, I looked at Ari in his sweet face, which now appeared different to me, and said,

"I've never done this before. I don't know the proper customs or reactions or process. You are going to have to help me so I don't seem lost."

Ari's smile consumed his entire face and his white teeth flashed in front me as he said,

"Does that mean you will be my girlfriend?"

"Yes," I replied with the smile of a little girl who just got in trouble on my face.

Ari had won me over.

"But let's not tell Olli or anyone for that matter, because I don't want them worrying about us with all that is going on right now."

"Agreed."

This time, Ari reached over, as we still sat on the floor, and gave me a hug. He held me so tight that I felt warm. I never wanted him to let me go. I promised myself as a newly orphaned child years before that I would never let myself be vulnerable to the pain of the world, but I just couldn't help it with him. He made me happy in a very angry and scary world.

After about ten minutes of him holding me in his arms on the floor of the library, I looked up at the clock, and to my dismay it was 12:30 a.m. I jumped up and said,

"Oh my God, look at the time. What am I going to tell Uncle Olli?"

"Calm down. We will figure something out on the way back to your apartment. Stefan is covering for me at my house, so I will make sure you get home safe."

We headed for the back stairs in a hurry. We rushed down the first three flights until we got to floor one and two, where we walked very slowly and quietly to avoid disturbing the sleeping patterns of the librarian. We weren't concerned about running into people. Austrians were too consumed with other events than to go to the library, especially at 12:30 a.m. In all probability we were in the safest place in Vienna, Austria.

Ari helped me put on my coat like a true gentleman, and then we peeked out the back door of the library and into the street to make sure everything was clear. We gathered ourselves and began to walk the back way to the apartment, attempting to avoid any hold-ups. As our feet rhythmically paced steadily across the cobblestone below, Ari reached over and took my tiny hand in his sending a jolt through my body that I thought only existed in fairy tales. I seemed to float.

CHAPTER 13

There are some truths in this world that most, if not all, people share; yet these things are rarely spoken of because people do not become self-aware of their natural thought processes.

For example, have you ever walked into a place for the first time and remembered that place in a very certain way? Maybe you remember a specific smell or the lighting. Once that place becomes part of your routine you get used to those characteristics, and they no longer stick out in your memory. Then something happens, and you reflect back to the first time you walked through the door of that place, and your first impression comes back as a flash from the past. The place that has become so familiar for a moment looks amazingly foreign.

That is exactly how I came to see Ari Prock. Walking with him home from the library with my hand in his that night, I looked at his face and had a flash back to the first time I saw him before we spoke or before he got punched in the face, and boy did he seem different.

"What are you staring at?" he said with a huge grin on his handsome face.

"Nothing, just looking at you for the first time," I said.

Then in an attempt to refocus on our current crisis, I said,

"What are we going to tell Olli? If he has been home for a while, then he will know my note was a lie."

"We tell him the truth; that we were at the library and lost track of time."

"Do you think he will buy it?"

"I think Olli is too overwhelmed in holding up appearances for the good of us all that he won't be able to worry about it. Plus he trusts your judgment."

We continued to walk and approached the apartment building. We quietly walked up the stairs, and when we got to the top of the fifth floor stairwell, I prepared to walk through the door, when Ari pulled my hand back and said with a grin,

"Let me kiss my girlfriend first," and then he gently kissed my lips.

As he stepped back from me after our encounter he looked at me and said with a wink,

"It'll be okay. I'm here to help you. Plus Olli will never believe that we wanted to be together."

"You've got that right," I replied.

We pulled our hands apart to avoid giving our secret away, and slid down the hallway until we got to the front door of the apartment. To the shock of both of us, my note still sat perched on the door. Olli had not been home yet. I looked at my watch and the time read, 12:58 a.m.

I usually fell asleep around 9:00 p.m. so I never knew exactly what time Olli came home at night, especially since he received his new role as Nazi researcher. I usually noticed the lights cut off in the living room around 1:00 a.m. when I would roll over in my bed or get up to get a glass of water. I assumed that Olli usually wandered in around 12:00-12:30 a.m.

Relief was my first reaction, but then fear overcame me. What could possibly be taking up so much of Olli's time? Ari could see the concern on my face and said,

"Let's go find him. We will then have the upper hand. We can tell him that you woke up and panicked because he was not home yet; that you came and got me so that he would not be angry that you went out alone. It is perfect."

I looked at Ari and said,

"You are smarter than you look."

The note this time read:

Uncle Olli—Woke up and got worried about you, went to look for you. Love,
JJP.

We headed back down the stairs, careful to avoid anyone who might wonder what two teenagers hoped to gain wandering around the city in the middle of the night. Ari again took my hand when we stepped into the cold, but this time he led. Somewhere along the way of growing up together, I had missed the part where he got taller than me and stronger than me. It felt nice to have him take care of me.

Thinking to myself, I still couldn't figure out why I appealed to Ari. I had never appealed to anyone before. Even the soldiers, who flirted with everything that walked by, completely ignored me. Before I knew it words flew out of my mouth.

"Why me?" I asked about half way to the University grounds.

"Why you what?"

"Of all of the girls in Vienna, why me? I know I am not as beautiful as some of your old girlfriends, not to mention how mean I have been to you for years."

"Your beautiful to me Julia. Every little detail, the scar on your forehead, the way your lower lip rolls, even your insults and demeanor are sexy, and over time, and with each day we have been together, my feelings have grown for you. Every time I see you, you are more wonderful. You are just different."

I smiled and squeezed Ari's hand as we continued to walk towards Hauptuni in silence.

By the time we reached the entrance to the building where Olli's office resided, the snow fell from the sky like rain in a spring thunderstorm, and with every second it seemed to fall harder than the moment before. Blinded by the white sheet that formed before our eyes and feet, we practically slipped through the door. Upon entering the building, I brushed the snow out of Ari's hair. It still amazed me that he desired me as his girlfriend. We separated hands again and walked up the stairs.

Olli's office door appeared in front of my eyes like a prison cell, as I peeked in through the tiny window. It seemed cold, distant, and empty compared to earlier years in Vienna. My eyes searched for some piece of who Olli used to be, but to my disappointment, no emotion existed in his private space. Even the Bible, which once existed as a permanent piece of Olli's desk, vanished into thin air.

"Where is he?" I asked aloud, more to myself than to Ari.

"I don't know. We would have passed him on the way."

"He's lying to me."

"I'm sure something came up Julia. Not to mention it is almost impossible for people to talk to each other openly right now. He has a lot going on, and he definitely has a lot resting on his shoulders."

My eyes looked toward the ground as I still stood in the hallway outside of Olli's office, and without any control, tears began to run down my face.

"What's wrong Julia? I'm sure he is fine."

"Don't worry about me. It is nothing," I sobbed.

"It's just that he is a stranger now, and I don't know when or if I will get my Uncle Olli back. He is somewhere doing something which excludes me from his life."

"In all fairness Jules, we are somewhere doing something which he is clueless about," Ari responded while rubbing my back.

A smile broke out on my face and Ari took off his gloves to wipe away my tears.

"You okay?"

"Ari just promise that you won't change on me. I need something to be real."

"I promise," he said as he took my hand once again and as we headed home in the thickest snow I could remember since living in Vienna.

This time when we reached the apartment, Ari left me at the door with a warm good night hug and a sweet and gentle kiss. My note still rested on the door, and as it approached 1:45 a.m. Olli remained missing in action.

"You know where to find me if you need me Julia," Ari offered.

"Anything, Anytime."

"I'll be fine. Of course I won't sleep until he gets in. I am going to go to my room and read to try and take my mind off of the subject. I'll see you in the morning?"

"Bright and early Beautiful."

We parted ways and I found myself all alone in our apartment, which over time had gradually seemed to decrease in size. In an anxious state of worry and concern for Olli's well-being, I decided to sit in the living room and wait for him to let him know just how much he had worried me.

The time flew by with all of the new things over which to obsess. My mind had not stopped since that morning at the cathedral, and with the new set of events that had recently transpired I had about ten different things to analyze in my mind. I kept skipping from thing to thing, first thinking about Ari and then worrying about Olli. I started developing scenarios in my mind, good and bad. What if Olli had been caught helping the Spiros? What if Ari and I fell in love and got married? What if the Nazi's took over the world? Where could Olli be in this snowstorm? The questions went on and on, and the longer I sat there, the more my muscles tightened.

Though I enjoyed thinking about my time with Ari over and over again, it also became an obsessive urge to replay all of the events in an attempt to feel the same butterflies, only this time through memories. I became so overwhelmed that I decided to employ the breathing techniques from my grandfather's letter, and by the time the front door opened, I had finally found enough peace to fall asleep.

"Where the hell have you been? It is 2:30 a.m.," I yelled as I opened my bedroom door.

"Jules, why are you up?"

"I'm the one asking the questions here. If you are going to come wandering in at 2:30 in the morning, then I need some kind of advanced notice so I don't wake up in the middle of the night worried sick about the location of my godfather."

"Sweetheart I'm so sorry for worrying you," Olli told me as he grabbed me up out of my chair and gave me a huge hug.

"I was working in my office trying to catch up on some grading and I lost complete track of time. By the time I realized how late it was, I didn't want to come in and wake you, so I waited until I thought you would be in a deep sleep. Obviously my plan failed."

Overwhelmed with guilt in the awareness that the lies went both ways, I just looked at Olli and said,

"You have got to let me know you are okay, especially with all that is going on in the world. Don't worry me again."

"Yes General Julia," Olli replied with a smile I had not seen in quite a while.

I finally made my way to my bedroom, almost jittery from the excitement of the day. I wondered where Olli had been, and why he felt that he had to lie to me about his actual locale. Of course it was likely I would never know, because I would have to admit my own escapades.

More so than Olli's whereabouts, my mind was consumed with Ari. I couldn't get past the idea that today had been a fluke, and that tomorrow he would have forgotten the connection we made. I worried that things would be awkward, and that we wouldn't know where to start.

If you have ever known someone and really enjoyed their company, and then been away from them for maybe a week, month, or year and come back together, you know that it sometimes takes a while to reconnect. You wonder if the other person remembers the good time you had together or if they forgot about you completely. You experience this a lot as a kid. You have friends that you play with in primary school, and then you go your separate ways. When you see them again, you don't know if they remember you and the fun you had together. You question yourself: Do they remember the same things you do, or did they completely forget about your presence in their lives?

I wondered these questions about Ari, although I would see him in less than eight hours. Maybe tomorrow would be different, maybe I had blown things out of proportion in my mind and he wouldn't be as I remembered. What if he pretended that the things that happened between us weren't real? I finally told myself I would just have to wait and see, and fell asleep from pure exhaustion.

CHAPTER 14

"Julia, are you awake yet? Ari will be here anytime to study, and I am leaving for work. I promise I will be home earlier tonight, probably around 10:30."

I came out of my room half asleep, realizing that I had slept like a rock, so much so, that I had allowed myself to oversleep more than an hour longer than usual. As I entered the kitchen, Olli looked at me and said,

"Well I am glad to see you got some rest after last night."

Immediately my mind went to the possibility that somehow he knew about the night Ari and I had together, but then realized that he referred to our early morning argument.

"Why do you look so dazed? Are you okay?"

"Just tired for some reason. Must be the weather."

Olli smiled at me and gave me a hug.

"There is food on the counter should you and Ari get hungry. Speaking of Ari, what have you been teaching him?"

"Austrian history. We went to the Votivkirche yesterday and talked about its heritage." Then to protect myself, I added in,

"I think it was way over his head."

"Jules be nice," Olli added when Ari came in the front door.

I had to look at the floor so that Olli could not see the huge smile that took over my face. I gathered myself and said,

"Speak of the devil. Here comes the boy wonder now."

Ari marched in saying, "Here is your work Drill Sergeant. Three and a half pages on how the military uniform will once again protect Vienna."

"So idealistic aren't you my dear boy," I replied.

I certainly had to keep up the appearance of despising and

demeaning Ari.

"Julia…" Olli eked out, simply out of the habit of protecting Ari.

"I know Uncle Olli, I'm sorry. I will examine his paper with complete impartiality, only correcting grammar and historical inaccuracies."

"Thank you," Olli continued.

"And Ari, please help yourself to the food on the counter, just in case Julia decides to let you starve as some kind of experiment."

Olli turned to walk out and then paused and turned to say,

"And Julia both of your science packets are due on Friday, so you need to make sure you take a break from being such a hard ass and work on your science together. It will do you some good to be the student."

"Love you Uncle Olli," I replied as Olli found his way out the door.

For once, I found excitement in being left alone with Ari. Of course, I had no idea where to start once we were alone. Should I start a conversation? Should I pretend yesterday never happened? Should I make some clever comment? Or should I just wait to see his reaction, since he obviously had more experience?

The moment the door closed, before I even had a chance to determine my course of action, Ari walked across the room toward me with an increasingly large smile until he reached my face, at which point he grabbed me and gave me a kiss. Immediately all fear escaped me, and I was in the same place he left me the day before.

"Good morning Beautiful," he said with his teeth glaring as he reached down to hold my hand.

"Hello," I replied shyly, trying to avoid eye contact with my face blushing uncontrollably. I could feel my temperature rise, and for once I had no control over my reactions. I couldn't help but smile.

"Wow, you are even more beautiful when you smile like that," Ari continued.

"So General Patterson, what is on the agenda for today?"

"I imagine those God-awful science packets. Let's head over to the library and get them finished, and then we can talk about your paper."

After about thirty minutes of nibbling on food and smiling at each other, we headed out the door. I honestly felt awe for Ari. When on earth could he have found the time to write his assignment after the day we shared; not to mention he couldn't have gotten home before 2:00 a.m.

We filed down the stairs without even making contact, realizing that any change in routine could blow our cover. When we reached the bottom of the stairs, the snow piles just seemed too tall to tackle. I looked over at Ari and said,

"Maybe this should just be an indoor study day."

We made our way back up the stairs and entered the apartment breathing hard from the cold and from the stairs. Once Ari caught his breath, he said,

"It must have just started coming down in sheets out there. I'm glad I got here while the streets were still passable. I hope Olli made it to work okay."

"If that is even where he is really going," I shot back.

"Lord knows what he is really up to."

"Give him the benefit of the doubt. You know he has a lot going on."

"I just don't understand where he could have been so late. I mean I understand if he is missing in action in the middle of the day, but who or what is even operating past midnight?"

"Keep in mind that we were both operating last night at that hour," Ari said with a smile.

I smiled back and simply said,

"Okay smart ass you win."

"I would have kissed you a long time ago if I had known I would actually win at an argument."

"Argument? What argument? I was just testing your ability to use logic, and you passed," I replied almost giggly like a five year old.

As I turned my back Ari came up from behind me and wrapped his arms around me giving me a bear hug.

"I guess, I'll just have to wrestle you into submission," he said as I noticed for the first time just how strong he had become.

I felt so warm and good that I never wanted him to let go.

For the moment I let him think he had control, I felt pure, uncontrollable, bliss. Then, in my typical manner of always seeking the upper hand, I grabbed his thumb and twisted it back. When he let go of me in pain, I took his arm, with his thumb still twisted back, and turned him around placing his arm behind his back. Once he was in my complete control I put him in a headlock and brought him down to the floor, well aware of the fact that he could regain control at any moment, but that he would never risk hurting me. I just figured it was one of my rights as the female in the relationship.

In the process laughing hysterically, we both lost our balance and fell over. When we finally caught our breath, Ari looked over at me and brushed the hair out of my face.

"Damn! Sometimes I forget that men raised you. At least you didn't punch me in the nose this time."

"I missed," I responded with a wink and a successful attempt to get myself up off the floor.

I flopped into the closest chair in the living room and said,

"Would you have believed yesterday morning that we would be acting like this today? It is amazing how fast things can change."

With his hand leaning over his knee still sitting on the floor and laughing, Ari said,

"I sure would have hoped."

My heart skipped in my chest and I suddenly had that same feeling of an indescribable loss of mental self-control. Suddenly, Ari was flawless. His looks were perfect, and even the things that once annoyed me magically seemed adorable. Every time I saw his face, it seemed like the first time, even better than the way I pictured it in my mind. The person I had despised more than anyone else in the world, besides Adolph Hitler of course, within twenty-four hours suddenly become perfect. I would later realize that was what people often referred to as love.

I regained consciousness and we made our way over to the counter to start our science work, which I had been dreading for way too long. I didn't understand it, I didn't want to understand it, and I had no interest in doing anything but memorizing enough facts to satisfy Olli and move on with information that actually enlightened my mind. Ari on the other hand breezed right through the assignment left by Olli and helped me along the way. It was probably the most pleasant science experiment of my life.

By mid-afternoon, science was a topic of the past. I read Ari's homework assignment and gave it back to him with grammatical corrections only, because his argument made perfect sense. Yes, it spewed propaganda and praise of the German and Austrian military machine, but it was all he could have possibly written in the society in which we found ourselves, constantly monitored, constantly under a microscope. Therefore, the content served as a perfect reflection of what a "Good Austrian" would have to say about Austria's military.

As Ari read over my corrections on sentence structure, verb tenses, introductory and conclusion paragraphs, and spelling, I looked out the apartment window to notice that the snow had dramatically let up and that the sun had come out.

"Let's try and go outside and throw the baseball in a few minutes. The snow has practically stopped," I yelled across the living room at Ari.

"Are you crazy? It's freezing out there, plus there are still piles of snow everywhere. What is your obsession with the baseball glove anyway? You are always carrying it around. Not that I mind, you must just really love baseball to want to play outside in this weather."

I immediately realized that Ari had no knowledge of my best friend in the world: Patrick. Reflecting on the secret he revealed to me yesterday, I told myself that it was finally time to share my biggest secret with him: Patrick's letter in the library; the very place where I decided to be his girlfriend.

"What do you say we go to the library now that the storm has seemed to clear? I have something I would like to share with you."

"What does it have to do with baseball?"

"You will see."

We waited until it got dark so that we could slip into the library once again past the night librarian. Thankfully the morning's storm only contained pure snow rather than ice. We were able to get to the library while only slipping on a few slick patches. I grabbed Ari's hand once we entered the back stairwell of the library and darted up the stairs dragging him behind me with my baseball glove still under my arm.

After five flights of stairs we stood in the same area of the night before, breathing heavily and rubbing our hands together trying to keep warm. Ari threw his coat around my shoulders and finally looked at me to say,

"Is this going to make sense soon? Not that I have a problem with all of this mystery, I think it is cute, but you are killing me with anticipation."

"Sorry," I replied.

"You will hopefully understand before we leave here."

My eyes had not looked at the leg of my cubicle since the day I put the note from Patrick in there, fearing that attention to the area would give away its importance, and I hoped with all of my heart that it still sat in there as pure as the day I hid it for safe-keeping. Although no one ever graced the fifth floor of the library or even moved the desks around, I still worried that somehow the note would be missing.

"Ari I have something to tell you. You told me something very special yesterday, a secret so intense that I now feel obligated to share something monumental with you. Although it can not compare to the intensity of yours, there is something that only two people in the world know, and I want to make that three."

Ari sat down in my cubby, and I knelt down on the floor beside the desk.

"This may not seem like a huge secret to you, but to me it is everything. Please don't tell a soul."

He looked down at me with his face blushing and said,

"Never."

I reached down to the bottom of the desk, unscrewed the leg, and quietly lifted the desk off the ground at an angle.

"Do you need help?" Ari broke in.

"No I am fine."

I used my tiny fingers to reach up in the leg and panicked, because I did not feel anything. My fingers searched around frantically until I put my face against the floor and looked into the leg. Sparing me from a heart attack, I saw the letter stuck to the inside of the leg. I quickly pulled it out and immediately put the leg bottom back on the desk. I felt like someone would enter at any moment and catch me, even though the possibility was slim to none.

I unfolded the letter and I lost my breath the moment I saw Patrick's handwriting again.   It had been a while since Patrick sent me a letter, understandably with the German's sniffing around everywhere looking for victims, and communication monitored with anything foreign coming into or going out of Austria. I forgot just how much I missed him.

"What is it?" Ari asked just in time before I completely forgot his existence beside me.

"I will answer all of your questions. Start with this," I said as I reached up to hand him the letter.

Dear Julia,

I must say, you completely lived up to the rumors I have heard about you for past four years or so of my life. My mother has talked about Olli's brilliant goddaughter since you moved to Austria, but I actually had to encounter you to absorb everything you had to offer. In other words, you did not disappoint.

If you ever need anything, anything at all, please just write me at our address in Paris. Julia, I feel like I have made an amazing friend that I can trust for the rest of my life. Therefore, I offer something to you that you must never share with anyone, even Olli. I know that is tough, but I trust and believe in you, that you will not let me down, because in my mind, you are someone General Pershing himself would trust. If you ever catch yourself in an EMERGENCY in this chaotic world and cannot find me, please find Soren Ambler in Paris and give him the key words 1,1,9,9,14,14,20,26. Julia, you must never give ANYONE this key word, you must never use it in conversation, and please pretend it does not exist. I do not seek to scare you, but I know that you understand the current situation in Europe, and in case you need life-saving help, I will be there for you, even if you cannot reach me directly.

Place this letter in a special place, where you will never forget it, but place the knowledge in the back of your mind. Do not seek this person, do not research the key word, do not even think about a situation where you would need to use Soren Ambler. This is just to insure you never find yourself without a friend in this crazy world.

Thank you for being a new friend in a lost world. Of all people it is you I would trust with my life.

Patrick Bellew
Paris, France
November 4, 1937

As Ari turned toward me, I found myself breathing irregularly and getting sick to my stomach. All of the excitement had thrown me into one of my famous panic attacks. I was pissed. The more panic and anxiety entered my life, I came to realize, panic seemed to target my happiness. Every time I found myself in a place of calm and excitement, just like in Paris, I would suddenly be interrupted with an uncontrollable sensation of disaster and impending doom, and to my utter dismay, it was happening again.

"Julia, what is wrong?"

"Just give me a minute," I said as I lied flat on the floor.

Not understanding the principles of panic, Ari hovered right over me asking me questions. I finally said,

"Just back up, I promise I'm fine-give me five minutes and some air. If I am not okay in five minutes, then you can worry. Five minutes Ari, just give me five minutes."

Taking deep breaths and thinking of only the moment at hand, I rolled over on the floor and let my face feel the cold. With every breath in and out, just as my grandfather's letters taught me, I re-entered reality and the panic subsided. After a few moments I felt like I had just vomited; I was sweating, shaky, and nervous, but I felt a hell of a lot better.

I sat up and looked over at Ari and said,

"I am so sorry. I understand if you think I am strange and don't want to be my boyfriend anymore. I have these spells sometimes, and I don't know what they are. I have done some research, and there are cases of other people who experience these same things. It just feels like I lose complete control for a few minutes, like I am going to die and then it goes away. It is the worst feeling in the entire world."

Ari responded with the only thing any human could say that could comfort me at that moment.

"No worries Sweetheart, that happens to my Mom all the time, especially when she is stressed."

"So I didn't scare you away?"

"It is going to take a hell of a lot more than a genius getting overwhelmed every now and then to run me off.

In that moment, the weight of the world flew from my shoulders like a newspaper flying out of the hands of a businessman on a windy Chicago day. I immediately stood up and grabbed Ari. I held him as tight as I could, and I cried for the second time in less than 24 hours. I thought for sure he would head for the hills; rather he pulled me down into his lap and held me, stroked my hair, and kissed my forehead.

The moment passed, and when I looked up from Ari's shoulder, he wiped my cheeks and said,

"Okay now?"

"You probably wish you could get rid of me. Do you think I am crazy?"

"We are living in a Nazi controlled country throwing its young away like toy soldiers. You are the least crazy person I have ever met. Trust me, lots of people deal with what just happened to you. Matter of fact I would be willing to bet that General Pershing experienced almost life-ending panic when eighty percent of his family died in one day. I know you don't think he is crazy. There is nothing wrong with you. I would say you are perfect now that I know you have real human emotion."

I felt completely vulnerable to the one person who I vowed to never let see my weaknesses. Still speechless, Ari continued,

"You know Julia, we all have our things."

"Is that so?" I asked.

"Yes Julia, that is so."

In that moment, I had never been so glad to let someone see what made me tick. I would be willing to bet that within seconds Ari knew more about me than I knew about myself. Having always looked at the negative when it came to Ari, I was shocked when my heart finally opened my eyes to see his good side. He was smart and practical; things I had chosen to overlook for so long. My God, was he more attractive than ever.

Before I had the chance to ask what "things" Ari had to deal with, he changed the topic again and refocused on the letter,

"Who is Patrick? Is he an old boyfriend? When did you go to Paris?"

"First of all, you are the first boyfriend I have ever had. Secondly, Olli and I went to Paris that week he cancelled all tutoring with you, which is where I met Patrick who gave me a gift with this very letter inside. The gift is my baseball glove, which I carry everywhere. It was a gift to Patrick from my parents on his last birthday before they moved from France to the United States. Olli and my parents were best friends with Patrick's mother Maria in the years before Olli received his professorship in Zurich, and before my grandfather got sick forcing my parents to move to the United

States. We went to Paris to get a book from Maria that she had found for Olli. In the process, I met Patrick who gave me insight into the life of my parents before they had me. I would say Patrick is my best friend in the whole world, although he is significantly older than me. He showed me everything in Paris."

"What does the letter mean?"

"I have always followed the directions exactly. It has been hidden in here since the day I got back from Paris. I have never tried to figure it out, out of respect for Patrick's wishes."

"Why now?"

"You shared something with me yesterday that I can never compare, so I wanted to show you that I trust you the same way. Also, Patrick promised to write me weekly, but he stopped, with good reason, when annexation took place. What concerns me more, however, is how Maria's letters have mysteriously stopped mentioning Patrick."

"Does Maria write to you?"

"No, she writes to Olli, and yes I read them secretly after he opens them and puts them in the shoebox in his closet. He loves her you know. He's never told her, but you can tell."

"Are you sure Patrick's absence in these letters has meaning?"

"Excellent question, and yes I am positive. If you look through every letter ever written to Olli, or at least the ones in his shoebox, they all mention something about Patrick until two months ago; since then, not one word that he even exists. My problem is, how do I know if it is an emergency? How do I know when, or if, to use this letter?"

Ari gave me a hug and said,

"You will know. You are the wisest person I have ever met. You'll know."

We separated from our hug, and without words I gently reached back down and put the letter inside the leg of the cubby. It wasn't time yet. We exited the library and headed back to the apartment, pretending again like we had no personal relationship.

"Maybe we will throw the ball around tomorrow, now that I know the meaning involved."

"That would be nice," I whispered as we approached the bar on the first floor of our apartment building.

With the weather so cold, the German soldiers had found a way of keeping their spirits warm: liquor. As they collapsed out of the doorway whistling and flirting with everything that walked by in a skirt, I saw Ari tense up. He knew that protecting my honor would mean outing our relationship. The protective look in his eyes said everything I needed to hear. His glimpse of jealousy made me feel like a woman.

In reality, however, Ari would never be forced to defend me. Men did not look at me with intrigue, even though the drunken Germans were not that picky. That is what made my relationship with Ari so special. He actually liked me, because he knew me, not because I sparkled like his previous girlfriends of choice.

We entered the building around 8:30 p.m. and to the surprise of both Ari and myself, Olli sat in a chair near the door to the apartment. I stood like a deer caught in a spotlight, like a little girl caught with her hand in the cookie jar, like an actor suddenly struck with stage fright; I did not realize that to Olli, nothing seemed out of the ordinary. Before I could come up with an apology about where Ari and I had been, Ari removed his galoshes and scarf and said,

"Those science packets were tough this week. You wouldn't believe how long it takes a genius to do simple physics."

Catching on to Ari's act, I replied,

"Well Wonder Boy, at least I have a weakness in only one subject rather than strength in only one subject."

As expected, Olli chimed in,

"Kids that is enough name calling. Julia, would you please excuse Ari and myself so that we can discuss something?"

"What are you going to talk about that I cannot be present?"

"For once let me be the adult. This needs to be between just me and Ari."

I stormed off to my room, not really upset, knowing that I could hear everything from my bedroom and knowing that Ari would fill me in on whatever I could not hear.

I slammed my bedroom door and made some racket, and then I put my ear up to the door to eavesdrop on the conversation.

"First of all, I want to thank you for helping me protect Julia. She is quite impulsive, and it is one less thing for me to worry about knowing that she is not alone. I know she can be difficult, but I have faith that you are benefiting as well. She is at the point now where she could teach me a thing or two."

I smiled to myself. I had forgotten how well Olli knew me. God, how I missed him, even when he stood beside me, the world had separated us millions of miles apart.

Olli continued,

"It has come to my attention that you are not yet enlisted in the Hitler Youth. Your older brother Stefan has been participating and preparing physically and mentally for a couple years now. I think that it would be in your best interest at this point to become an active participant. I think that you understand the necessity of you to join. Do you understand me?"

"Yes sir," Ari replied with a knot in his throat.

"I understand that this choice will be in the best interest of my family and FRIENDS."

"I will talk to Julia later to inform her that she does not have permission to leave the apartment without my approval if you are at training sessions. I think that you need to be involved at least once a week."

"Yes sir. Are my parents aware of this?"

"Yes. They asked me to discuss it with you. I'm sure they will also bring it up when you go home. Speaking of home, I think you should head on. Julia has monopolized enough of your time today with books and riddles I'm sure."

"Have a good evening," Ari replied.

"And I will make sure my participation in the youth organization is clear before I arrive tomorrow. I don't think it will literally kill Julia to miss and hour in the library."

Life changed very little in the following months. Ari and I studied during the day, keeping our relationship secret. We had our private discussions at night in the library, talking about Patrick and my trip to Paris, Maria and Olli's relationship, Ari's recent activity in the Hitler youth movement, Ari's family, my grandfather's letters, and even my parents. I did not realize until we started talking about our lives, our dreams, our likes and dislikes, how very little Ari knew about how and why I was an orphan.

Ari once said to me,

"Gosh, I bet you miss your Dad. It was just the two of you for so long."

Amazingly, I never even thought much about those statements. Since I had written that letter to my father trying to forget all of the pain, I rarely thought about my life before I came to live in Austria. It seemed like a completely different lifetime. Sometimes I even questioned whether or not anyone in the United States would even remember that I once existed there. My first eight years had been significant to only two people, my father and myself, and my father no longer had a voice.

I loved being around Ari, talking to him about things I had never let out of my mouth, but it always seemed to bring on a flood of emotion. I learned quickly the difficulty involved in sharing one's life with the world.

As little changed in the daily pattern of life, the world found itself turning somersaults. Every person in Europe had to make a choice of good or evil, and the lines were not black and white. Like Ari and Olli, one's actions did not, could not, reflect one's heart.

So when Germany took control of Norway and Denmark in the middle of the year, I pretended that life continued as normal while trying to figure out how to disturb German operations. Little opportunity presented itself, so I again felt stuck in a world I wanted to change, but could not find the vehicle to do so. The Procks and Olli had figured out a way to help without being obvious traitors. I also had to figure out a way. I had to find my own way to make General Pershing proud. For some reason I thought Olli's letters from Maria or my grandfather's letters would provide answers to my questions, a portal to guide my soul.

CHAPTER 15

I jumped out of bed to a startling noise. Thinking someone aimed to break in the front door of our apartment, my heart started to pound and I ran towards the door. I soon realized that someone was actually knocking. Completely disoriented, I looked at the clock as I entered the living room. To my utter dismay, the time read 4:37 a.m. I peeked through the hole to see a man in complete German officer dress. I opened the door, remembering that Olli appeared to the naked eye to be this man's superior in the Third Reich, and with Olli in the apartment, I had protection

"I need to speak with Professor Zingre please," the officer barked at me.

"Give me one moment please," I said as I turned toward the hallway rolling my eyes without him seeing.

I walked toward Olli's bedroom as fast as I could, desiring to get away from the intimidating man at the door, and wondering why Olli had still not responded to the sudden noise.

"Uncle Olli," I whispered toward Olli's bedroom door.

"You have a charming visitor."

Olli and I decided years ago that "charming" would serve as a code word when referring to any Nazi in our presence.

When Olli did not answer his door, I cracked the door and immediately saw a perfectly made bed with neatly folded pajamas on top, bedroom shoes underneath the bed skirt, and missing snow boots. With a pit forming in my stomach, I turned around to see that the mystery guest lounged in a seat in the living room.

"It appears the professor has gone out."

"I need to speak with him now," the officer spewed.

I can't shit him out, I thought to myself, but I gathered myself to say,

"Did you check his office at Hauptuni?" I offered as I looked toward the door.

I wanted him gone. He made me feel incredibly uncomfortable. Something was not right about this twenty-something Nazi alone in an apartment with me at 4:30 in the morning.

He got up out of the chair by the door and started to walk toward me.

"You will lead me there. Go get dressed now," he said as he grabbed my arm.

Without even thinking about blowing cover, Olli's position, or proper customs I spouted out,

"That's what you think asshole," and before he had the chance to realize what was happening, I grabbed his arm and held it against my side and jabbed both of our elbows into his ribs and then threw my head back into the center of his face.

He released my arm and grabbed his stomach. Before he had the chance to grab hold of me again, I kicked him below the belt as he fell to the floor. Then I shoved my knee into his face. At that moment, Olli walked through the front door. I wish I had a picture of that moment.

"What the hell is going on?" Olli said as he rushed toward me.

He picked me up and ran me out to the hallway. With tears in my eyes and anger in my throat, Olli asked me,

"Are you okay? What happened?" I explained everything with fury in my voice.

"Wait here," Olli demanded as he marched back into the apartment.

"Get the hell out of my home and don't you ever come back. I will be speaking with your superiors tomorrow, and you can expect a demotion of rank. And if I ever see you near my daughter again, you will be the victim of more than just a beating from a teenage girl."

With his head down, the soldier ran past me and down the stairs. I re-entered the apartment and with confusion in my voice I screamed,

"Where the hell have you been? You make Ari follow me around to protect me, and then you leave me alone in the middle of the night without telling me. Still writhing in terror, I started bawling and crouched down on the floor and said, "Where were you?"

"I am so, so sorry. You are right. My actions are inexcusable. I had to run over to the University, because I forgot my most recent ethnic analysis, which I need for a meeting first thing in the morning. I didn't want to wake you. It will never happen again. I promise."

Olli smiled, wiped my tears, and said,

"At least we know you can take care of yourself."

Still half sobbing and half laughing, I asked,

"What did he want that was so urgent anyway?"

"I don't know, but I'll find out tomorrow. Whatever he wanted, there is no excuse for his actions. Don't you worry, I'll take care of him."

With those words, Olli actually sounded for the first time to my ears like a Nazi.

The next morning, Olli actually cooked for me. I knew he felt responsible, because it was the first time I could remember him actually making food with his own two hands since we returned from Paris where he cooked for Maria. When Ari arrived, Olli headed off for his important meeting. As he headed towards the door, he looked back to me and said,

"Everything will be okay. I'll give you an update this afternoon. I promise I'll be home by 5:00, and I'll cook supper."

"What was that about?" Ari asked as Olli headed out in the snow below the apartment.

163

It took me thirty minutes to explain the events of the early morning.

"It's a good thing he didn't hurt you, because I would have killed him. Nobody puts their hands on my Julia."

His words made my heart melt. No doubt about it, I was in love with him. It was the first time I let myself say that and believe it in my heart.

Ari continued,

"Maybe it has something to do with France."

Coming out of my love comma, I turned in complete panic to say,

"What happened in France?"

"Oh, I thought you would have heard, but I guess you haven't been out yet today to see a newspaper. Germany began an invasion of France yesterday."

"What about Patrick?"

"We don't know anything yet. Let's wait until we see the French response. We don't even know if Patrick is still in France."

"You're right. We must be patient," I said reassuring myself.

With the events of the day before us, and with the recent news about France, I didn't even feel like going to the library. I just wanted to be held and talk. In other words, I really wanted to feel like a girl, no fronts, just pure emotion. Ari could sense my nervousness and vulnerability, and he obliged my wishes without even using words. He just grabbed me and started talking while brushing the hair out of my face.

"So did you make him bleed?"

"My adrenaline rushed so high, I don't remember much past throwing my head back and Olli dragging me into the hallway. Do you think Olli is in trouble because of me?"

"Not possible. He is ranked so high because of his research. There is no way they would blame him."

"I want to show you something," I continued as I grabbed Ari's hand and pulled him towards Olli's bedroom.

"Please tell me there is a good reason you are dragging me toward a bedroom," Ari said with a devilish smile.

"You wish," I responded as I opened Olli's closet and pulled out a box below the shoebox full of letters.

I opened the box and pulled out stacks of paper on top of paper. Ari flipped through the papers,

"My God what is this?"

"Extermination," I replied.

Ari held in his hands lists of names, thousands and thousands of names, categorized by race, age, skills, political party, and worth to the German Reich. These were the lists of occupied peoples, and a classification of their values as if they were breeds of dogs. Olli had these lists to determine whom he could pick for test subjects in his research on racial superiority.

Thank God he didn't actually torture or kill anyone like the Nazi's expected him to. That was his fight against Hitler. Fake reports, intelligence, and a serious demeanor kept him inconspicuous. I came to believe that God's grace put him in that position.

"I have an idea, but it is risky, and I will need your help."

"You're brilliant," Ari replied.

"I trust you."

"He has three lists here," I continued as I flipped through the names.

"He has a list of those in confinement from occupied countries, a list of wanted political enemies who do not know they are political enemies, and a list of those scheduled for execution. The latter is the list he usually keeps in observation for his research, no doubt to save them from certain death."

"So what is your plan General Patterson?"

"I want to figure out how to inform the people on the 2nd list that they are in danger. Maybe they will have a chance to get out."

I took a deep breath and said,

"I just want to help at least one person in this world gone to hell, so I can live with myself."

"It's too dangerous," Ari spoke back before even thinking.

"Julia, you can't," he continued holding back his voice to a whisper.

After a pause I looked Ari in the eyes and said,

"If I can't use my own humanity Ari, then I am already lost. Will you please help me?"

Putting his head down, he wrapped his arms around me and said,

"I can't say no to you. We live together, we die together. I'm not going to let you do this alone, but we have to talk about everything before either one of us does anything."

"Agreed," I replied.

As five o'clock neared, Ari and I pulled out the books and began studying. We knew that Olli would be home on time, and we needed to appear to have actually hated each other all day, which was getting more difficult with every breath.

I sat at the counter, he sat in the chair by the door, and we both anxiously awaited Olli's entrance and news about the events of the early morning. At almost exactly 5:00, Olli walked through the front door. I looked at him from the counter and said,

"Wow, it is possible for you to be on time."

"Just like your mother, you are always giving a professor a hard time about punctuality."

I just smiled. It had been so long since my Uncle Olli had slipped through the seams of his Nazi uniform. He placed a bag of groceries on the counter near me, and looked over to Ari to say,

"I'm sure you have had your hands full today. You are excused from your duties early."

With a look of disappointment at the denial of information about the morning events, Ari got out of his seat and headed for the door.

"Thank you sir. I'll see you in the morning Drill Sergeant."

"Not with any luck," I replied.

Still sitting at the counter, now across from Olli, I waited to hear about the ripple effect of my morning actions.

"So how was your day?" Olli began.

I immediately jumped in and said,

"Cut the crap. Are we in trouble?"

"Of course not. I can tell you, however, that one over-reactive officer has been demoted, and that your godfather is very sorry for putting you in such a horrible situation. Thank God your father taught you how to beat the hell out of people, but quite unfortunate for Ari and the man coming to tell me that I needed to report to Berlin."

"Berlin?"

"Yes Jules, Berlin. I have been asked to make a trip through the recently occupied countries to help determine the classifications of the races. The young officer from this morning decided to make a name for himself by being the first to tell me of my planned 7:00 a.m. departure. Of course when he made an ass out of himself, my plans were delayed until tomorrow. You, however, are the current talk of the headquarters. The joke is that you should be Hitler's personal bodyguard."

I smiled on the inside about my ability to put a grown man on his ass, but in the same moment I knew just how lucky I had been. He never expected me to fight back. If he had, the story could have turned out quite differently, and all of that suddenly hit home.

"Will I go with you to Berlin?"

"I have arranged for you to stay with the Procks. You must follow all of their directions, and try and be nice to Ari. I will be gone about 5 days. Do you understand what I need you to do?"

"Of course Uncle Olli," I replied with a twinge of excitement about sleeping in the same house as Ari, although the knowledge that the Spiros were in hiding on the same premises sent chills through my entire body.

I tried to wrap my mind around the idea that two people were hiding in some tiny space, while I continued to live my life. For every move I made, conversation I had, or time I slept in my bed, they remained trapped indefinitely, not knowing if they would be found the next day. My God how selfish I felt.

Olli and I had a magnificent evening together. While he cooked and boosted my ego for protecting myself, the adrenaline from the day slowly seeped out of my body. We talked about the pride my parents would feel toward me, the weather, my health, and the memories we held together. For one evening in 1940 Austria, life returned to the good old days.

As I headed toward bed, Olli called for me and said,

"I'll take you to the Procks' in the morning before I leave. Also, I would like for you to teach my class while I am gone. I trust your judgment Jules. Just make sure you take Ari with you and remember where we are and who you are talking to."

CHAPTER 16

"You'll be staying in Ari's room. He can bunk with Stefan while you are our guest," Ms. Prock said as I entered the front door of the Prock residence with Olli on one side and my suitcase on the other.

"I can sleep in a sleeping bag on the living room floor. I don't want to put anyone out," I said politely.

"Oh you know the thought of inconveniencing Ari is a dream come true for you," she replied with a sly smile.

"Right this way Sweetheart."

As I settled myself in Ari's room, with my stuffed monkey and baseball glove, Olli stood in the living room with Mrs. Prock thanking her for the favor and telling her about his trip.

"I really do appreciate this Annaliese."

"Don't even start Olli, after all you have done for Ari, this is the least I could do. Not to mention that Julia is an absolute pleasure. It will be nice to have an in-depth conversation with someone about history."

"Well if you need anything just..."

"Olli, really she will be fine."

"I know, I know. It is just that from the day she came to Austria, we haven't been apart. Goodness, it has been over seven years."

"You have done a great job, so relax and be safe."

"Thanks Annaliese for everything," Olli said as he headed toward the door.

"Come give me a hug," Olli yelled back in the house toward me from the doorway.

I ran out and gave Olli a hug like I would never see him again. In my mind, I actually wondered if he would come back. Something about the circumstances bothered me. I held back tears and released him, thinking back to the last time I saw my own father. My God, I couldn't stand to lose him. It would kill me.

"Five days," is all I said to Olli.

"Five days," he replied wiping a tear from his own eye.

Although I had already seen Olli more time that day than I normally saw him in a week with his new position, I felt all alone when he walked out that door. No word could describe how I felt better than the basic word: sad. I sat in the Procks' kitchen in self-sorrow as Mrs. Prock talked to me about Napoleon and Jefferson, when Ari came popping in the front door. Mrs. Prock immediately said,

"Go change the sheets in your room for Julia and make sure everything is picked up please."

"Is it not good enough that she stole my room, now I have to wait on her hand and foot?"

"Young man, do not talk back to me."

"Yes Ma'am," Ari replied as he turned by me to walk toward what usually served as his bedroom.

On the way he winked at me, with his back turned to his mother.

"I saw you smile," Mrs. Prock said to me.

Panicking thinking she knew our secret, I froze. She continued,

"I can forgive you for enjoying my son's torment. He no doubt finds every opportunity to do the same to you. I can imagine it is quite tough for you to be trailed around Vienna every moment. Maybe you and I can spend some time together while Olli is out of town. It could be a refreshing change for you. What do you think?"

Only using common courtesy I smiled and said,

"That would be nice."

Internally, I despised the idea. I liked Mrs. Prock well enough, however, the idea of doing girly things made me feel incredibly uneasy. Although I loved feeling pretty and attractive for Ari, I had no idea how to be a woman, and I had accepted that. I loved ignoring gender stereotypes and just doing what made me happy. Growing up around men of course reinforced this nonchalant view of physical and emotional appearance. My God I missed Olli.

Mrs. Prock interrupted my thoughts and began talking about Olli. She went on and on about how wonderful Professor Zingre was, what a good man he aimed to be, how sad it was that he didn't have a girlfriend, etc. I chimed in about the wonders my godfather possessed, and before I knew it, my anxiety about being left at the Procks' house eluded me and the day was gone.

When night arrived, I found myself exhausted and ready for bed. As I headed towards Ari's bedroom, I passed Stefan's room where he and Ari were making up the other twin bed for Ari to sleep on. When I looked in the door, Stefan turned toward me, released a huge smile, and said,

"Hello Julia. Sleep tight."

Kind of creeped out, I walked faster and entered Ari's room. I couldn't believe that Ari had ratted out our relationship. That was the only sensible explanation as to why Stefan acted like he had magical insight into my life.

After my irritation ended, it made me feel incredibly happy to know that someone had awareness of our relationship. I felt validated and special. It made my heart skip a beat to think that not only was I good enough to be with someone of Ari's attractiveness, but that he gladly told the person he trusted the most about me.

Planning to pretend to be infuriated with Ari at the library the next day, I snuggled under the warm blanket. Ari's natural scent overwhelmed me, although I had never noticed he even had a scent before. Truly consumed with a sense of peace, excitement, and comfort provided by knowing I slept in the room next to Ari and immersed amongst Ari's being I quickly fell asleep.

I dreamt all night of Nazis banging down the doors and finding the Spiros, dragging me away, and murdering Olli in Berlin. As my subconscious spewed my unspoken fears, I sat up in bed with my hands around my knees shivering. I would have given anything to have Ari hold me, but I knew that could not happen. To help myself through the night, I pretended that Ari sat beside me rubbing my hair and telling me funny stories to distract my mind from my dreams. These imaginary scenarios along with my baseball glove eased my fears just enough for me to get patches of half-awaken sleep.

"Good morning Sleepy-head," Ari said as he obnoxiously banged on my bedroom door.

"I knew you were dumb, but I didn't know you were lazy too," Ari spouted so everyone in the house could hear.

Of course he followed his flurry of insults with a wink and kiss quickly blown through the air.

As I awoke to Ari's voice and face, I knew I loved him. The boy I had once despised was turning into the man who felt perfect in every way. I still struggled to believe that someone who made me feel so good, who I had such a crush on, actually liked me back. I would look into his eyes and wonder how someone like him could possibly have fallen for someone like me: and that feeling was priceless and indescribable.

I loved him in that way, when you see a man's face, each time he becomes more and more attractive, until you think he couldn't be more handsome, that is until you see him again.

"Ari Prock, don't you talk to that nice young lady like that.

"If you are going to call her stupid and lazy, than I would hate to find out the words that describe you," Mrs. Prock scolded Ari as he came into the kitchen for breakfast.

"Julia, don't think twice about my baby boy's words. We are still working on his manners."

It was at the Procks' house that Ari and I began our quest to inform the people on Olli's lists of potential enemies and prisoners, so that with some miracle, they still had time to escape. We had determined previously that we would start with Jurgen Sina, a local Austrian artist.

Put on a list of Nazi hatred simply by supporting local Jewish artists in his gallery in the years preceding occupation, Jurgen found himself accused of degenerating classic art by displaying modern Jewish art, a characteristic Adolph Hitler personally despised. Poor Mr. Sina had no idea that he had become an enemy of the state, and he became my first attempt to make General Pershing proud.

After going to have tea with Mrs. Prock to satisfy her need to provide me with "girl things", we returned to the Prock home, where Ari and I then headed to the library.

Tickled on the inside, yet appearing furious that Ari proudly claimed me as his girlfriend to his brother I said,

"So why the hell did you tell Stefan about us? I thought we promised not to tell anyone."

"Sorry Beautiful. He started asking me questions about why I was out so late, and why he had to cover for me so much. He told me I would be on my own unless he got some answers. So I told him. Not to mention I have been dying to tell someone that the smartest girl in all of Europe is dating me and not him. Trust me, he will never tell our secret."

"I hope you are right," I said as we approached the library.

Shivering on the inside from my intensifying feelings for Ari, I couldn't even look him in the face without blushing. The little asshole made me truly breathless.

We waved at Ms. Gerg as we entered the library. I could see the disappointment spread across her face when I did not have any of Olli's local leftovers for her, so we stopped by the counter, and I explained Olli's current situation. She nodded with her typical half-smile. I gave her my list of books, on science of course, so that she could tattle back to Olli that I actually cared about my science education, as Ari and I headed upstairs to wait for the books she would bring shortly. It was of upmost importance to keep up appearances.

Ms. Gerg delivered our books as I barked orders at Ari about the daily lessons, and then she headed back downstairs to surely talk to the other librarians about me and my need for a woman's real influence. Lord knows she probably took every opportunity to call Olli about me, because she simply hoped he would ask her on a date.

We studied for a few hours, actually doing what we were supposed to do for once, and then we made our way to Liechtenstein Palace to talk about our plan of action in a public place, surrounded by lots of people, making lots of noise. We seated ourselves in the same place where we had our first decent conversation and I began with,

"So how are we going to deal with number 1?"

We decided to refer to those we sought to help as numbers to avoid leaving any trails.

"You tell me General," Ari replied.

We started talking, and before we knew it, we had been discussing our options for two and a half hours, until we finally came up with a plan to save our first future victim of Nazi hatred.

We decided that we would use the facade of Nazi support and Ari's contributions and training in the Hitler Youth, also known as Jungvolk, to our advantage.

The Jungvolk were often encouraged to stand guard of Jewish owned businesses, to prohibit anyone from shopping in Jewish owned stores. Since all Jewish owned businesses in Vienna had already been obliterated, we decided to use the same premise to hurt the business of Mr. Sina.

Because he supported Jewish art, although personally not Jewish, we could pretend we aimed to incite a boycott of someone with such a lack of "taste". While Ari and some of his evil "friends," he trained with daily, guarded the front door on a day soon to be determined, I would slip in through the back and talk to Mr. Sina about the immediate danger he faced. If he chose to follow my advice, his disappearance would provide no suspicion, because of the recent boycott of his store. Ari would appear as the perfect Nazi in training, and yet we could save the life of an innocent man.

Meanwhile, while I put Ari to the task of planning our mission, I still held the responsibility of teaching three of Olli's lectures while he was in Berlin. Olli had arranged for "my" substitute lectures to take place after Ari's Jungvolk training, so that Ari would be present to insure my topics were toned down and Third-Reich approved.

Struggling to come up with a topic that would not turn me into a traitor, yet would not reinforce Nazi ideology, I talked Ari into going to the apartment to get a letter or two out of Olli's shoe box from the past. I came across a letter which opened with a poem and found the words to be intriguing. I grabbed it so that Ari and I could get out of the building before being noticed and reported to Olli upon his return.

We had our evening meal at the Procks', and then I headed to bed early. In the morning I would have to perform my first lecture, and the following day Ari and I would help our first victim perhaps avoid annihilation. Still struggling to figure out how I would teach Olli's class without betraying my own ideals, I opened the newly liberated letter from Olli's closet.

Dearest Leeana,

Silhouette of black silky hair,
A wry smile seldom to appear,
The magic of wisdom underneath,
Angels smile on the simplicity,
Of a woman of solid earth,
Who entered this world as my first,
Calm, structured, and assured,
Worldly bothers undisturbed,
All alone yet with everyone,
Her values not to be undone,
The child the gods took away,
But a gift to the world every day.

Have I ever told you child just how much I miss you. I know you get tired of hearing that, but I never want you to doubt that I will ever forget you. Should I never see you again, I will still cherish every moment of your life.

Enough of that, however, because you are no doubt ready to be done with this mush.

My child, you are no longer a child. Unlike your siblings who see the world in black and white, you view the entire spectrum of color, and although that brings you a tremendous gift, it also brings you a huge burden. Having thought about the question you posed in your last letter, I want to simply respond by saying those who want a way will find a way. Leeana, you could make a square fit into a circle or thread a camel through the eye of a needle, you just have to use your gifts and believe in yourself. If you believe, others will follow, because they will be enchanted before they become aware. You read people without your own understanding or their knowledge, and for that you will make a difference in the world. You will find a way to make things work. You always have.

I apologize for the brevity of my message, but I think that you already know the answer to your question, you just must find a way to make it work, and of all people, you can and WILL find the path you are looking for.

As always I love you and miss you dear child. Write me soon.

Love Always,
Papa
April 18, 1920

Papa's words sounded so familiar to me, as if I had heard them time and time again. As I laid my head on the pillow, snuggling again under the comfort of Ari's imaginary presence, it hit me. Regardless of whatever problem my mother had posed to my grandfather, the words of advice sounded exactly like the words my father always spoke to me.

"You determine how people feel Julia. Believe in yourself and others will believe in you. Make a plan and follow it, everyone else will fall in formation."

It seemed as if my grandfather's letter provided a channel to the psyche of my father. No wonder he and my mother fell in love. He understood her, and he understood me.

The mission for my debut in teaching became crystal clear. I would have to figure out a way to make the students understand my plight without them knowing what was happening to them. I would have to be strong, calm, and in control. I fell asleep in complete confidence and with a plan of action.

CHAPTER 17

"Sit your ass down if you want to pass this class. Go ahead try me," I yelled at the first student who tried to skip out of Olli's class when realizing he sat moments away from being taught by a fifteen year-old girl.

"Dr. Zingre has put full trust in my abilities and if you decide to step out of this room in my presence, then I will take that as an automatic withdrawal from this class, because not only will you have put your ego above your education, but you will have also insulted me."

Needless to say the arrogant Nazi jerk found his seat, and I will never forget the smile that broke out on Ari Prock's face.

I kept reminding myself to maintain control, patience, and composure. Somehow passion and destiny kicked in, and I felt completely at home. I was ready.

"I will be teaching you for three lectures. Each lecture will require certain responsibilities on your part. Do not disappoint me."

My plan focused on three parts, with all facets converging to instill one basic principle in the students seated in front of me. I would make them empathize with their fellow members in humanity, with or without their will, and hopefully they would never know the difference. The students would be exposed to the following layout:

Julia Josephine Patterson Lecture Series I
The Geographic Shift of the Jewish Problem

Class Session 1--Lecture on the movement of the Jewish population throughout the world, the problems faced, and the eventual convergence on and disturbance of Europe.

Class Session 2--Round table discussion of answers to the Jewish problem. Have the students discuss and debate ways to find Jews in hiding. Class will end with essay assignment: Imagine you were born Jewish, what would you do, where would you go with the situation in Vienna?

Class Session 3--Collection of essays. Lecture continuation to conclude with evaluation of the world without the Jewish problem, including analysis of adjustments that will be required in society.

I would use all three class sessions to convince the students that I was anti-Semitic. They would truly believe that I understood the plight of the Nazis and that I aimed to help them understand how the Jews operated so that they could better attack them. In reality, however, my purpose was to simply make them sympathize with the Jews in Europe. The culmination assignment, the essay, would force them to use their anti-Semitic purposes, of seeking out Jews in hiding and destroying one of the world's oldest cultures, to put themselves in the position of being born Jewish in Vienna. I held just a glimpse of hope that in all of the propaganda and hate speech, someone would see the light of humanity at the end of the tunnel, that someone would understand that a Jewish child never did anything to anyone. I wanted to force them to relate to the victim, to imagine the world sat just beyond their grasp.

In class session one, things went smoothly, once I made my lack of amusement at being treated with disrespect apparent. I actually forgot Ari sat in the room and became engulfed in my lecture. Although I had taught Olli's classes before, it had been a while, and I had never been left completely to myself to insure classroom management. It was a bright day in a dark time, one I would never forget.

"I will see you the day after tomorrow," I told the class at the very end.

"Come prepared to thoughtfully discuss the Jewish problem."

Afterward Ari and I headed back to the Prock house for lunch. Mr. And Mrs. Prock had surprisingly left Stefan in charge to run some "emergency" errand.

"They will be back in the morning, so don't get on my nerves, stay out of my space, and be home by midnight," Stefan spouted out his version of a pep talk when we sat down to eat a sandwich for lunch.

"Don't forget Ari you have Jungvolk training this afternoon. Julia, you can stay here until he gets home, and then you can go to the library or wherever it is you really go," he added with a wink.

In all actuality, the sudden change in plan occurred in perfect timing. Having the ability to stay out late would allow Ari and I the chance to go to the library during the night librarian's shift where would be able to finalize our plan to help Jurgen Sina the next day.

Once Ari left for training, the awkward silence between Stefan and I overwhelmed the Prock residence. We sat at the kitchen table saying nothing, avoiding eye contact, and pretending like we were individually consumed in deep thought, while fidgeting.

"So..." Stefan started to break the silence.

"Don't worry," I interrupted.

"You don't have to make small talk with me. I know you have stuff you would rather be doing. I am going to go read in the bedroom."

Stefan smiled slyly at me and said,

"Okay Julia."

As I turned to walk away he continued,

"You are quite a charming little thing, you know. I get what my brother sees in you. I would like to meet a girl who has no problem running past the mirror to learn something new. I never thought I would see the day he cared about something or someone more than himself, and for you I think he would do anything. And don't worry, I won't tell anyone about the two of you."

Completely smitten, shocked, flattered, and surprised that someone like Stefan would say such things about me, I couldn't help but smile uncontrollably. I tried to control it, I tried to turn my head downward, but no doubt Stefan could see all over my face just how magnificent he made me feel.

"Thank you," I said as I almost jogged to the bedroom where I spent the entire time I waited for Ari obsessing about the situation.

I replayed the scenario over and over in my mind trying to recreate that flutter of self-esteem in my stomach. Again and again, in slow motion, pausing and restarting, with pleasantry and misery at the same time I thought about Stefan's comments until it felt just right. I conveniently finished with my typical recitation of the Constitution, which just so happened to be two and one half hours later, shortly before Ari walked through the door.

"Your brother is pretty nice," I said to Ari as we headed to the library for the night shift discussion.

"Sure," Ari replied, completely distracted in the process.

"Listen, we are entering the point of no return here. Are you sure you want to proceed? I need you to think about it, and tell me when we get in the library."

I had never seen Ari so serious, so I stopped talking and walked by his side as the sun began to set. Still maintaining the appearance of utter disdain in public, I wanted to give him a hug, but that act of compassion could not happen.

Once settled in our normal spot with books pulled out and opened to serve as our cover (just in case of an unlikely intrusion), I took a deep breath and looked at Ari.

"Are you okay?"

"Fine."

"Ari, you are not fine, and I don't like it."

"I'm sorry. I am not as brave as you. Tomorrow's mission is creating a great deal of unexpected stress. It became very real to me today at training when I proposed the idea to my fellow members of the Hitler Youth. They are prepared and willing to help me lead this boycott of Mr. Sina's art shop starting first thing in the morning. Are you prepared to sneak in and break the news to him that he is one of the Reich's enemies?"

"I am more ready than ever to make General Pershing proud. I am ready to stop sitting on my hands and to actually stop the bleeding in Vienna."

"Alright. Well, tomorrow is set."

With those life-changing words Ari smiled, walked across the room, and kissed me. And for the first time he didn't just kiss me. He touched me, he embraced me, and he truly felt me, sending shivers throughout my entire body. I didn't want him to stop, but he stepped back right when I needed him to without even using words. He took my hand, kissed it, and said,

"Let's head on back so that Stefan doesn't panic, so that I don't get tempted to do anything else, and so you don't punch me in the face."

I squeezed him as tight as I could and then we headed toward the stairs. I stopped him right before we separated to hold up appearances and said,

"I want to say a prayer."

Ari nodded and I began,

Lord hear my prayer. I come to You tonight in faith, not in myself but in Your will to save the innocent and strengthen the weak. Lord I am not perfect, though sometimes I forget that, so I need your help tomorrow. I need my actions to be for someone besides me. Lead me Lord and protect me, walk with me and hold my hand as I enter into danger. I thank you for all of the things you have given me in this world, for this person standing here with me, and for Olli who is the greatest man I have ever met. I am so blessed and yet act so selfish sometimes. I ask that you give Ari and I the wisdom to defeat the poor in compassion and the patience to do so in a manner of your approval and planning. Thank you for this life and this opportunity to do your work. In the name of your son Jesus, Amen.

"Amen," Ari whispered as we headed down the stairs.

By 5:00 a.m. I sat wide awake, dressed, and about to burst at the seams. Ari's Nazi youth led boycott would begin at 8:00 a.m. Stefan had class all day and the Procks wouldn't be home until 5:00 p.m. or so.

I had to sneak into Mr. Sina's business before the boycott started, because the door would be sealed once the boycott began. So by 6:00 a.m., I initiated our plan by crawling through a window near the back alley of the art shop. Ari and I had scoped out the area a couple days before. Thank God I was so tiny. It took everything in the world to get me through that window short of grease, and when I found myself safely inside I had a bad scratch on the back of my right arm and a twisted ankle from my jump from the window to the ground in the storage room of the shop. I settled myself on some crates in the back room.

The art shop did not open until 9:00 a.m. Hopefully, Mr. Sina would show up to work after the boycott started. He would shuffle through the Jungvolk and enter in a confused and flustered state, or so the plan entailed.

As I sat waiting, nursing my ankle, I reflected back upon the days that I would have the occasional conversation with Mr. Sina. A customer at the Spiros' bookstore, I usually sat on a stool behind the back counter when he entered. With luck, he would still view me as a friend.

My knees banged together in anxiousness, I could not wait for the day to be over. It made me wonder how on earth the Spiros remained in hiding day after day. Without even a glimmer of their experience, I thanked God I was not Jewish. Then it occurred to me what a horrible prayer I had made. Compulsively asking for forgiveness, I heard yelling outside, and within moments I heard the bell on the front door ring, followed by the door slamming shut. It was show time.

I peeked out into the art shop and waited for Mr. Sina to close the window shades to his shop and catch his breath. He flopped down in his desk chair like a rag doll, pulling his hat off of his bald head, and wrenching it in his hands. He looked completely defeated.

I questioned myself. Should I tell him? I would be saving his life, but would he want it this way? I was in too deep now to step back. I thought of General Pershing, of the burden of command, and of my duty to not be a bystander. It was at that point that I stepped out into the studio to confront Mr. Sina.

Acting like a meek little mouse, I simply whispered, "Mr. Sina?"

He jumped out of his seat and ran across the studio floor as if he needed to extinguish a fire. He grabbed me by the shoulders and said,

"We must get you out of here Julia. It is not safe for a girl like you here."

My first reaction was actually relief that Jurgen remembered me. I so often felt invisible, minding my own business and lacking social skills beyond my comfort zone. To have him recognize me immediately actually made me feel like a significant part of Vienna. I actually mattered.

Within moments, I realized this was not an appropriate time for self-consumption and spouted out as loud as possible, yet without being heard beyond the internal walls,

"This is my fault. I did this to you."

Mr. Sina paused, let me go, and said,

"What are you talking about?"

"We need to go into the back room."

We walked to the back storage room, where I pointed to the window, through which I entered moments before, and through which I had exactly forty-eight minutes to get out, when Ari would make a distraction from the area for my secured escape into a back alley. By the time we seated ourselves on crates in the back, I had forgotten about the pain from my ankle, as the adrenaline had kicked in full blast. I looked into Mr. Sina's deep and saddened eyes and I started,

"Please, just let me explain."

"What do I have to lose at this point?"

"Your life," I replied.

"Julia, please tell me you do not have a gun on you or that you plan to beat me up like you did that officer in your apartment."

Again I felt so important and dignified that Mr. Sina not only remembered me, but that he also knew of my exploits. I did exist and I did matter. I again left my distractions and continued the conversation.

"No. You are in no danger from me. I am simply here to warn you that you must leave Vienna. Matter of fact, you must leave Austria. You must do this today."

"Aren't the men standing at my front door enough for today? What makes you think that you know something I do not?" he asked with respect and concern in his voice.

I reached in my pocket and pulled out the list with his name on it. I placed it in his hand and closed his fist around the paper.

"Mr. Sina, I am responsible for staging this fake boycott of your store. Yes, those are real Jungvolk, but they are only out there because I know someone on the inside. I asked my contact to set this up so you and I could talk, and so I could convince you to leave Vienna, before you simply became just a number or a name on some other list that will be forgotten forever."

"And does the Professor know that you are here today?"

"No, and you must understand the dangerous implications this makes for us all. Uncle Olli will never blow his cover to outwardly save you. He has too much work yet to do. He has no knowledge of this effort to help you, and he can never know that I compromised myself for this purpose. Mr. Sina, this is all very simple. Pack what you must have to survive only and get out of town tonight. No one will question why you left, because of the threat on your store."

"Must I leave tonight or do I have more time to tell my friends and my life goodbye?"

"It must be tonight. On average people only remain on this list for one to three months, and this list was released three and a half weeks ago. Better safe than sorry."

He paused and looked at the floor without saying anything for an awkward two to three minutes. It seemed as if I was watching him die right there. All of his dreams were vanishing, and I only had thirty-seven minutes left before my escape.

After a pro-longed and painful silence, he looked up at me, stared directly in my eyes, and as he reached out for my hands, he said,

"You are an angel. Even God has angels that must deliver unwanted news. You are like Gabriel telling Mary she will have the baby Jesus, delivering a message that will one day make more sense to me and the world. Thank you."

I held back tears and grabbed Mr. Sina around the neck and squeezed. Within seconds the flood began, and I was sobbing. I felt so foolish, until I looked up to realize that he was crying just as hard as I was.

What had seemed like an easy task on paper had become an emotional quagmire. With helping this seemingly innocent man, I realized saving people was going to be harder than I planned. I had conveniently forgotten to figure human emotion into the equation of saving lives. My God, I thought to myself, how on earth did people like General Pershing make the decisions he did every day? How did he watch young men die at his command? I would soon realize the first experience is the toughest, and from there one must become numb to survive.

After my time expired, Mr. Sina quite politely helped me climb back up to the window, this time more carefully and with less adrenaline. I waited to see Ari peep his head around the corner at the designated time, which acted as my cue to jump down and get out of the area. I blew Mr. Sina a kiss and found my way to the alley, again realizing my ankle was hurt when I hit the ground, yet still running on enough adrenaline to sprint to the Prock residence without limping on my hurt ankle, yet limping the entire way with my broken heart.

CHAPTER 18

Olli's first move upon his return from Berlin, that is after giving his goddaughter a hug and playing a game of catch, was to "clean-up" Mr. Sina's business. When it became public knowledge that Jurgen Sina had disappeared after the boycott of his store, Olli took control of the property and everything left inside, informing the Reich that any profits made would be given to sacred Germany and its mission.

His second move included giving me a forged birth certificate, changing my father's country of origin to Austria, just in case questions appeared about my American heritage. Ms. Gerg was the only person left in Austria who knew my true heritage besides the Procks and Spiros. Despite her melodramatic and sulky demeanor, she would never do anything to hurt Olli.

As the days rolled on and as Olli returned from Berlin, the world and Vienna continued to change, and my concerns for Patrick continued to rise. By early June, the Germans had begun to bomb Paris; by mid-June the Germans entered Paris, and by late June France signed an armistice with the Nazis. To add insult to injury, Adolph Hitler decided to prance his silly little ass around Paris like he owned the place, nauseating most of the free world.

I tried to focus my attention on helping others as I had Mr. Sina. And with the passing months, I became more confident in my ability to change Vienna one unsuspecting victim at a time, though each situation held possibilities for disaster and ruin.

General Pershing's words in his Pulitzer Prize winning book, *My Experiences in the World War*, reassured my mission. Written in 1931, he dedicated his book to the Unknown Soldier, and because every part of my life had become top secret, I felt like I made a direct connection to the General as my list continued to grow, and would grow throughout the entire war. I began keeping a personal list of those helped in the side margin of my journal, so that one day I could look back and remember that I chose to live.

The list I made would include fourteen lives by the end of the war; fourteen people with families, dreams, property, fears, daily worries, work problems, birthdays, illnesses, and knowledge. I imagined my own life and everything in it, and then I thought about it all disappearing in an instant. I would eventually save all of that fourteen times over.

Julia's List
In Honor of General John Joseph Pershing
In Memory of Those Already Lost

#1--Jurgen Sina

#2--Clemenz Warmisch

#3--Armin Quinl

#4--Sabine Pedarzolli

#5--Liesl Fink

#6--Brigatta Gruber

#7--Lukas Reiter

#8--Mariella Schuster

#9--Tobias Janosi

#10--Josef Mika

#11--Eike Happ

#12--Leonie Bietak

#13--Sebastian Zweig

#14--Franz Wirth

Needless to say, I kept myself very busy, trying to occupy my time, which conveniently helped me move past the obsessions. Not to any surprise, I found myself consumed more with activity and less with reciting the Constitution to myself.

With or without my help, the war raged on, and it became acutely obvious to the world that Hitler's appetite could never be satiated. Bombing on Britain began later in the year and soon war raged stronger than ever in North Africa.

Olli, even more consumed with work, inhabited the apartment less and less, and found himself traveling more and more. His absence gave Ari and I time to evolve in our relationship, and before long I felt like he knew me and I knew him better than anyone in the world, including Olli.

I knew in my heart that Olli's job required that I find a place on the back burner of his life, but my heart felt abandoned, especially when he found himself in Poland on my sixteenth birthday, leaving me again at the Prock's with nothing but a card.

Devastated and sulking the entire day, despite a beautiful heart necklace from Ari and a strand of pearls from Mr. and Mrs. Prock. I threw Olli's card on Ari's bed at the Procks' house with my other gifts just before Mrs. Prock cooked my birthday dinner. I always felt a little mellow on my birthday, and with Olli gone and the knowledge that the Sprios could not celebrate birthdays on the very premise in which I stood, I headed to bed early.

I settled in running my fingers over the beautiful strand of pearls. Although I knew I would never feel appropriate wearing them, I treasured them in their box. They were too perfect to take out. I then placed the necklace Ari gave me around my neck. It felt perfect. I kissed it and let it drop against my chest. I imagined I could carry him with me everywhere, which gave me great comfort, even though he was always with me anyway.

Finally, I decided to open the card from Olli. No doubt it would say the usual; have a great day, remember to smile, love you Jules.

I opened the envelope and pulled out a very plain card, typical Olli fashion. Inside read,

To my beautiful daughter on her sweet sixteen. May the beauty of your spirit spread light upon this world. Thank you for making me a better man and for always being my Jules.

P.S. Your father asked me to give this to you on this very day, and I am sorry I am not there to give it to you in person.

I smiled and started to tear up. As I reached up to wipe my eye, I still had the envelope in my hand and a smaller envelope fell to the floor. I picked it up and noticed that it was strangely faded. "Julia" appeared on the front. Thinking I held another letter from my grandfather to my mother, I flipped it over and reached to pull out the letter, however, this envelope was sealed. Across the seal was written: "To Be Opened January 30th, 1941 by Julia Josephine Patterson."

The letter began,

Dearest Julia,

I hope by some stroke of luck that you are opening this letter having met me at some point in your life, although the stars seemed to be crossed in such a way that I fear this might be my first contact with you. I am your grandfather.

If directions were followed, this letter has been sealed for ten years and you are now, beyond a doubt, a beautiful sixteen year-old young woman just as your mother once was. Sadly you never knew her, but I can assure you that you come from good stock. She was beautiful, brilliant, and captivating; and from the communication I have had with your father since your birth, you are exactly the same.

I don't know if I will ever meet you or see a picture of your face beyond baby pictures, but I know that the world will cherish your life as it did your mother's. There is no doubt in my mind that you were born to fulfill the dreams of your mother, to change the world, to show humanity that passion and intelligence can accomplish anything. You are sixteen now, so young; almost the age of your mother when she left Russia. This letter, however, is not about your mother, it is about you.

Although I probably seem so far away, in a distant land, I think of you every day, and if I am still alive when you open this, I will be thinking of you. The world has thrown obstacles between us, as it is becoming more difficult to write than ever, but on your sixteenth birthday, wherever you are reading this, I will say a prayer for you and your life. I have faith in you Julia, as did your mother in the short time she had you on this earth, and I know she is still with you from heaven. Your father is an amazing man, who touched your mother in a way I thought she was incapable of experiencing. He gave her life Julia, and I don't know you, but I want to tell you that she would desperately want that for her only child.

You have cousins very close to you in age. Your Aunt Zouriat has twin boys, Pasha and Nikolai. They have a younger sister two years younger than you, Olga. This year your Aunt Kristina had her first baby, Stanislav and two months later Kiril's wife Alexandra gave birth to a beautiful girl Ana (named in honor of your mother). I wish you could meet them, as they are now no longer babies but teenagers like you.

I wish I could be there to hug you and hold you and tell you the stories of your mother, but I cannot. On your sixteenth birthday Julia, please know that I have thought about you every single day, as I will for the rest of my life. For you are the only grandchild I have not yet met, yet the one I believe has the most opportunities thanks to the choices of your mother from an early age.

Be the gift to the world your mother left. And leave the pain of the past behind to find the person you were born to be.

Love Always,
Your Papa
September 8, 1931

After a flood of emotion, my first reaction was amazement, first that my grandfather had contacted my father after my mother's death, something my father never mentioned, and secondly that my grandfather was thinking of me in that very moment. I always dreamed that he knew of me, and thought of me, but I had settled for the idea that he had more immediate family to fill his time. He loved me, and with just a few sentences he became very alive to me.

I wondered if I would be disappointing to him if I ever met him. I wasn't as beautiful as my mother. Maybe he wouldn't like my personality. He built me up so high that I could only go down. He placed his dreams, my mother's dreams, and even the world's dreams on me. I thought I put enough pressure on myself to make my father and General Pershing proud. I would have to add one more.

My sixteenth birthday letter also gave me the first realization of how old my aunts and uncles had become. In the old letters I read Kristina was a tomboy and Vitali was his Momma's baby. I viewed them up to that point as younger than me, when in reality they had children my age. I froze them in time, and I preferred to remember them that way.

I struggled to fall asleep that night, thinking of all of the things from the day; the gifts, the letter, Uncle Olli's absence, the way the Procks had become like my family. Everything swirled in my mind, inhibiting me from any sense of calm that could possibly lead to a decent night's sleep.

And to make the situation worse, I grew increasingly frightened every time I stayed at the Prock's house because of the knowledge that the Spiros sat within feet of me, miserably thinking of how each breath could be their last. To be quite honest, it seemed creepy being in the Prock house; creepy, terrifying, and uncomfortable.

I just wanted the damn war to be over, although I knew things would never be the same. The war would change us all, create irreversible scars, and more importantly would age us, so that when everything went back to normal, nothing would be normal.

Years later, I would look back and miss those times. Although scared and constantly wishing for the future, for something or some better time; I would think back to the pleasant memories. At the time, I felt like my world had gone to hell, but years down the road I would forget the pain and remember running around Austria with Ari, teaching Olli's classes, living in the apartment in Alsergrund, walking past the original home of Sigmund Freud less than a mile from our home, idolizing General Pershing, meeting Patrick and Maria, and falling in love for the first time. It took me years to truly understand that happiness is always around, even when things drastically change or fall apart; it is simply our job to figure out how to enjoy it at the time rather than when it is too late.

Part III: GENERAL JULIA

CHAPTER 1

Where will life take us? Where will we go? What will we see? Who will we love? Who will we hate? Who will enter our lives? Who will suddenly leave?

Who am I? Am I singer? Am I a dancer? Am I a writer? Am I a painter? Am I an athlete?

What am I? Am I a lover? Am I a loner? Am I funny? Am I troubled? Am I all alone?

There are moments in life when our true being seeps out, and as much as we try to deny it, as much as we seek to be something else, the same thing always finds its way to the surface.

No matter how beautiful a dress I put on, how much make-up I covered my face with, or the beautiful jewelry I decorated myself with, I never felt pretty or girly. I was always just Julia, raised by men, confident in my knowledge, and more secure in conversation than social gestures.

I was always Julia, eager to please others, never pleased with herself. A perfectionist that always found something that had to be better, where disappointment could not exist.

I was always Julia, afraid of embarrassment, so much so that I immediately eliminated anything that could cause failure.

I was always Julia, tougher than hell, and yet not as tough as I hoped my image projected to the world.

I was always Julia, hell-bent on avoiding pain, of avoiding uncontrollable emotion, and of letting anyone see that pain hurt me too.

By December of 1941, the Nazi's bailed out the Italians in North Africa and betrayed the Soviets. Personally, I had come into my own. I taught myself to accept my panic as a tradeoff for my genius. More importantly, I learned to not only accept who I really was, but to also embrace it and enjoy it. I would never be a beauty queen or an opera singer, but being smart and witty, making people laugh, and holding intense conversations suddenly made me incredibly happy to just be me. What amazed me most, however, came with the understanding the more I accepted myself, the more I naturally acted like a general, the more I would have made my father and grandfather proud.

Now to make myself clear, I still had the occasional obsession and panic attack, and the Constitution had not yet become a stranger from my ritual of removing unpleasant thoughts, but for the most part I could use breathing exercises and writing to help me move past my worries. Other letters from my grandfather taught me that writing out the worst case scenarios coming true could make me realize how silly and irrational some of my obsessions had become. In other words, I was learning to function in a world where I could never escape being obsessive-compulsive. And thanks to my grandfather, I would function rather than become paralyzed with worry and fear.

Finally ready to change the world, the question became, was the world ready for me?

CHAPTER 2

December 7th, 1941 served as not only the scariest day of my life, but also the day that provided the most hope. As the last stronghold of world democracy reeled from a date which would live in infamy, that same stronghold entered into a war and a world, which needed them. Although terrifying to see the final piece of independence struck in a battle of good and evil, the idea that the United States could be the answer to defeating Hitler gave increasing hope with every breath. Within a few hours, the Japanese awakened the sleeping western giant, creating the final question. Would this be the end of democracy in the world or the end of Fascism? Regardless of the answer, I enjoyed the fact that the answer finally sat around the corner. It wouldn't be long before we would know.

And so the tough times began. Olli being gone, pretending I was a different person, watching friends and neighbors suffer, worrying about safety and humanity, seeing the evil come out in people, and eventually severe food shortages seemed to overwhelm all sense of security.

Over the next year, I consumed myself in music. There is something soul capturing about beautiful words mixed with sound, which makes a person feel an emotion indescribable with words. Every thought and obsession a million times over could not create the same feeling the right song creates in a split second. Music turned me even more into a hopeless optimist, but that was okay, because it kept me going through the shortages, the fear, and the uncertainty.

I pretty much came to live at the Prock's house and became a full-fledged professor with Olli's traveling. My lectures became more and more frequent through the ongoing war over North Africa, through the Soviet adjustment to betrayal, through the rebuilding of the British air force, and through the conclusion of my teen years. Truly coming to grips with what love meant beyond the butterflies and kisses and continuing to grow up way too fast, I found some sense of peace out of the chaos. Hopeful that the war was on the downswing with success in North Africa, the standoff at Leningrad, and the awareness of Italian military weakness, hope tugged at my heart again that stability would once again enter my world. My life, however, changed forever, pulling out the true general inside, in the following winter of 1942.

Of course I continued to be a snoop, going through Olli's mail, lists of names, and old letters in the few days out of the month I actually got to live in our apartment. Olli always made sure he spent Christmas with me, and it was then, right before my eighteenth birthday, that I discovered a name on a list of enemies of the German Reich.

"It Can't Be!" I shouted aloud to myself standing in Olli's bedroom closet.

My heart felt like it would explode when I saw the name "Patrick Bellew--suspected of espionage and treason."

Ari was right about me knowing when to follow Patrick's advice from the letter. No question existed in my mind that the time had come to pull Patrick's letter out of the library and take action. He would have to be number fifteen on my list of innocents saved. We would either leave France together or I would die there, however, this one would be tricky. I would have to figure out how to get out of Austria. Not only that, I would have to figure out how to get Patrick out of France.

Completely dumfounded by the knowledge that Olli intended to make his next business trip to Yugoslavia, with no doubt the awareness of Patrick's presence on the list, I turned to the one person I now trusted more than anyone else in the world, Ari Prock.

Hysterical beyond words, we finally found time to be alone in the library, where Ari just kept telling me to breath and calm down. Once I had regained consciousness and the ability to produce rational thought, Ari suggested we make a plan.

We decided that we would have to act within one month to be absolutely sure we could get everything we needed figured out, yet to hopefully have time to get to Patrick before someone else did. Ari suggested that whatever our plan developed into, it should be initiated on my eighteenth birthday, January 30, 1943.

Rather than go to the library to do our planning, we found more comfort in the empty apartment, making a daily appearance at the library just to satisfy Ms. Gerg. Although we risked being seen by neighbors, the chance to be alone together for a month before I risked my life for Patrick was priceless. Internally Ari and I both knew that going to France by myself to save an enemy of the German state had immense ramifications, so large that we never even discussed the negative possibilities. We just soaked in every moment with each other. Often tempted to spend our time as teenagers, discovering the other, and truly expressing our love, we could not waste a moment. We had only one chance to save Patrick. We had to remain focused.

Almost daily Ari tried to talk me out of my plan, distracting me by kissing me on the neck or pulling my hair like a little boy. He would say something like,

"Julia we will find another way to help him. Who knows if you will even find him? I hate to say it, but he could already be dead."

And I would always respond,

"My father always taught me that only I could change the world. We all have the potential as human beings, but if we want something to turn out the way we want, then we must take action ourselves."

Ari knew he would never change my mind so he didn't try too hard to convince me to forget Patrick, he only made me promise never to forget him.

Our plan grew into one long list:

1. Ari would book my train ticket and hotel room

2. I would decipher Patrick's letter

3. I would research possibilities for locating Soren Ambler

4. Ari would help me create a cover story as to my entrance into Paris

5. Ari would secure my "new" papers with Zingre as my last name

6. I would figure out how to navigate Paris on my own

7. Ari and Stefan would create a cover story to tell the Procks

8. I would continue to read Olli's mail and lists looking for possible clues

And so the planning began. Consumed with myself and helping Patrick, I relied on Ari to continue to be with me and help me day in and day out. He had given his life up for me, and I had come to expect it.

Things went smoothly, and two weeks away from my eighteenth birthday and the big day I would leave Austria alone, Ari handed me a letter in the apartment. As I reached to open it, he yelled,

"Stop!"

Then composing himself he continued,

"I mean stop please. I want you to open it tonight while you are alone. Okay?"

"Yes, anything you want. What is it?"

"Just wait and see."

That night, as asked, I opened the letter.

Dearest Julia,

So many letters you have read, and so many you have shared with me from family you have never known. I think the time has finally come to give you a letter from me. Knowing what lies ahead for you, I desire for you to have something to carry with you, something tangible that you can pull out and touch and hold.

Sometimes I know you live in your own world, with your thoughts and your ideas, and I accept that because that is the person who is my best friend. When you need something else, however, which I am sure will happen when you least expect it, you will have this letter. Maybe one day your children will read this and try to figure out who the hell Ari Prock is, just as you attempt to solve the mysteries of your mother's letters. And as you stand there holding your grandchildren in your arms, wherever you may be, I hope you tell them that I was the first man you loved. It is so amusing to think how far we have come.

I have never said it to you directly before, although I try to imply it every day, so here it is officially: I LOVE YOU JULIA JOSEPHINE PATTERSON, and no matter where life takes me or where it doesn't, I want you to know that I will ALWAYS love you. And tomorrow, I will say it to you the first moment we are alone, even though I wish to scream it from the mountaintops.

So, I want to express everything to you, holding nothing back. I know you look at yourself as average looking and boring, but I want you to see yourself through my eyes for just one moment:

Julia with her dark brown eyes,
Drains the pain of the war,
Her soul-capturing glance from across the room,

Takes away the shivering of the core.

Julia with her beautiful smile,
That rarely shows its upward ends,
Making me laugh without her knowledge,
Away with pain she sends.

Julia with her brilliant mind,
Dumfounding those she meets,
Destined in the world of the wise,
Enchanting her listeners as she speaks.

Julia with her comical wit,
Insulting away lesser minds,
Protecting those whom she loves,
Peace with herself she finds.

Julia with her tough demeanor,
Pushing the wicked to the edge,
Raised by men of honor,
Never failing on a pledge.

Julia with her confident appeal,
Content to be by herself,
Underestimating the beauty she possesses,
Underestimating the power of her stealth.

Julia with her iron fists,

Punching a mean boy in the face,
Standing on her own two feet,
Making that boy stop in place.

Julia with her distant charm,
Mesmerizing those she meets,
Making even the toughest foes,
Fall in love at her feet.

I will always love you Julia. You have captured my mind and ravaged my soul, and you will always be the General of my heart.

With Love Always,
Ari Prock
January 15, 1943

CHAPTER 3

I held Patrick's letter in my hand. I could not believe the date. It seemed like just yesterday he gave me my baseball glove and made me feel like we would be best friends forever. In reality it had been six years.

I worried about him constantly, and I wondered if he still thought about me or remembered me. What if all of this effort was for someone who barely knew of my existence? I would tell myself that was nonsense, because the letter he gave me certainly demonstrated a deeper connection; a connection of trust and true friendship. Not to mention how he got me gifts on my birthdays until communication became too difficult. Yes, he would definitely remember our time together in Paris, and worst case scenario he would no doubt appreciate a little bit of help in his situation.

1,1,9,9,14,14,20,26 blurred before my eyes. At first I assumed I could just give this series of numbers to the Soren Ambler person as the secret code, but what if the code led to a password or another clue? Patrick no doubt knew of my intelligence, yet he would want to make it easy enough for me to figure out without any doubt left in my mind. Within five minutes I had tried the most obvious choice: Each number stood for a letter.

1-A

1-A

9-I

9-I

14- N

14-N

20-T

26-Z

It would have to be scrambled. Unsure of my method, I continued, thinking that I had to exhaust each try so I could rule out failed attempts. The "Z" continued to catch my eye. Only so many words have a "Z" in them. The most prominent word at the time being Nazi. I could make the word Nazi out of the letters provided. Now what about the rest? If Nazi was one word than the A, I, N, and T were the letters left. Unscrambled, that would form: Anti. Together the pass code could be Anti-Nazi. I tried a series of other patterns, but nothing made as much sense as Anti-Nazi. Of course it could simply be the numbers I needed, but I would carry my unscrambled code in my mind just in case. I had to be prepared.

As time whittled away, I studied maps of Paris. I vaguely remembered places, markers, and monuments, but I would need a complete mental image. I definitely could not look like a tourist.

Ari guaranteed me a hotel room and documents for my trip. He said he would keep them hidden until he walked me to the train station. He didn't want any info to leak out in the meantime. No doubt at this point I trusted him.

My story for entering Paris would be study and research for teaching Olli's course. I worked on forging papers using Olli's signature from old letters so that if stopped, I could claim that Professor Zingre sent me to study the human geography behind the resistance in France.

We would tell the Procks a different story. We would simply tell them that Olli gave me permission to stay by myself when I turned eighteen, and if they had any concerns they could ask Olli upon his return. By that time I would be back and say that I was scared to stay by myself and wanted to continue to stay with them while Olli was gone, never having to involve him. If the Procks protested, I would simply say that I just wanted some privacy from Ari and his constant presence in my life. The Procks might question Ari, but they would never question my honesty.

And so, within five days of my eighteenth birthday, all of the logistics had been settled. Although nervous, I also found myself mentally and spiritually prepared. I knew I could stay calm, I knew I could take care of myself, and I knew I could sacrifice without looking back. General Pershing would be proud of me, and more importantly, so would my father. General Julia seeped out of my skin. It was time.

"Julia, I would like to go the Votivkirche today. Is that okay?" Ari asked with four days to go until the big day.

"It is a special place for us, and I would just like to sit in peace there for a while before you leave me."

"You know I am not leaving you for good Ari. I love you and will feel the same about you when I return safely. Remember to use the power of positive thinking. But, sure we can go there today."

"I don't know what I will do without you while you are gone. It is amazing, Patrick always seems to pull us apart. The last time we found ourselves apart for more than a day or two occurred when you and Olli went to Paris. Are you sure you don't love him?"

"Of course I love him, he is my best friend. But do I love him the way I love you? Of course not. I can't imagine loving anyone the way I love you," I said with a wink.

Ari smiled and looked at his feet. I couldn't believe I had finally embarrassed him. I had never seen him actually blush, like I so often did.

Later that afternoon we fulfilled our plans and walked quietly into the Votivkirche with our heads bowed and our hearts open. Ari took my hand and lead me gently to the bench where he first kissed me. We sat down and he said,

"Julia will you say a prayer?"

"Of course," I replied slightly stunned. Ari never mentioned religion. He only prayed, that I knew of, when we were together and I asked. And so I began:

Lord hear my prayer. May the words that leave my mouth be pleasing to your ears and may the thoughts that leave my mind be in your will. I am about to embark on a very dangerous mission, but of course you know that. I ask that you give me strength and wisdom, and I pray that you bless Patrick. Lord let him be okay and let me find him in one piece. So many have gone before me making much greater sacrifices Lord, so I feel almost selfish asking for personal protection. What I do ask is for your presence in my life. Please hold my hand in the steps I take. In the process I ask that you bless Ari. I know sometimes I take him for granted and focus on my own desires. Before I leave Lord, let him know just how much my strength depends on his. Thank you for him in my life. We come together in this place of worship today to ask for your grace. In this time of war and pain for so many, we know you are still with us and will take care of us. Thank you for my life and for all the gifts I have to share with the world. Help me to use the blessings I have received to bless others. Thank you, in Jesus' Name, Amen.

"Amen," Ari simply replied.

"Are you ready to go now?"

"No, I just want to sit in this holy place for a little while if you don't mind. It brings me a little peace. You can walk around outside if you want, but I would like you here with me."

"Okay, I'll stay," I said.

We sat in the back of the chapel watching worshippers wander in and out, some looking at the architecture, some kneeling at the altar, some simply sitting in the pews staring forward, and some obviously in mourning, seeking comfort. Ari kept his head down with his lanky and firm arms leaning on his knees. With his hands crossed he fidgeted with his fingers, only occasionally looking up from the floor to watch a new person leave or exit. I could sense the importance of our presence, so I didn't say another word. For once I wanted to be there for him as he was always there for me, so I sat quietly enjoying the calm before the storm.

When the chapel cleared for the second time, Ari turned and looked at me.

"What?" I said. "Are you okay?"

Ari took my hand, kissed it, and brushed my free-for-all hair out of my face.

"My God you are beautiful."

As usual I blushed and looked to the ground, and before I had the chance to say some smart-ass comment, I felt Ari move. When I looked over he was down on one knee. Grasping for words and in absolute shock, my hands shook as Ari held them in his and started:

Julia Josephine Patterson you have been in my life every day for the past two thousand three hundred and seventy days. With each day my life has gotten better, because I have grown to know you more. You are everything I have ever wanted without realizing it, and somehow in this very place God allowed you into my life. Our first kiss took place on this sacred ground where you first explained to me how the Austrian uniform once saved Franz Joseph, and I truly believe that this is the exact place where you will save the Austrian uniform. I love you Julia. I have loved you since the day you punched me in the face. You are like no woman I have ever met, and unlike any woman I will ever meet. This

moment is not about four days from now, it is about the days that have
preceded us and the days that will hopefully follow in years to come.
Julia Josephine Patterson will you marry me?

Tears overran my face running across my lips leaving the taste of salt on my tongue. I felt as if I would never speak again. With so much emotion I looked at this man, yes man, on his knees before me asking for my hand in marriage. I couldn't believe he was such a man. My mind often captured him as a little boy or teenager, but he was a man. With sturdy shoulders and strong arms, he was lanky but incredibly firm and muscular. The Jungvolk training had made him a military machine, and he epitomized handsome. And nothing made me feel more like a woman, than having this man seeking me for the ultimate commitment by making himself completely vulnerable.

For once in my life I didn't think about all of the possibilities, I didn't weigh the pros and cons, and I didn't even rationalize my choice. I simply yelled,

"Yes."

"Yes! Did you say yes?" Ari said with a huge smile.

"I said yes," I responded back as I reached down and pulled him up off the floor, realizing the importance of getting him up before anyone entered.

Ari grabbed me and threw me up in his arms and as I slid down he kissed me in a way I didn't realize existed. He then reached in his pocket and pulled out the most gorgeous ring I had ever laid my eyes upon.

"Where did you get that?" I asked in awe.

He reached over and put the hair behind my ear and whispered to me,

"When the Spiros came to live at our house Mrs. Spiro only walked in with a few personal items and her mother's wedding ring. She told me she wanted me to have it, since she did not have any children herself and didn't know if she would live to see freedom again. She told me to give it to my wife one day. I can only imagine how pleased she would be to know that it will forever rest on your finger."

"It's perfect," I said as he slipped it on my finger.

We sat back down in the pew, and then rational Julia kicked in.

"How are we going to do this? I mean hell yes I love you and want to marry you, but no one knows about us. Are you ready to tell everyone? I don't think we can right now."

"I've been thinking about that for a while and I have a complete plan, starting with you trip. I want to go with you. At my house I have two sets of tickets, one for you going by yourself and one with tickets for both of us, with your new name, Julia Josephine Prock. I figured you would want to keep your same initials in honor of your father and General Pershing."

In awe, I continued,

"Okay but how will we get married?"

"I have arranged for us to go the Registry office and be married. Stefan has agreed to be our witness.

"You really did have all of this planned. Stefan knows already?"

"Yes."

"What did he say?"

"He said he wanted you to say yes and that he hoped to find a woman like you one day."

My insides turned to mush. So many good feelings at once seemed like too much to swallow. I gulped and said,

"What will we tell your parents?"

"Your story will remain the same. Olli gave you permission to stay alone when you turned eighteen. Stefan will cover for me, telling my parents that I am off to complete my final training for Jungvolk before I am eligible for the military. We can travel together as a young Nazi couple, plus we have your forged note. I have already adjusted it with my name added. We will worry about the rest when we get back."

"Okay," I said, I think for the first time in my life.

Something felt quite nice about Ari taking charge of me and my protection. For just one day I let go of everything and it felt amazing.

CHAPTER 4

My sixteenth birthday strand of pearls, a white skirt, a plain purple blouse, with a white cardigan made up my wardrobe as Ari, Stefan, and I walked to the train station from the Registry in the 1st District, where moments before I vowed to be Mrs. Ari Prock.

"We have a train to catch," I said as the three of us picked up speed on my eighteenth birthday.

Jumping on a train to go to Paris with my new husband would have never been anywhere on my radar of possibilities ten years ago when I found myself living with a professor in Austria. Thank God life takes us on journeys we never expect. If all of my childhood tragedy led to me to finding Ari Prock, well then it might just have been worth it.

"So when's the honeymoon lovebirds?" Stefan joked as we walked.

I just blushed. I couldn't even look at him.

"Shut your mouth Stefan. You know we have more important things to do. And don't talk about inappropriate things in front of my wife."

I couldn't wait for Ari and I to be alone on the train. I found it difficult to talk in front of Stefan, and even though our marriage did not serve as the most important thing in our lives for the next couple days, I wanted the train ride to savor the moment of being a bride with the love of my life, before putting us both in danger.

At the train station we both hugged Stefan goodbye, and he whispered to me as he took my hands,

"You are a beautiful bride. Take care of my brother."

We boarded the train with no problems. We found our seats and Ari took my hand.

"Finally, I can show my affection in public," Ari said as he put his hand on my knee just under the edge of my skirt.

My body tingled all over as Stefan's words continued to play over and over again in my mind, but I would have to put that aside. I had to remain focused on Patrick.

"So, I thought that when we get in to the hotel we get a good night's rest and then tomorrow we can begin our search for Soren Ambler."

"Sounds great."

I put my head on Ari's shoulder and just soaked in every moment with my new husband. Nothing seemed boring. Matter of fact, the ride flew by, because of the anticipation of the days to come. We talked about our hopes and dreams, our future, and especially the story of how we would break the news to our parents. When we arrived in Paris, we still had not quite figured that one out yet.

The biggest fear of course revolved around the idea that Ari would be placed into the German Army in light of his completion of the Hitler Youth training. We decided, however, that we just couldn't worry about such things. Ari carried my things up to our room on the fifth floor of the hotel, fitting as how our late night meetings also took place on the fifth floor of the library.

"I'll go get the rest of the luggage. I'll be back in a minute," Ari said as he headed out the door.

I went to the shared bathroom on the hall of the hotel to freshen up from the train ride and then I quickly slid back into our bedroom. I put on my long plaid nightshirt and slipped under the covers. When Ari returned up the stairs he put the luggage down and put forth a devilish little smile. He was adorable.

"I know you want to go to bed and get some rest, being that it is so late, but I would be honored to have just one dance with my wife on our wedding night. Just one dance please Mrs. Prock?"

"Of course Mr. Prock. I would be delighted," I said as all meaning behind the words Mr. Prock changed.

As I worried about what movements to make, Ari put one hand on my waist and the other in his. Thank God he always knew the right thing to say or do. He lifted my chin, with our hands clasped, so that he could look down into my eyes and our feet began to move magically in unison. After three or four minutes our feet stopped moving and our bodies simply swayed.

"I really love you," Ari whispered.

"I love you more," I replied.

Ari smiled and reached down to kiss me. His lips felt so warm, so comfortable, so much like they were made to touch mine. I still stood swaying as our lips did not part as expected and as Ari's hand went under the back of my night shirt.

In that moment, happiness to be a woman overwhelmed me and let the man before me love me. Passion took over, and I stopped thinking.

The pleasure was too much for my brain to handle as Ari gently laid me down on our hotel bed in Paris, the same place where my parents fell in love.

Completely a different experience than expected, Ari's strong muscular frame over me, I couldn't get past his beautiful shoulders and rigid frame. I lay in awe of the most gorgeous creature to ever come before my eyes.

When I finally let myself close my eyes, Ari stopped. I opened my eyes in confusion to hear him say,

"Are you okay? I am not hurting you am I?"

"No, please don't stop," I said as tears from nowhere filled my eyes.

"Are you sure? We have a lifetime of this."

"I am positive."

And what began as our first dance turned into our first night as a married couple, our first time experiencing one of this world's greatest gifts, our first moment caring more about the other than ourselves. Nothing could have made a night better in 1943 Paris than falling asleep in the arms of the man I was born to hate but grew to love, my husband Ari Prock.

CHAPTER 5

My feet floated to the floor as I crawled out of Ari's arms in our hotel room bed.

"I want to stay in bed with you all day, but we have to remain focused and get started on our search."

"Julia, suppose we find Patrick. How will we get him, a wanted man, out of Paris?" Ari asked as he rolled over in the sheets on his stomach.

"We will just have to figure it out when it happens. I can't worry about it quite yet."

"Okay, well you know that I am there every step of the way."

"You had better be after last night," I said with the smirk of a schoolgirl.

Before we left our hotel room, I had to fill Ari in on our current situation. As he sat down to put on his socks and shoes I began,

"So here is what we know. Paris is dealing with severe food shortages and curfew, which means we eat only as much as we need and that we are back in this hotel room no matter the circumstances before the sun goes down. Should we get separated, we will meet back in this room before dark, no excuses. You know we are dealing with the Vichy government, not much different than Vienna. In public, we are proud Nazis. Got It?"

"Yes General, I am ready to serve," Ari replied with a salute and click of his heels.

With a long kiss, a hug, and a hand around my waist, Ari and I strolled out of the hotel room as man and wife, and for the public's information, passionate and loyal Hitler supporters researching to help one Professor Zingre at the University of Vienna. It felt amazing to be able to display ourselves without hiding our true emotions.

We almost ran down the stairs and skipped into the lobby with anticipation, excitement, and nervousness wrapped into one. We planned to walk around Paris, going to key locations, looking for information or clues as to the whereabouts of Soren Ambler on our first day. With little pressure on day one, we could ease ourselves into our surroundings with a little reconnaissance before we made a major move. Knowing that we would be out in the open air for most of the day, I stopped at the ladies room on the bottom floor of the hotel before we began our journey. I hurried myself so that we could get started, and I burst out of the bathroom door with a thought I just had to tell Ari.

"Ari, I forgot to tell you last night..." I started to say when Ari interrupted me.

"Julia, I think you should know," and before he could finish his sentence I turned around to see Uncle Olli standing fifteen feet behind me.

I squinted my eyes twice and for a matter of what seemed to be an eternity, but only added to a few seconds, I felt completely disillusioned. Slightly dizzy and trying to regain my bearings, Olli walked past me to the front counter of the hotel lobby.

"I have a family matter to deal with Monsieur, could you please make sure no visitors are sent to my room until I come back down stairs?"

"Of course Monsieur Zingre."

Without words, Olli turned toward the stairs and began to walk up to his room. Ari took my hand and we followed, knowing that we could not discuss our predicament in a public place. We entered Olli's room on the third floor, which he booked entirely for himself. Still holding hands we entered the room as one as Olli held the door for us. After sweeping the hall for any stray bodies, the door closed and I, in my typical outward way, yelled,

"Why aren't you in Yugoslavia?"

"Excuse me Miss Patterson, why aren't you in Vienna?"

"Eighteen Uncle Olli, our pact was eighteen, and actually it is Mrs. Prock," I said without thinking as I held out my ring finger.

Olli sat down on his bed in shock. The room filled with awkward silence until Olli took a deep breath and finally said,

"I mean I knew you were in love, but I didn't think you would run off and get married."

Then with a long pause he added,

"Ari could you please excuse Julia and I for a moment. You can stay right outside the door to make sure no one wanders up here."

I looked over at Ari and nodded and then reluctantly released his hand as he opened the door.

As soon as the door closed I started in on Olli in typical Julia fashion,

"What did you mean by, 'I knew you were in love'?"

"Julia, for once let me ask the questions. You are just a child."

"Excuse me but I have a correction to make. I am a woman, or did you forget that I had a birthday?"

"As always, you know what I mean Julia. Regardless, go ahead ask me the questions. Whatever it takes to get you to talk to me in an honest and calm manner."

"Okay then, number one, what did you mean by 'I knew you were in love'?"

"Do you remember the night you sat up until 3:00 a.m. waiting for me to come in from work?"

"Of course."

"Well the next morning when Ari walked in our door, I knew on your face you loved him, and every day since then, I knew that you were completely safe in his hands because he loved you too. I haven't seen a look like that since your father looked at your mother."

"How did I look at him? Like you look at Maria? The way you react when she sends you a letter? Or your posture as you stood in her kitchen cooking?"

Olli bowed his head and cut his eyes to the floor. I could tell that he was composing himself. Slightly choked up he whispered,

"Exactly."

Taking the time to then compose myself, I continued,

"Okay, then since we are speaking honestly for the first time in years, question two, where were you that night you came in so late? Ari and I went to your office and you weren't there."

"What do you mean you went to my office!"

"Uncle Olli, come on..."

"Fine. I have been using my cover as a professor for the Third Reich studying Eugenics and Ethnic Hygiene to select subjects. The Reich believes that I do my research and then dispose of the bodies. I conduct fake research, which supports the Nazi belief in Aryan superiority and in the meantime I help those selected escape using an underground network. Some of them end up hidden in Vienna, while some I am able to get out of Europe."

"Okay then, question three, why did you lie to me about Yugoslavia?"

"Because I didn't want to scare you."

"Scare me about what? I am living in damn Nazi occupied Vienna. What could possibly scare me?"

"Jules, Patrick is in trouble. I have information that he is wanted by the Nazis for participating in the resistance."

"Well why the hell do you think I am here? I saw his name on one of your lists and knew he was in trouble, and I came to help him."

"And how do you plan to get him out of Paris?"

"Well I could ask you how you plan to find him if he is part of the underground?"

"Jules, I love you, but to be quite honest you don't really know anything about the mess you are getting involved in. This is dangerous stuff."

"Well, let me be quite clear Uncle Olli, up to this day I have saved fourteen innocent people on your lists. You could actually name them if you tried because those are the names that gradually disappeared from the face of the earth. I am not a child, and I am certainly not helpless. I know you remember Mr. Sina, you took over his business, he was my first, and if you don't get in my way, Patrick will be my fifteenth."

Olli paused, seemingly contemplating the new information. He wiggled in his seat and finally said,

"Again I propose the question to you: How do you plan to get him out of Paris?"

"And again I ask you, how do you know where to find him? By the way, what is your magic answer of how to get him out of Paris?"

"I have my connections. I can capture him as a subject to experiment on, bring him back to Vienna, and then secure his safety. How do you magically plan to find him?"

"He told me how to find him in case of emergency when we came to Paris together. He wrote me a letter explaining where he would be if I EVER needed him."

"So together maybe we can really save Patrick," Olli said taking a deep breath and rubbing his chin in thought.

After a moment he continued,

"Well General Patt...I mean General Prock, it is time for you to really be my General. I am at your mercy. Lead me Julia, help me to save him."

"Absolutely," I said with pride beaming on my face. I felt for the first time like my name served as a true self-fulfilling prophesy. Dad, Papa, and General Pershing would be proud. What was important, however, was how proud I felt of myself.

"And I am sure Maria will be forever grateful," I continued.

"Speaking of Maria, I need to tell you something."

"I know, I know, after the war you are going to marry her. All of this tragedy has made you aware just how much you need her," I said with a hint of sarcasm.

"No Julia, there is something else."

Completely intrigued I just stared at Olli waiting for him to talk.

"Jules, there is something that only two people alive in this world know, and when you leave this room, it will be three. It is about Patrick's father."

"Oh my God it all makes sense now," I interrupted.

"You are Patrick's father."

"Actually Jules, Patrick is your brother, or half-brother rather. Maria asked me to let you know when I felt the time was right, and I think that is now. You obviously feel a deep connection with him."

"I don't understand," I said with my mind reeling trying to come up with every possibility. "Did Daddy cheat on my mother?"

"Not in a million years sweetie. He loved your mother more than life itself. You see your father never knew Patrick was his son."

"Please explain," I said starting to feel a little queasy and leaning back on Olli's bed.

"Are you okay?"

"I'll be better if you will just tell me the truth."

"Okay, here it goes. In January of 1920 your father and I became best friends. I was in school and he was working odd jobs around Paris. In April of that year your father had a one-night stand with Maria Bellew. Though remaining mutual friends, they realized that one night of passion definitely did not equal love. A month later your father met your mother, and the rest of their love story that you are familiar with was history. By the time Maria found out she was pregnant, your mother and father were knee deep in love, and Maria chose not to tell him he was the father. She knew his heart belonged to your mother and that telling him would solve no problems. Patrick was born in December of 1920, while Maria was eight months pregnant. Because he came early, your father never questioned if the baby was his, and Maria never told him. Julia, he would have been honorable, but Maria didn't want to be with a man in love with another woman. She named him Patrick in honor of his father, your dad, Jacob Patterson."

I sat thinking over the entire situation. My father had a son he never knew about, giving the baseball glove he gave Patrick a whole new level of meaning. I had a brother. I felt so connected to Patrick, and now it made sense. We had the same father.

"Are you okay?" Olli interrupted.

"Fine, just trying to take everything in. How long have you known?"

"Just since our trip to Paris to get that book from Maria. I am sure you know by now that the trip was not simply about a book. Because Patrick was almost grown, she wanted to make sure that someone else knew in case something happened to her. I told your father I would take care of his child, and whether he knew it or not when he died, that included Patrick."

I kept taking deep breaths on Olli's bed, processing all of the new revelations.

"Well, let's go get him," I said.

"Sure, just as soon as I have a little talk with my son-in-law."

"Uncle Olli, promise you will be nice."

"I am not promising anything. You can't argue with me on this. This talk is between the men only. Go change places with him in the hall."

"But..."

"No exceptions Julia. Now."

"Okay, but while it is just the two of us, can I ask you for one favor?"

"Sure, Jules, anything within my power."

"Uncle Olli, promise me you will stop keeping your life from me trying to protect me."

"I promise, because obviously the last thing my silence has done is protect you."

Despite all Olli and I talked about, my heart didn't really start to pound until he asked for Ari. I walked into the hallway and updated Ari on all of the developments including, my new brother, Olli's true alliances and mission, and Olli's desire to have a "talk" with him. Ari kissed me on the cheek and said,

"No worries, it will be alright. He can't kill me."

Ari entered the room and closed the door, and I put my ear up to the door.

"Dr. Zingre, I would first like to say that my intentions with Julia are absolutely pure. I love her as I have for the past four years, and I would give my life to protect her. She is now my wife, and although I could not ask your permission to marry her for obvious reasons, I do not regret my actions. I know it is too late to ask, but I feel that I must do it anyway. Dr. Zingre, may I have your permission to have Julia as my wife?"

I could tell Ari's voice cracked with nervousness. I could hear the quiver in his voice, but there was nothing more noble than him standing up for me. Surely Olli would respect that.

"Ari Prock of course I will bless your marriage. I have seen Julia find increasing happiness with every day she has known you. Even before she fell in love with you, she seemed more alive being around someone her own age. You are both young, so you will have to work through a lot together. I trust you not to give up."

"Thank you Dr. Zingre," Ari replied as I heard him head back to the door.

"Wait just a minute though," Olli chimed in.

"Just one more thing."

"Yes sir."

"If you hurt her, I will kill you. I can find you, I will hunt you down, and you will regret ever entering my life, but only for a split second, because then you will be dead. She is special as I am sure you know. Don't ever forget just all she possesses for you and this world, and don't ever underestimate the power of this professor."

"Yes sir. And just so you know, if anyone ever hurts her, I will kill them myself."

"Glad to hear it. Go let Julia in."

CHAPTER 6

Within moments my entire life changed again, propelling me to be the general of Patrick's, my brother's, rescue. We all sat in the room together, and in order to pull off our biggest save yet we had to put our knowledge together.

"So tell me what you've got," Olli said as we put the awkward discomfort in the backdrop.

"I have the name Soren Ambler. Patrick said to find him if I ever needed him."

"Soren Ambler's is the name of a bar on the other side of Paris," Olli said with the troubled look that always seemed to grace his face.

"Well, let's start there."

"You should know that during the day it is graced by German supporters. We should go now before the bar gets busy."

We began walking, the three of us, Olli carrying a briefcase to prove his credentials. It was tough on me, being back in Paris, seeing that all of my memories no longer existed in reality. It made my heart crumble on the inside to think that all I would ever have of my brother again would have already existed, without him even knowing the biggest secret of both of our lives. We continued walking in silence, and within five or six blocks of our hotel, Ari reached over and took my hand. Olli looked over and grinned, the first grin on his face in a long time, and then turned his head back forward focusing on the road and no doubt his thoughts.

Our steps became monotone, with the nervousness and anxiety standing before us in the air, like a shadow moving before we could catch it. As we neared the Louvre, I bit my lip to keep from crying. The thought of all of the culture stolen, abandoned, and destroyed in the war, I couldn't even fathom. The pieces of art, which I had once discovered and shared, no longer sat in the museum we passed. Damage stood, for the lack of a better word, all around us as we walked. Lives, dreams, and hopes gone to hell, haunted me with every step I took until we reached the bar. Goose bumps filled my arms as I walked right past the door. I couldn't even let myself believe I walked through Paris. It wasn't the Paris I remembered.

"Julia this is it," Olli said.

We agreed, or I should say that I demanded, that I would be the one to go in and that the men would wait for me outside. They would wait for the bar to clear of any riff raff and give me forty-five minutes to take care of business before they made a scene. Luckily, or by the fact that the clock read 9:00 a.m., when I entered by pushing open the ridiculously heavy wooden door no one sat inside. Only the bartender behind the counter graced Soren Ambler's.

"May I help you young lady? I am not sure you are old enough to be in such a place. Do you have some form of identification?"

"I am not sure you are old enough to be here either," I replied.

"Sassy. I like it," he said with a wink and a smile.

"Shame you are married though. I bet your husband doesn't know you are here," he continued with a glance at my ring.

"Bartenders will flirt with anything with two legs and long hair."

A brief pause filled the room. I felt like I had built some rapport with this ragamuffin, so I went for it.

"1,1,9,9,14,14,20,26."

"Are you having a seizure?" he asked.

I questioned myself. Was this the point of no return? Should I go forward or should I say sorry and step out? Before my mind decided, I said,

"Anti-Nazi."

He looked at me with a soul searching stare that I thought would never end, and as I turned to walk away he said,

"Downstairs, third door on the left--knock twice--wait exactly thirty-three seconds and then knock once. When you are done leave through the basement. If we ever meet again you don't know me. Got it."

"Thank you. I think I will go to the restroom now," I said as I headed down the stairs to the cellar.

Praying along the way that a trap did not lie before me, I unconsciously felt the words of the Constitution going through my mind calming my nerves. I followed the directions given to me moments before and the door opened. Someone grabbed me and yanked me in. As the door slammed, I felt someone grab my hands and begin to bind them. With a blistering head butt I flung my head backwards watching blood begin to drip down my shirt as I glimpsed down.

"What the hell is this? I screamed.

"Where is Patrick Bellew?"

"What the hell are you doing?" the man whose nose I broke asked wiping blood from his face as others entered the room from a back passageway.

I ran back to the door and I heard a voice say,

"Stop it!" and then with a pause I heard, "Julia?"

I turned back around and dropped to my knees. It couldn't be, I thought to myself. Although my mind told me it was possible, hearing his voice seemed like a dream.

"Patrick?" I screamed, as he ran forward and lifted me up off my knees.

Although not much taller than when we had met before, the strain of my new found chubbiness created no obvious discomfort on his face.

"Just like old times," he said as he kissed me on the forehead over and over again.

After a few moments of me sobbing he said,

"What are you doing here?"

"I've come to save you."

"From what?"

Before I spilled my guts I needed an explanation of why I had almost been handcuffed a few moments before. Patrick explained to me that the knocking pattern on the door indicated that I had provided all of the correct information, but that intelligence indicated that I did not come alone. For security's sake, it was the process to restrain anyone under those circumstances until clarification could be provided about those accompanying the guest.

I explained to Patrick that Olli escorted me, and then I explained how my letters last mentioned how much I hated Ari Prock, but how I had fallen in love and married him. We laughed about the situation and then Patrick said,

"Damn Sweetheart, you still can take care of yourself. You have some of the same skills I have that your father taught me when I was a little boy."

"You mean your father," I replied.

"What?" Patrick asked with a confused look on his face.

And that's when I told him our true connection. He grabbed me again and threw me up in the air. He had the strength of an ox and really reminded me of Daddy in that moment.

"Well Sis, what exactly are you here to save me from?"

"I have accurate information that you are wanted by the Nazi's for conspiracy against the government. I have come to take you to safety."

"Damn it. I thought I got out of dodge on that last mission. I guess

I didn't."

"What mission?"

The other boys in the room asked Patrick to step back and talk with them privately in the back of the room. I'm sure they were concerned about him divulging information to me, but he guaranteed them of my loyalties. Then Patrick began to explain,

"I am part of the resistance here in Paris. As our part of the French underground, I have been helping downed American and British pilots escape through Spain. I take them to a safe zone and pass them on to another network closer to Spain. On my last trip someone followed me, but I thought I lost them before they got a look at my face. I guess not. So what is your plan General? Whatever it is, I truly do hope you make General Pershing proud."

I went into great detail explaining Olli's position and power to get Patrick out of France. In the end I said,

"Basically you will be captured for the sake of the German government's information. Then Olli will write up fake research, declare you dead, and put you into hiding. Most importantly you will be safe."

"Julia that all sounds great, but then I will be of no use to defeating Hitler. I can't quit now."

"You won't be of any help dead. What if I can promise you that Olli will allow you to conduct research and provide information while you are in hiding that will help him continue to save innocent people including your wanted friends? And by the way, we have eighteen minutes until Uncle Olli and Ari come barging in looking for me."

"Okay. I trust you Julia," Patrick replied.

After a few conversations wrapping-up some loose ends, Patrick said goodbye to his friends with handshakes and hugs, and together we walked for the door, stepping over a pool of blood on the way.

"Oh yeah, sorry about that," I said to Patrick's fellow resister still holding his nose as we made our way to a back alley on the other side of the bar.

And so I became General Julia Josephine Prock, JJP, just as my father would have wanted, but I did so under my own name and under my own conditions. The only thing that could have led me to change the lives of fifteen innocent people, including my brother Patrick, was my spirit, that string that tugged at my heart when I tried to pretend I was something else. And it was not until I embraced the fact of who I was born to be, that I truly harnessed all I had to offer. It took everything in the world for me to let go, which then gave me everything in the world. By letting go, I became Julia, and I can tell you, if felt pretty damn good to be me and to not give a shit about how others chose to view me.

CHAPTER 7

War changes everything. Reality becomes non-existent, morals change, and sin does not exist. Although I knew that in theory, I did not really experience it until we found ourselves back in Vienna.

After we returned to Vienna so many things changed. For one, Olli finally recognized that I had grown up before his eyes, and I think he regretted missing some of the recent years. After our trip to Paris, I also think he came to see me as my own person rather than the child of my parents.

The most humorous new occurrence after our return came with explaining to Ari's parents our new unification as man and wife. Completely dumfounded, they accepted me immediately, but it took them a few days to overcome Ari's many deceptions. With Stefan's coaxing they came around, and Ari moved into our apartment in Alsergrund. Olli was never there anyway, so we had plenty of time to ourselves, not much different than before. It made me realize just how much I loved Olli. Unlike most parents, he understood and remembered what it meant to be young and in love. He understood the delicateness of my emotions, my need for space, and my obsessive worry; and he made every effort to make me comfortable.

Uncle Olli even did me the favor of a lifetime, guaranteeing that Ari would not be drafted. 1943 served as the year for the maximum conscription of Austrian men into the German Army with over eight hundred thousand Austrians drafted. Olli petitioned for Ari to stay with him declaring that he had an essential job helping him find "wanted" traitors to the state. He had done the same for Stefan a few years before, and now he kept my husband from more than likely never coming home.

Not all changes were good, however. For when we returned, war truly came knocking at our doorstep. Yes, Patrick and all of the people I cared about were finally safe, or at least as safe as a person could be under the circumstances, but it was then that the word sacrifice came to have a real meaning in my vocabulary.

By the end of 1943, the support of the German Army and Hitler in Austria had all but crumbled, especially with their failure at Leningrad and then with the defeat of the German and Italian armies in North Africa. On the positive side, the allies were coming, on the negative side I found myself surrounded by their enemies.

Food shortages continued to grow, and as Hitler's little pansy ass moved closer and closer back to Berlin, the threat of attack became more and more real. I prayed more than ever as we entered into a pattern of life that included bomb drills, alarms, and hunger. Always searching for the nearest cellar, waiting for the moment that Vienna, also known as, "The Reich's Air Raid Shelter" no longer served as a safe haven.

My worst fears became a reality on March 17, 1944. As bombs crashed around us, and as I sat in a cellar with Ari's arms wrapped around me, my father's voice ran through my head. Specifically, another Napoleonic quote brought me comfort, although this one did not involve dominance and control as others I heard as a child. I can remember Daddy saying to me as he told me a story of the First World War and tucked me in to sleep,

"There are only two important forces in the affairs of men. One is the sword and the other the spirit, and in the long run the sword will always be conquered by the spirit."

I often felt like Napoleon was a liar sitting in a cold, damp, and dark basement almost daily for the next year as Vienna was bombed fifty-two times. In the end, eighty-seven thousand houses were destroyed and most tragically for me, twenty-six bombs hit the University of Vienna including my treasured library reading hall, where the glass roof shattered.

The D-Day invasion followed shortly thereafter, and although the war seemed all but over, we had several realities to face. First of all, we had to come to terms with whether or not our liberators would be kind, and secondly whether or not they would let us explain how we helped their cause from within rather than act as an enemy.

The answers to our questions came in April of 1945. After a year of bombings, near starvation, and living with the working technology of the Middle Ages, the Soviets entered Vienna via Hungary. Eleven days of resistance followed to have the Soviets officially liberate us on April 13, 1945.

War is a hell of a thing and sometimes it brings out the best and bravest, but more often it brings out the worst and savage. Liberation did not equal freedom, it equaled anarchy, hence fear. Knowing that I would be protected by the men in my life provided no relief, because I knew they would die for me, and I didn't want to face death, not this late in the war. My bravery was running on empty.

A provisional government came to power and seceded from the Third Reich. Staying out of the way and avoiding any possible conflict became the philosophy of Olli, Ari, the Procks, and myself. The Spiros chose to remain in hiding until stability secured their safety. Every day seemed like forever as we sat waiting for the war to end everywhere in the world.

CHAPTER 8

"We need an interpreter. Does anyone speak Russian?" a soldier screamed out in Russian running down the street with his gun lowered by his side.

"Please, if you can understand me, I need your help."

"I speak Russian," I responded from our porch, which I stepped out upon when I heard noise outside.

"Julia, what are you doing?" Ari asked me as I headed for the front door.

"Olli, please tell her not to go. This is not her problem."

"Shush now," I replied before Olli could chime in.

"They need my help. I don't think they are looking for someone to hurt."

"Okay, but I am coming with you."

Ari and I reached the ground floor and we stepped out into the open where the screaming soldier stood with tears running down his face.

"Please come help us. Please."

"Of course. But what is wrong?"

The soldier did not answer, he just grabbed my hand and gently tugged me behind him with Ari following right on my heels. We ran about half a mile before we reached a group of spectators all standing around some scene we could not see from the outside. The soldier broke through dragging us with him.

"Here! Here is the interpreter," he said breathing deeply.

"What is wrong?" I said.

Immediately I realized that my words were in vain because a soldier with a gun and a Viennese man stood fifteen feet apart screaming at each other, one in Russian the other in German. Between them a baby wrapped up in sheet sat crying. Probably fourteen months of age at the most.

"Please one at a time," I first said in German and then repeated in Russian.

Then I looked directly at the Austrian man and said,

"What is happening? Why are you upset at this young man?"

The Austrian man went on to explain to me how he came across the Soviet soldier watching the baby. He recognized the baby, because he knew the baby's mother, who recently died in a bombing raid. He explained to me how he had no idea what had come of the baby until he was taking his morning walk to see a soldier letting the baby crawl around in the dirt. He moved to pick up the baby and take it home, but the Soviet started screaming at him in Russian and eventually picked up his weapon.

I then turned to the Russian to get his version of the story.

"Excuse me sir," I began.

"Could you please tell me the problem?"

Like the man a few moments before, the soldier gave his account of the situation. Apparently, they came across the baby a few days before with an elderly woman who was very sick and could not get out of bed. The soldier decided to take the baby with him, figuring a better chance of survival than leaving the baby to starve. He became adamant that he would not leave the baby to starve or be thrown aside. He explained to me that he had already witnessed too much of that in the war, and that he would die or kill before watching another child get hurt.

That is when I did my job. I translated the stories for each man in his own language. The Russian lowered his weapon, and after long sessions of translation, I walked forward and picked up the baby in my arms without saying any words to either man. As I held the little baby against my chest, I turned to look at Ari. He would tell me years later that the look on my face said a thousand words for everyone standing among us.

After the resolution, I took the baby in my arms and Ari and I turned to walk away when I heard in Russian,

"Excuse me young lady. You are now translator."

At first I wanted to resist, not wanting to get involved in any possible complications, but it then occurred to me that by helping the Soviets, they would protect me. All of a sudden, I had become a valuable commodity to all parties involved.

I placed the baby in Ari's arms, told him I would be okay, and followed the soldier who sought me out. After about a mile and a half of walking in silence, we came to the soldier's commander. In Russian he informed him of the situation and my part in resolving it.

"What is your name?" he asked me.

"Julia Josephine..." and before I could finish my name another soldier in the unit turned around and said,

"Patterson?"

"How would you know that?" I asked in shock that some stranger knew my name.

"Is it you? Are you really Julia Josephine Patterson? Are you the daughter of Leeana Serenova?"

With a complete loss of breath, I sought words to respond. Searching for noise to come out of my mouth the man with thick, dark black hair kept talking, partially in Russian with a word or two in English.

Disillusioned and searching for answers I said,

"Who are you?"

"I am Nikolai Khovansky. My mother is Zouriat Serenova, your mother's sister. We are cousins. I can't believe it I actually found you. Is it really you? I can't believe it. Grandfather told me you lived in Austria, but I had no idea I would actually find you. Is it you?"

And that was just the beginning. He went on and on in a complete train of chaotic thought. I found my bearings mentally and physically and said,

"Yes, I am Julia Josephine Patterson, or actually Prock now. How do you know about me?"

"Grandfather has told me of you my entire life, since I was a boy sitting on his knee. He said the last time he heard about your location, your father had just died and all he knew is that you were going to live with a family friend in Austria. I wish he could be here. I wish he knew that our unit would end up in Austria. He could have sent a personal message."

Chills ran up and down my spine, and without thinking I ran over and gave him a hug. I didn't care what anyone thought, my mother's blood ran through him, and I had to feel his pulse. I had to be that close.

The commander agreed to let him come back with me for the evening to meet Olli and Ari. In exchange I would stay with the unit during the day as a translator should any other problems arise. I didn't even argue or question the agreement. I wanted to spend every possible moment with a cousin I may have never met if it had not been for a world war.

"Julia you can't just run off..." Olli began to say as I walked back in through the front door of the apartment.

"Who is this?" he said when he noticed a strange man walk in the door behind me.

Nikolai took off his hat and slightly bowed to Olli. Completely ecstatic I looked at Olli and Ari, who still held the baby in his arms, and said,

"Can you believe it? This is my cousin Nikolai."

"You are Zouriat's son," Olli said in Russian.

"You are one of the twins. You resemble your Aunt Leeana. Please come in, have a seat."

Meeting my Russian cousin ended up as an amazing blessing. Not only did I get to experience a piece of my Russian heritage, but I got an update on my mother's family. Most tragically, I found out that my Uncle Mikhail had been killed in the military when the Germans invaded Leningrad, and that my Uncle Kiril had named his youngest son Mikhail in honor of his brother. I had loads of first cousins running around, and I wanted so badly to have them know me.

Nikolai also guaranteed my safety and the safety of my family and friends in occupied Vienna. The first wave of Soviets that entered Vienna, including Nikolai's unit, had behaved well under the circumstances of a collapsed society with no police force. The second wave of troops, however, were exhausted by the war, and like so many before them, lost their reason. Assault, looting, and violence became real daily threats as our city sat in ruins. Nikolai protected me like a big brother, telling me stories of my family the entire time, picking on Ari like a brother-in-law, and serving as my bodyguard when the Russians needed me to translate.

By September of 1945, Vienna faced the same fate as Berlin, divided by the four victors in the war, and Alsergrund found itself under the control of the United States rather than the Soviets. Nikolai secured me an inter-allied identity card that allowed me to move from zone to zone as needed. He vouched for me as a significant translator, and so I continued to help the Russians translate, but I also helped the French, English, and the Americans in the other areas of Vienna.

Placed in temporary custody of the Americans as a possible war criminal, Olli's name was cleared by Christmas of the same year. Enough papers, testimonies, and witnesses existed to exonerate him as a Nazi and prove his true allegiances and purpose.

The Spiros finally came out of hiding to enjoy life once again. I remember hugging Mrs. Spiro for the first time. When she first noticed her ring on my finger, she hugged me even harder and said,

"I couldn't have dreamed it would be anyone better."

Mr. Spiro actually slept outside for his first night of freedom. He wanted to see the sunset and the sunrise. He wanted to feel the air and breathe in the world. Both of the Spiros ran outside the first time it rained after freedom, playing in the mud like children. I came to believe they appreciated life more than anyone else in the world.

As for Mr. Sina, Olli banked all of the assets from his art shop that he took control of when Ari and I had made him number one on our list. Although Jurgen never returned to Vienna, or Austria for that matter, he did receive a life changing check in the months following Olli's release from allied custody.

After a reunion of familial proportions, Patrick returned to Paris and his mother, who had not seen him since the start of the war. I walked him to the train and just like he had once done for me, I re-gifted him the baseball glove from my father, or I should say, our father. Inside I placed a note as he had for me years before.

Dear Patrick,

I must say that I am sad and glad to see you step onto a train for Paris. Of course I am saddened that we are once again being separated into different worlds, but now we have a common denominator, one that will bind us for all of our lives. We share the same father, and unlike before where I struggled to understand the nature of our friendship, I now know that in a world where everyone related to me seems to die, I have a brother. This brother of mine is strong and will not let the world beat him down. It is he who I believe holds the key to the value life can hold.

I am also glad. Foremost in the fact that you are boarding a train for home, which means two things. One, the war is over. And two, you survived. Adjusted to watching the things closest to me disappear or change form, this war has given me the gift of you, the same as the day I met you in Paris, and a friend for life.

If it took a war to give me back a piece of my father, the sacrifice was well worth it. Take your time, recover, and start your life anew the way it should have always been, and remember that when everything is how you want it, you have a sister who will always be there for you as you were for her when you didn't even know it.

See you soon!
With Love Always,
JJP

And so everything changed again, except this time every experience would be new, as the Vienna I had grown up in and watch change before my eyes would never again hold the same presence. My life in Austria would only exist in memory as the library sat in rubble and shattered glass, and as the people I loved most had been broken by the destruction and pain of war.

In early 1946 Nikolai returned under military orders to Russia, and with him I sent a letter for my grandfather. Knowing I would likely never see him again with the increasing American-Soviet tensions, and with the development of the "Cold War," I chilled myself to human emotion. The thought of losing yet another person to pure stupidity on the part of the world's leaders proved too much to handle. In my heart, I feared that the moment I wished Nikolai goodbye might be the last moment I would ever communicate with my mother's side of the family.

And so in the summer of 1946 using my still valid American citizenship and my value in helping the Americans with translation in Vienna I secured a trip for four to the United States of America. Seeking a new beginning with my husband and our adopted war orphan, who we named Jacob Serenov Prock, and who led me to my Russian cousin, we planned to start a new life in America. The fourth guaranteed seat belonged to Olli, to whom I owed the world. Uncle Olli, however, chose to finally do something for himself. Rather than tag along with the young Prock family, he moved to Paris to be with Maria.

PART IV: ACCEPTANCE

CHAPTER 1

Invictus

Out of the night that covers me,
Black as the Pit from pole to pole,
I thank whatever gods may be
For my unconquerable soul.

In the fell clutch of circumstance
I have not winced nor cried aloud,
Under the bludgeonings of chance
My head is bloody, but unbowed.

Beyond this place of wrath and tears
Looms but the horror of the shade,
And yet the menace of the years
Finds, and shall find me, unafraid.

It matters not how strait the gate,
How charged with punishments the scroll,
I am the master of my fate:
I am the captain of my soul.

-- William Ernest Henley

CHAPTER 2

I picked up my remote control and flipped on the television, as was part of my morning routine; the "Dream Team" again. Everyone knew Michael Jordan, Larry Bird, and Magic Johnson all on the same team provided poetry in motion, but couldn't there be more important news? I guess not, and what a good thing after all of the horrible news that had graced my presence in my sixty-seven years of life.

"Sweetheart we have to meet Patrick at the airport in an hour. You know how Raleigh traffic is on Friday afternoon."

"Okay," I replied to Ari grabbing my shoes and purse.

After forty-nine years of marriage we got in our station wagon and headed for Interstate 40 from Durham to Raleigh. Tired from my medication and work schedule I reclined my seat back and stared out the car window as Ari drove. With my eyes closed I reflected on how on earth I had gone from being an obsessive orphan in World War II Austria to the mother of an obsessed Vietnam Veteran in Durham, North Carolina.

When we boarded the plane for the United States, I gave Ari the option to live anywhere he wanted in the United States for the sacrifices he made for me during the war. I only wanted a University nearby. He chose North Carolina, because of its proximity to Mountains, the Appalachian Chain, and the Atlantic Ocean. North Carolina also had several universities, providing me with choices galore. Durham became our home, and eventually Duke University became my educational mecca as I specialized in teaching European History, at first the Napoleonic Wars and later the Holocaust. I also taught history courses at other local colleges such as The University of North Carolina and North Carolina State

University. Ari worked construction while Jacob was young and eventually became a general contractor.

The baby we pulled from the ashes definitely did not share my love for knowledge and slipped through high school with the least possible effort truly enjoying the chaos and turmoil of 1960's America. But that was okay, he was my baby, the only one I would ever have, and I loved him as my own.

After high school he worked for Ari until he joined the army where he would eventually serve with Richard Warren Pershing, grandson of John Joseph Pershing in the 502nd Infantry. Buried beside his grandfather, Richard sadly never made it home from Vietnam. Even more tragic for me, Jacob never really came back a whole person either. Vietnam broke him more than World War II could have ever affected me.

I worried more about him than I knew possible, more than I worried about Patrick in World War II, more than I worried about my father as he drank himself to death.

Another war that made me sacrifice my family taught me a little something more about my obsessive disorder. Unconsciously still saying the Constitution in my mind to rid myself of unwanted thoughts, I came to better understand the waves of my worry. It always seemed that I could weather the storm just fine. It was the downtime my brain couldn't handle. When things seemed to be just right, that was when irrational thoughts overran my mind, when I would spend ninety percent of my day trying to convince myself of the things I already knew to be true in my heart.

When Jacob returned from the war a broken man, I took him to get help readjusting to society, and in the process I finally helped myself. Although I managed my OCD to some extent, I could no longer live with the pressure of worry riding upon my soul. My grandfather's letters and helpful tips kept me functional in society, but with an excuse to help my son, I finally freed my own soul with therapy.

"What time is the flight supposed to get in?" Ari asked, interrupting my reflections.

"Uh, 4:45."

"And what time will Jacob be at the house?"

"He is supposed to pick up your mother and Nora from school, and Helen from work. He should be at the house around 6:00."

"Sounds good."

CHAPTER 3

At the airport I jumped out of the car full of excitement, leaving Ari pushing quarters into the parking meter. I found the correct flight number and ran to the window pressing my nose against the glass like a child. It had been a year and a half since I had seen my brother and his family, and just as important, it had been equally as long since I had seen my Uncle Olli. I had not been to Paris since Maria's death in late 1990.

Ari joined me at the window and took my hand. His rough fingers from years of work still comforted me.

"Are you ready for this?" he asked.

"I've been ready for this since we left Vienna."

Ari just bowed his head and said,

"I know."

I absolutely lost my breath when I saw my Uncle Olli step off the ramp leading into the terminal. Walking just as good as ever, my ninety-one year old godfather immediately recognized me. He brushed his hand across his forehead, where his hair used to be, out of habit and gave me his typical half smile.

"You know I can live by myself General. You don't have to take me in like a lost puppy," he said as he hugged me and shook Ari's hand.

"Just think of me as the lost puppy. I need you to come take care of me. Remember you promised my father."

"Well if you put it that way," he continued as Patrick joined us in the terminal with his wife, Galiene.

"Hey Sis," Patrick said dropping down his carry-on bag.

We all exchanged hugs, picked up the luggage, and then headed out to the car.

After the war Olli finally chose to follow his heart, which led him to Paris, and to Maria. Although they never married, they lived in bliss until Maria died in 1990. I visited France every year after moving to the States, sometimes with Ari and Jacob and sometimes by myself. Patrick and his family, Maria, and Olli came to see me just as often, providing the kind of family I never thought I would have. Patrick's kids grew up thinking of Jacob as their brother, and over time I came to cherish the holidays, and I never again felt alone on my birthday.

Patrick chose to stay in Paris after the war. He became an engineer and helped rebuild Paris, just like our father had once done after the First World War. He married a woman just like Maria, sweet and patient named Galiene, and they had three children.

Now that Maria was gone, Olli had nothing holding him to France, and I wanted to soak up every moment left in the life of the man who shaped me, who raised me, and who taught me to stand up for what I believe, and most importantly, accepted me for me.

When we finally reached home, Jacob came outside onto the porch.

"Did you pick up Mom?" Ari asked as he helped Patrick, Olli, and Galiene with the luggage.

"Of course I did. I am almost fifty years old for crying out loud. Do you think I would leave Grandma high and dry?" Jacob spouted as his wife Helen, daughter Nora, and Mrs. Prock joined him on the front porch.

"Listen to that lip," Olli chimed in.

"He most definitely learned that from you Julia."

"Hello Annaliese," he continued.

Mr. And Mrs. Prock came to live in the United States after Soviet occupation of Austria ended in 1955. They lived nearby in the small town of Hillsboro, North Carolina. Stefan married and started having children by the time occupation ended and stayed in Vienna, visiting the States every other year. In the early 1970's Mr. Prock suffered a massive heart attack and passed away leaving Mrs. Prock a widow. After that, she came to our house every Sunday for afternoon lunch.

"Turn on the television," Nora yelled across the living room carrying Olli's luggage into his new bedroom.

"What is the hurry?" I replied.

"Your great-grandfather and great-uncle just arrived from Europe."

"I just want to see an update on the Olympics."

"I can guarantee you that it is not nearly as exciting as Duke's two National Championships in a row in basketball," Jacob contributed.

"I personally prefer the North Carolina State Wolfpack. I sure miss Jim Valvano's spirit."

"We know, we know," Jacob said as he helped me set the table for dinner and as Olli and Annaliese sat down to talk in the living room.

Everything seemed to be right with the world.

CHAPTER 4

All alone in the house while Jacob and Ari took Olli to the doctor to get his medical records updated to American standards, and while Patrick, Galiene, and Nora went to a college baseball game, I sat back in my recliner. A smile came to my face as I watched Ethiopian sensation Derartu Tulu run to Olympic gold, becoming the first African woman to win an Olympic gold medal. I laughed on the inside thinking of my once ignorant comments about Jesse Owens.

The 1992 Olympics provided other firsts as well. The Barcelona games served as the first Games in three decades without some kind of boycott, and of course, the first Olympics since the dissolution of the Soviet Union.

The Olympics amazed me. Something about athletics transcended race, ethnicity, religion, or transgressions of one's own country. The Olympics made me believe that world peace really could exist.

Watching the world move past the Cold War through healthy competition, while fighting an afternoon nap, I heard a knock at the door. I crawled out of my recliner to see the mailman standing in front of me.

"A package for you Mrs. Prock. This one is actually from Russia, the first I have seen since the collapse. I bet it's still censored."

"Thanks," I said taking the package and closing the door in the mailman's face without even realizing it.

I sat in my chair and held the thick, padded envelope in my fingers. I had no knowledge of how to contact any of my family. The last time we communicated was when Nikolai took a letter back to Russia for my grandfather. I ran my hand over the address, preserving the perfection for as long as possible, or at least until I couldn't stand it anymore. That is when I opened it and pulled out a loose letter.

Dear Julia,

I gave grandfather your letter upon my return to Russia, and he made me promise that one day, when the iron curtain collapsed, that I would send to you his letters. When I reported to him of your life in Vienna, he decided that he would write you a letter every week for the rest of his life, and I can tell you that he fulfilled this promise. Not knowing if or when Communism would collapse, he desired for you to know what truly filled his heart.

Now that he has been gone for over twenty years, it is hard for me to write this to you. I had long put his boxes and boxes of dusty memories aside, believing that the day would never come when I could freely write you or that I could even find you again as fate had once done for us. By a completely unexpected aligning of the stars, I again have found you after seeking out help from recently emigrated Russians from our community.

And so the time came to pull Grandfather out of the trunk at the foot of my bed and fulfill his wishes for you and your mother. Julia you have impacted my life in many ways and to this day you impact my life still. Please know that although you have always been so far away, you haunt all of our hearts daily. All fourteen of grandfather's other grandchildren know about you-the long lost Julia of mythical proportions. I pray that this letter and Grandfather's letters can give you a piece of your Russian family that this world has so cruelly denied you.

On my own behalf I plead of you to write me. Let me know of what has become of your life. And enjoy being the only child of Grandfather's dear Leeana by having a complete memoir of the last thirty years of his life written for your eyes.

With much love,
Nikolai Khovansky

I reached back into the envelope to find a pouch of letters wrapped in rubber bands and plastic with a note on top in Nikolai's handwriting which read, "Start on top, it is the first in a series of hundreds of letters to come."

Dearest Julia,

Oh my child, how Nikolai's stories of you just melt my heart. You are everything I could have ever imagined plus more. Without ever having spoken to you, I can tell that you seep your mother, but that you are distinctly your own. His stories about your translations, about your witty jokes, about your intelligence and independence, make me wish I could hold you and show you off to the world, but something tells me you will do that for yourself.

I plan to write you every week for the rest of my life, so that even if you are old and gray, you will still know from where you come. Julia I am charged to love you by default, but I love you because of what you have become. Take the advice I always gave your mother, and remember to choose happiness before structure, although I know you will always choose security over bliss.

Enjoy the pictures until the next letter.

Love Always,

Papa

December 11, 1946

Inside the first letter were thirteen pictures, pictures I had never seen; my mother playing with her puppy as a child, my aunts and uncles, my grandfather with his mad scientist looking hair, and their home before the Revolution.

Just as my father had come back to me through Patrick, my mother now came back to me through my papa's letters

I immediately pulled out a pen and wrote a letter to my grandfather in honor of the spirit and strength he maintained for so many years for me. Maybe one day I would give it to my own granddaughter Nora as I shared my story.

Dearest Papa,

I am sad that we never met, though I know our spirits have connected throughout my entire life, perhaps before either of us ever walked this earth. You were no doubt a pillar of strength for my mother and now me. I can't believe that I am now a grandmother just as you found yourself a grandfather when Nikolai and Pasha were born. It is unbelievable how suddenly life changes and how fast we age once our lives truly begin.

I know that I will see you again and for the first time in heaven one day. Until then I leave these words:

Scruffy beard,
Curly hair,
Lanky arms,

Skin so fair.
The wisest man I never knew,
Giving peace to my chaotic mind,
Simply stating the obvious,
To help me out of a bind.

Loving with an open heart,
Writing with hope and grace,
Standing strong against all odds,
Trusting in war's face.

Giving strength from across the world,
Committing to the children you loved,
Finally at peace above the skies,
Soaring around as a dove.

Thank you for teaching me patience and peace. Thank you for never giving up on me. And most of all thank you for teaching me to listen to my heart without recourse, and to understand that fate exists when people get the hell out of the way.

With Love Now and Forever,
Julia Josephine Patterson Prock

THE END

Acknowledgements

I would like to sincerely thank the following people for their help, kindness, and expertise in the writing process:

Karen Carotta

Caden Spooner

Samantha Stichter

About the Author

Christian Strayhorn Spence holds a Master of Arts degree in History from the University of Nebraska-Kearney and a Bachelor of Arts degree in History from North Carolina State University. Originally from Asheboro, North Carolina, she currently teaches history in Greensboro, North Carolina. In 2011, she received the honor of becoming a Horace Mann Abraham Lincoln Fellow, one of fifty teachers selected to study the legacy of Abraham Lincoln. *General Pershing's Other Daughter* is a reflection on a shared sense of the human condition. The grandchild of a Russian immigrant and the grandniece of a World War II veteran who served in Austria, Christian weaves together parts of her own history with her passion for writing.

Made in the USA
Lexington, KY
21 May 2013